The Last Victim

A Ryker Townsend Novel

By
Jordan Dane

The Last Victim
Copyright 2015
ISBN: 978-0-9855132-5-2
Cover Art by Croco Designs
Formatted by Wizards in Publishing

The Last Victim

When a young hunting guide from a remote island in Alaska is found brutally murdered, his naked body is discovered in the Cascade Mountains outside Seattle—the shocking pinnacle to a grisly Totem of body parts. Nathan Applewhite is the fourteenth victim of a cunning serial killer who targets and stalks young men.

With the body count escalating, FBI profiler Ryker Townsend and his specialized team investigate the gruesome crime scene. They find no reason for Nate to have mysteriously vanished from his isolated home in Alaska before he ended up in the hands of a sadist, who has been taunting Ryker and his team in a sinister game of 'catch me if you can.'

But Townsend has a secret he won't share with anyone—not even his own team—that sets him on the trail of a ruthless psychopath, alone. The intuitive FBI profiler is plagued by recurring nightmares—seen through Nate's dead eyes—that slowly chips away at his mental stability. Is he burning out and losing his mind—becoming unfit for duty—or is the last victim reaching out to him from the grave?

Townsend sees horrific flashes of memory, imprinted on the retinas of a dead man, the last image Applewhite saw when he died. Ryker must piece together the fragments. Each nightmarish clue brings him closer to a killer who knows how to hide in plain sight and will see him coming, but when the dead man has the skills of a hunting guide, he has the perfect ally to track down a killer—the last victim.

Dedication

To John - You are missed.
JD

Dear Readers,

The Last Victim is special to me since it is set in Alaska where I lived for ten years. Many of the outdoor float plane and hiking experiences of my FBI profiler, Ryker Townsend, were from the many trips I had taken, a city girl exposed to true wilderness for the first time.

Although my life is simple when compared to Ryker's, I hold my Alaskan memories very dear and the biggest adventure of my life. A mother moose charged me on an isolated trail with only a small birch tree to separate us and I've had more than one close encounter with bears. I was also a checkpoint operator for the Iditaski Race, held along the Iditarod Trail during the dead of winter. I've had my share of fun. I dearly love Alaska and hope you'll enjoy *The Last Victim*.

Jordan Dane

Chapter One

The soothing murmur of an ocean ebbed through Nathan Applewhite's mind until he felt the waves and made them real. Now as cool water lapped the sandy shore to make frothy lace at his bare feet, he looked up to a cloudless sky—the color of a robin's egg—that stretched its reach to forever. Fragments of his senses came together. Every piece made him yearn for more. When warm skin touched his, he knew he wasn't alone and he smiled. He held a tiny hand. His five-year old boy Tanner walked the strand of beach beside him.

The memory came to him often, but it never stayed long enough.

The saltwater foam swirled over white sand and triggered another memory of the tablecloth in his mother's dining room, something from when he was Tanner's age. White lace. The smell of Thanksgiving turkey and pies in the oven. The memories were vivid. Nate wanted to stay in their comfort, but he was too weak.

The pain always yanked him back.

He couldn't escape the reality of where he was and must've lost consciousness again. Blood loss made him lightheaded and the hallucinations had grown worse, but his past was only a fragile refuge. The sting of gaping and bleeding cuts kept him prisoner to his waking nightmare.

Were his eyes open? He couldn't be sure at first. Everywhere he looked he stared into nothing but blackness. When he took a deep breath, he smelled the thick fabric over his nose, tainted with his sweat.

The hood. He still wore a hood on his head.

He didn't know how long it had been since he'd been taken. He had no sense of time, but his corner of hell came in a rush like rising flood waters. The dank odor of humidity, and the steady drip of water coming from a sink near his head, closed in on him. When he moved, he felt the chilling touch of the metal table under him. He was naked, vulnerable and exposed. His bare skin tightened with goose flesh and his teeth chattered. He couldn't stop shaking.

Sprawled spread eagle and bound, he tugged at his arms and legs and a rope dug into his skin—deep cuts that would never heal. He wasn't going home. He would die here. A tear drained down his cheek as he thought of never seeing his ex-wife and little boy again. He'd made a mess of everything and it didn't look likely he'd get a chance to make things right. When he heard the hollow sound of music echoing from the ductwork over his head, his body tensed. He grasped what had awakened him.

Music. He's coming.

His gut twisted with panic. In his delirium, he didn't know how much time he had now until he realized he hadn't heard the song. The bastard always played a special song before he came down the stairs—a song Nate's ex had picked for their wedding. Nate listened for anything that would tell him where the man might be. When he heard the hollow thud of footsteps over his head and dusty grit from the ceiling dappled his hood like rain, he knew it wouldn't be long, but it wasn't until Ray Charles sang "What a Wonderful World" that he knew he'd run out of time.

Oh, God.

That song had been another way the man tortured him. Once it started, it would play on continuous loop. The lyrics reminded him of everything he had to lose. Every time the guy worked on him with the knife, he prayed to die. Picturing his son's face forced him to endure the grueling agony, but he wasn't sure how long he could go on.

Giving up felt like the coward's way out. Nate couldn't give up on his boy. His son was the one thing he had worth the pain, but if he couldn't fight it anymore—if he didn't have a choice—he'd have to find a way to say good-bye to his boy. If that happened, he may as well be dead.

After he heard the creak of a door and footsteps on the wooden stairs, he thrashed harder at his restraints and the rope dug into his skin, deep. Fresh blood came from the wounds—warm and sticky—and a coppery tang mixed with the stench off his bare body.

His abuser made the music erupt louder on overhead speakers at the flip of a switch. Despite the noise, it didn't cover up the sound of him approaching. His feet scuffed across crinkling plastic on the floor.

"Did you miss me, lover? I missed you."

His captor used a device to disguise his voice into something mechanical. When Nate first heard the gruff tinny sound, he thought it meant the man was afraid of being recognized, like he'd know him. He hoped once the man was done with him, he'd let him go. He tried talking to the guy, telling him about his son, but that only made things worse. The man degraded him and the mutilations came next.

Too much had happened for him to walk away.

"Have you figured it out yet?"

Nate heard the voice by his ear, but he'd learned not to speak. Saying the wrong thing brought more pain.

"Death is the only thing that will free you now. That makes me your savior."

Nate tugged at his restraints, knowing the man spoke the truth. When he heard the stretch of latex gloves, he knew what would come.

"Soon, everyone will know your name. You'll be the pinnacle of my greatest creation...and I'll be the only one who knows how you earned the honor."

"Why are you doing this to me?"

For his boy's sake, Nathan had to risk asking one more time, even if it cost him. The man never answered that question, no matter how many times he'd begged for a reason. Nate listened to the clatter of him rooting in a drawer for his instruments, not knowing how he'd punish him next.

"Pain or a tender send off. What'll it be, lover?"

He cringed when he felt a gloved hand on his body and a cold drizzle of something slick and oily.

"Stop it. Don't." Nate would've given anything to get lost in his memories—for good this time—but he didn't have the strength. Not anymore.

"But how else will you understand that every part of you is mine?"

As the man worked on him, robbing him of his last dignity, Nate thought of his son as a distraction to what was happening. *His home. God, his poor mother.* He prayed he'd never be found—not like this. Another tear drained down his cheek when his body shuddered and the man got rewarded for his abuse.

"You have what you want," he panted. "Get it over with."

He was done bargaining with the man who would kill him.

"You're right. It's time."

Without another word, the man climbed onto the table and straddled his belly. Nate felt the weight of a body on his hips and hands pressed down on his chest. In an unexpected move, the hood got stripped off his head and he squinted into shadowy darkness.

Nathan blinked and strained to see anything. A silhouette loomed over him and blocked a flashing red light. As his vision cleared, his captor's face took shape and came into focus.

"You..." he gasped. "Oh, God. Why?"

Before he said anything more, Nate saw the red light glint on the blade of a large knife, held high over his head.

"No! Please...don't. *Please!*"

Nathan stared into the eyes of his killer as the knife plunged into his heart. The loud thud echoed in the room as the blade cut through muscle and sinew. His eyes watered with the excruciating pain and a warm liquid filled his lungs. The ocean frothed and swelled to his throat.

He couldn't breathe. He was drowning.

"Come on. Give it to me. That's it. *Yes.*"

Nate blocked out the cruelty of the voice. Only one thing mattered now. As the familiar face above him blurred, it got replaced with another—the sweet smiling face of his little boy Tanner—and the rumble of a wave hitting the shore. Sunlight made Tanner squint when he looked up at him. His son let go of his hand and ran down the beach with a giggle trailing behind him.

Hey, little man. Wait up. Daddy's coming.

With sand caked to his feet, Nathan took off running after his little boy. The two of them splashed in the waves and made shimmering diamonds with their feet. He never caught his son. Time had ticked down to its final precious seconds. He only had one way to say good-bye to Tanner. Nate watched him run and he listened to his little boy laugh until—

Pain let him go and set him free.

***

Cascade Mountains
Outside Seattle
The next day after midnight

Moonlight cast its slate glow onto a lifted hand, fingers gracefully posed toward the dark heavens. They would point to the worthy pinnacle of the masterpiece. The bare skin of a sculpted leg made a beautiful silhouette against the full moon, toes perfectly poised to catch the glimmer of the night. Frozen flesh glittered under the stars in the right light. The crystalline webbing of ice turned blanched skin into an intricate texture with a shine that reflected the dark sacred night.

Too bad the meat had to thaw. To rot.

Every metal stake played its part to hold the Totem together. Now all that was missing was the best part. The adornment on top of the whole creation. The inspiration to it all. A sturdy chain cranked through a metal hoist, a rig with back stops to make the lifting sure and easy. Every aspect had been carefully planned and practiced and would soon be rendered.

Splayed arms and legs inched up the rough bark of a spectacular Hemlock tree. Seeing the naked body being lifted to its final position brought tears. Not sad tears, but tears of glorious joy. Of unadulterated pride. The tree had been selected with great deliberation.

It had to be perfect. It *had* to be.

Set in a clearing that wasn't easy to get to, the tree would showcase well from the ridge where Golden Boy would first see it from a likely access point. A special note would accompany the creation, one that Golden Boy should appreciate. Watching him as he read it would be priceless. That would have to happen.

Under the light of a full moon, the dead body was

hoisted into position and locked into place at the top. It had never been part of the plan to sever his arms and legs like the others. This perfect one had earned his place of honor. Death had freed him, but seeing the empty shell of cold raw meat brought the rage and the reminder that not everyone had been freed by this one's sacrifice. It wouldn't stop here.

Not here. *Not ever!*

It wasn't enough. It was *never* enough.

Only one thing left to do. Flashes from a camera ruined the perfection of the moon, but that couldn't be helped. The camera clicked over and over in the eerie stillness of the night. Around and around. Dizzy. Magnificent. Seeing every detail was addictive. Mesmerizing. A record had to be made, to relive every minute again after the inevitable emptiness came. A foot, a hand, the skin of a face brought back adrenaline-filled, impossible memories.

Cutting a scream loose, the warmth of a blood shower, the thrill of seeing the soul leave the body and knowing God's hand played no part in it—those were rare and powerful addictions—but none of those things matched the final moment when hope left their eyes and they accepted their fate. Sated and drunk on memories, the driver tossed sturdy work gloves aside and climbed into a truck when it was time to go, started the engine, and turned on the music.

The voice of Ray Charles sang. "What a Wonderful World" brought a fitting end as the truck jostled along the gravel service road toward the busted gate few people knew about—heading through the trees into the dark sacred night.

One final glance in the rear view mirror made it hard to leave, but the stunning silhouette of the Totem against the moon stirred the question that remained. Who would top the next creation? There would definitely be a next time and it had to be someone worthy. It wasn't enough to kill perfection once.

Hitting stride, the Totem Killer had only gotten started and had crosshairs on the next one. A name. Another perfect one. Everything had been planned with each detail thought out. Nothing would be rushed.

The driver had a pick up to make and wouldn't go home empty-handed.

Chapter Two

Ryker Townsend

Flies. Hundreds of them swarmed into a frenzied buzz. I couldn't escape the sound...and the smell of violent death. My footsteps echoed in the murky dark, but I couldn't picture where I was. Too dark. The only light came from behind a burgundy velvet drape that hung in front of me. A red glow pulsed in erratic beats. Whenever it flickered out, it plunged me in total darkness, but that didn't stop me. I kept moving, even though I didn't want to.

The flies got louder. I wanted to hate them, but they were only feeding.

A shadow moved behind the curtain. When I got close, my hand reached to pull back the fabric and I tensed.

No! Don't!

My body fought the impulse to look, but something made me reach for the curtain. As I drew back the drape, the red light blinded me. The last thing I saw was the shadow of a faceless body...before the suffocating stench of blood smothered me and I couldn't breathe.

Death was everywhere.

***

"No!"

I heard the familiar panicked cry in my voice and a chill skittered across my skin. With my body drenched in sweat, I thrashed and rode out another dream. My arms flailed as I fought dank sheets and my heart hammered as if it were punishing me.

I must've looked like a defeated cod dying on a beach, too desperate for air to simply stop flopping. Anyone else—anyone *normal*—might've been alarmed at the intensity of the dream, but once I quit sucking air, I accepted what had happened.

My nightmares were a part of me.

I'd grown all too familiar with straddling the thinly veiled line between twilight sleep and whatever reality was. Until I figured out which side I was on, I didn't always rush to wake up. Both sides had their peculiar merits. Sometimes my strange dreams helped me puzzle through my life. Most times they kept me on the wrong side of normal. Gasping, I looked around and couldn't remember where I was— another side effect of my work.

Too much travel. Too many hotel rooms. Too many little soaps.

My eyes searched the shadows of a large room that had a library with countless books. I flipped on a lamp for a better look. A lucky stiff lived here. That stiff was me.

"You're losing it, Townsend, if you ever had *it* in the first place."

Odd how I didn't recognize my new loft in Woodbridge, Virginia. The industrial look of it had appealed to me, but apparently I hadn't gotten used to it. An exposed red brick wall ran the length of the space that could've passed for a warehouse. A transient quality I rather liked. On one end was a cook's kitchen in stainless that fed my culinary fantasy. Between the bed and the well-equipped kitchen were sofas and a dining table in one open space. Spring cleaning would merely require good water pressure and a long garden hose, if I ever wanted to test the theory.

Except for a pile of moving boxes, the place looked like an upgrade I didn't deserve.

"Shit."

I raked a hand through my hair and when I felt the cool of my damp bed, I yanked off the T-shirt I'd soaked with night sweats and glanced at the clock on my nightstand. Four-thirty in the morning. I gave thought to sleeping again, but I suspected my mind wouldn't let me rest now. It harbored too many dark places to hold me prisoner.

I got up, stripped the sheets from my bed, and tugged off my boxers. Naked, I hit the shower to wash off the tainted remnants of the dream. With my hands braced on the tiled wall, I stood under the showerhead and let the hot steamy water run down my face and shoulders, as if it would be easy to forget.

"There's no light without the dark."

I repeated what my mother always told me as a kid, after I'd wake up shaking. In the intimacy of shadows I still heard her on quiet nights. She got me to understand I could hate and crave my dreams, but my internal struggle turned my mind into a battlefield where opposing energies fought inside me. The way I dreamed had taken over my life like an undiagnosed mental condition to which there was no cause and no cure. All that remained was acceptance, but everything in my life had gotten complicated.

After I got out of the shower and toweled off, I decided more sweat would be a thing of beauty and put on my running gear. Living alone had its drawbacks, but not having anyone around to tell me that I was crazy for taking a shower and washing off the spoils of my dream before I ran, wasn't one of them.

My new loft apartment butted up against a lighted trail system that snaked through a greenbelt and wetlands preserve. Ten miles of hills usually left me exhausted at the right pace. Abusing my body with a punishing run beat the alternatives of forced therapy if anyone at my work found out why I couldn't sleep.

I'd chosen to move not long ago, outside Washington DC and nearer to Quantico, for a shorter commute. If I didn't travel so much, I might've appreciated setting down roots, but after I laced up my running shoes, I stood and stared down at a stack of unopened moving boxes. They were in plain sight as a chronic reminder. The absurdity of those boxes had become symbolic—a cardboard testament to my nomadic, unencumbered, uncommitted personal life. With my work, I was all in, but when it came to taking care of me, I had turned into an abandoned pile of unopened boxes filled with contents I didn't want to see.

Before I got out the door, my cell phone rang and life beckoned. I looked at my watch. *Five-twenty.* It had to be work—and this time of morning, the news would never be good.

"Townsend."

"SSA Townsend? We've got a request for assistance. A familiar one, I'm afraid. I'm sending you and your team to Seattle. The jet leaves in two hours. You'll be briefed en route. Your team's being notified as we speak."

I recognized the voice of Anne Reynolds, my unit chief of the FBI's Behavioral Analysis Unit 4 under ViCAP. She'd recruited me fresh out of college from the University of Maryland, but it wasn't until three years ago I ended up under her seasoned supervision in the Violent Criminal Apprehension Program, hunting serial offenders. I led my own team under her watch as a Supervisory Special Agent.

Seattle. I knew what that meant. Our UNSUB, that the news media had dubbed the Totem Killer, had erected another work of art, but I couldn't help feel our Unknown Subject's hunting ground had been fate messing with me. To hear I'd soon be landing in Seattle brought more significance to the puzzle of my dream.

I had personal connections there I'd been avoiding. Apparently providence had other ideas.

"Is it TK?" I asked.

"Yeah. Wear good boots. I hear the terrain is a challenge. This one's bad, Ryker. Worse than the others."

"Worse is hard to fathom. Thanks for the heads up."

The call soon ended, but her words stayed.

This one's bad.

Her warning lingered in my head as I went to my closet to grab a few things. I had a ready bag that I kept at work, carry-on luggage filled with everything I'd need to stay a few nights. Whenever a call came for FBI assistance, I didn't have to go home to pack. I could hit 'wheels up' time without breaking a sweat.

It struck me that I must've had the dream for a reason, one I would find out about soon enough. I'd stopped questioning the timing of my nightmares and my peculiar ability to conjure them—and since the death of my mother I never talked about my so-called gift—or visions, as she'd called them.

Over the years I'd covered up my ability and amassed my secrets. I explained my leaps in logic to colleagues as the science of profiling, but I'd learned to trust the elusive messages hidden within my dreams—even when they taunted me.

I accepted them like death and taxes.

***

Snoqualmie Pass- Cascade Mountains
Outside Seattle
Ryker Townsend

I sidestepped down a steep embankment with my boots cutting into dirt and tufts of grass. Dressed in khaki tactical pants and a navy polo with my Glock 21 in a holster, I wore my uniform to crime scenes when I could. The stench of decomp had a nasty way of bonding to fabric. Since I didn't always know how bad it would be, I'd taken precautions and had a heavy duty plastic bag in my luggage to seal the smell until I could sterilize my gear. As the terrain leveled out, a dense canopy of Hemlock and Fir trees towered over me and blocked the steel gray of an overcast sky as a fine mist dappled my FBI windbreaker and cap.

"This is random...and remote."

Why here? The UNSUB picked an isolated spot for his body dump. That sent up a flare that our unknown subject had become bolder in stretching his boundaries.

No one on my team spoke as we trudged through the wet brush toward the crime scene. Like me, the others were steeling themselves for what they'd find. Every investigator had their thing—a way to mentally prepare for what they would see—for what they would bring home.

When the flash of a dull fleeting shadow crossed my path, looking like a wisp of black smoke hovering over the ground, I glanced up to catch the dark wings of a raven cutting through the trees and the computer part of my brain kicked in.

Raven. A Trickster god. Prevalent myth in the Pacific Northwest. Poe. Edgar Allan.

My mind acted like a hard drive of stored random facts, especially at stress times. Sometimes they hit me hard and I blurted them aloud. That made dating a challenge. I'd always been drawn to intelligent women, but once I let them into my world, crossing that line usually ended any relationship. I simply had no interest in hiding who I was.

At the sight of the raven, keywords pummeled my brain to trigger imagery and I flashed on pages in a book I'd read, but spotting the bird meant something else. Scavengers would've already hit the crime scene and done their damage. All things considered, I preferred thinking of mythology and Edgar Allan Poe. If I had more of an appreciation for the circle of life, I might've embraced the synergy of being nothing more than walking worm food.

"We caught a break this time," Special Agent Lucinda Crowley said as she walked alongside me. She was my number two and another profiler on my team. "The local field office dispatched agents to preserve the scene before the locals trampled over it."

"Yeah, good," I said.

I stopped and gazed toward the next rise. I didn't have to ask how far the crime scene was. A circle of ravens and crows had gathered. Their black winged bodies cut across the gray sky like an ominous Hitchcock montage. The eerie echo of their squawks and their frenzied aerial acrobatics told me all I needed to know.

My body tensed and I emptied my mind to brace for what I'd see as I hit the crest of the hill.

It never failed. When I looked down to the clearing below, standing shoulder to shoulder with my team, a familiar twist hit my gut. I stared at the grisly work of the Totem Killer and forced myself to look beyond the shocking horror. Every severed limb was someone not coming home—a brother, a husband, a boyfriend, a son. The violation clenched my belly, but I owed it to each of the victims not to turn away.

I would have to speak for them now.

"Dear, God," someone muttered.

A monolith of bloodied flesh stood fifteen feet high like a statue to be idolized. Dismembered legs, arms, and faces were tied to a tree to make a macabre tower. As exhausted as I was, my eyes tricked me into seeing severed limbs that twitched and slithered like entwined snakes under the circling cloud of ravens. When I blinked, the bodies stopped writhing and I let out the breath I'd been holding, but I'd gotten a taste for the dreams that would punish me later.

"We are your sons. We are your husbands. We are everywhere. And there will be more of your children dead tomorrow."

I couldn't take my eyes off the bodies as I recited the quote.

"Who said that?" Crowley asked.

"Ted Bundy."

I wanted to believe in God, but standing there, I couldn't. With what I see, I don't hear him anymore.

I didn't want to look, but I couldn't turn away. Seeing the depraved display from a distance gave me a perspective that would haunt me. Body parts were broken down to their artistic elements and artfully strapped to a tree, making a mockery of real Totems seen throughout the Pacific Northwest. Where most people would only be revolted, I forced myself to see the symmetry and the attention to detail of a meticulous mind. I saw the artist behind the work. It's how I compartmentalized the shock and kept my objectivity.

The way I saw the scene spoke volumes of the killer.

I ignored what it said about me.

I headed down the slope, unable to take my eyes off the Totem. The peeled skins of faces were stretched and nailed in a neat row down one side. I suspected TK did the faces as an inventory list—his version of a head count. A line of bent legs were attached upside down, flaring out to make a visual ledge, and a ring of butt cheeks and two severed penises dangled at the base. A spray of arms were fixed as if they were raised in prayer, exalting the freshest body at the top.

A fleeting thought hit me.

"The way they look in moonlight. The memories...and the power of your creation."

I said the words aloud to give my first impressions gravity, but it felt as if someone else had spoken. A distant muffled voice filled my head. My voice, yet *not*. The moon and its shadows painted folds of dead flesh. Questions struck me. I wondered how the Totem of severed limbs would've looked at night—how the intimacy would've *felt*—when the UNSUB must have fashioned it.

I let my mind go there. I never liked it, but I couldn't afford to filter the darkness. For the victims, I had to allow the killer in.

"He left you whole," I said these words aloud, not caring if anyone else heard me. "You must've been special, my unlucky friend."

I found it helped to speak to the dead. It was an ice breaker for when they returned the favor during the autopsy where they shared their secrets in the only way they could. Talking to the dead at the scene reminded me they were someone's child or lover...or lost brother.

This time our UNSUB gave us a gift.

A whole body would allow us to examine what the killer did to his victims. We could enhance our profile. The autopsy would be key, but beyond the evidence my team would uncover, the killer had deliberately flaunted his ability to get away with murder by giving up an entire body for us to study.

Pure arrogance.

"This is one sick son of a bitch," a local cop said as he glanced at me. He expected me to agree, but I didn't confirm or deny.

I simply resisted the temptation to demonize the human beings I hunted by calling them names. Most people did it, but I couldn't afford to give in to the impulse. I had to get into their heads and keeping an open mind helped me to understand them. The fact I could do this instinctively had been one of the reasons Unit Chief Reynolds had recruited me.

"The stuff of nightmares," Crowley said as we got closer.

She looked up and so did I. Death cast its pallor on both of us and the whine of flies escalated—the sound from my sleep.

It's happening. Again.

I'd quit being surprised at how similar my dreamlike visions were to actual crime scenes I'd not seen before. I'd never told anyone about my disturbing episodes with déjà vu. I chalked them up to bad memories leaking out. There were places in my head—deep seated in my brain—that were hidden behind closed doors of my making. The barriers, the way I compartmentalized, allowed me to cope and do my job.

But my dreams *opened* those doors.

Seeing the horror never got easier. I looked at dead bodies as if they were an intellectual exercise to analyze. I used to think that helped, but lately I've had my doubts. My mind housed the memory of countless dead faces. From my own hellish repository, the dead rose up and visited me in my sleep, coiling from my head as gruesome puzzle pieces when cases were similar.

"We should've stopped for coffee." I winced.

Without a caffeine fix, I'd hit empty.

"What's wrong with your face?" Lucinda Crowley

asked.

I shot a sideways glance at her. It hurt.

"You'd be the better judge, but if you must know, I'm engaged in a mêlée with an arduous headache. My back's to the wall."

Crowley gave me a look I'd seen before.

"Drop the ten dollar words. This isn't Jeopardy," she said. "Take one of your chill-lax pills. I'm sure it's not terminal...*yet*."

'Your optimism gives me strength."

"I'm here to serve."

From inside my windbreaker, I pulled out a bottle of aspirins and popped a couple to choke down dry before I grabbed my sunglasses and put them on. The brightness of the overcast sky hurt my eyes, but I had another reason for needing my shades. The dark lenses distanced me from the shock as I let my gaze drift to the faces nailed to the bark.

"Five this time," I said.

Four skinned faces lined the pole beneath the full body of a naked man at the top, splayed to look like Da Vinci's 'Vitruvian Man.' The victims were all men. I stared up at the last kill—the special one the killer had chosen for the high point of his creation. Dead eyes were filmy white. As I stared into them, random particulars helped me deal with my natural revulsion.

Corneas became cloudy and opaque after death. It's natural. It happens. It's pure science. Takes a few hours if the eyes are open. Twenty-four hours if the eyes are closed. Cause: Potassium concentration in the vitreous humor. A thick jelly-like substance in the eyeball.

I took a slow measured breath and my gaze shifted to the mouth that gaped open to capture the terror of his final minutes. He'd been stabbed in the heart. He would've drowned in his own blood from a severed artery, but not before his body had been carved as if he were a human *Etch A Sketch*.

Poor man.

"Did you hear me, Ryker? I got us a meet and greet. Come on."

Crowley had interrupted my link to the bodies. Unlike other investigators, I used more than my eyes and my mind to take in a crime scene. My sixth sense had a tenacious grip that was often difficult to shake off. Being interrupted felt as if Crowley had shoved me into the deep end of the pool, when I couldn't swim. She didn't know how profoundly I connected to the dead.

I didn't trust *anyone* with my secret. Not even Crowley, a woman I considered to be a tolerable friend.

"Sorry, yes." I waved a hand to let her pass. "You play the brilliant flash and I'll be the thunderbolt that follows."

Her eye roll told me she recognized my version of the bastardized quote. No doubt I'd used it before.

"It's definitely too early for Voltaire. Let me do the talking."

"My aching head thanks you."

After introductions with the locals who had requested the FBI's help, we set up a game plan for the investigation and my team got to work to lend their expertise and resources. Dr. Julian Martinez was a Medical Examiner and would oversee the autopsies once we got the bodies back to home base. That would give us continuity across the jurisdictions our UNSUB operated. Special Agents Devin Hutchison and Camilla Devore were my evidence recovery techs and the last member of my team had stayed in DC, my computer specialist and resource diva, Sinead Royce.

When I could focus again on the crime scene—after pressing flesh with the locals—I had questions for Lucinda Crowley.

"Did this masterpiece come with a note?" I asked. "Our boy loves taking credit."

"Yeah, it's already been bagged and tagged." She held it out to me. "First thing I asked for, but this one is different."

From the expression on her face, I wouldn't like the difference. I pulled on my latex gloves before I took the bagged piece of evidence in my hand. At the last two crime scenes, the UNSUB had left a generic message, taunting the FBI in a brazen display of superiority.

This time, the letter had *my* name at the top.

"He's fixated on you now," she said.

I felt her eyes on me, but I didn't meet her gaze. The typed message on the page was personal, directed at me. I read every word.

This one is for you, Ryker Townsend, Golden Boy of the FBI. My best work yet. It'll be hard to top, but you know I will.

A voice and a touch yanked me back to reality.

"Are you okay?" Crowley reached for my arm. "I'm sure this is nothing more than our UNSUB following the case in the media, but still. It's creepy."

Seeing my name in print, in a message from the killer, had been unsettling, but as leader to the investigating team, I couldn't let it show. I had to remain objective. My reaction wasn't about saving face or being the tough guy. My show of strength was for my team, for Crowley who would one day be in my shoes and lead her own investigations.

"I'm fine. The job is still the same." I handed her back the killer's note. "Who found the bodies?"

"Local cops got an anonymous tip to 911. If it's like the others, tracing the call won't give us anything. TK loves prepaid burner phones, but we'll go through the usual paces."

Crowley's dark hair was tied in a pony tail that jutted out the back of her FBI cap and her pale blue eyes squinted as she stared up the Totem of dead bodies. She had a quiet intensity, but her eyes never hid her humanity. That vulnerability had been her strength and weakness. No one walked away from a crime scene like this without being indelibly marked by it.

"I saw tire tracks from the ridge," I said. "Did the locals have any ideas how our killer gained access to such a remote location?"

"Yeah. They said whoever did this, they must've known about the service road. This is private property, but there's a gravel road that gives access to a cell tower." She pointed toward a stand of trees and a metal structure jutted above them. "The road's only used when there's service trouble. The lock at the gate was busted with a bolt cutter. No traffic, no interruptions would've given TK plenty of time to work his perverted magic."

The Totem Killer had been operating in the Pacific Northwest for nearly two years, abducting and killing several men at a time to create a grotesque steeple. Late last year, there were two discoveries, a few months apart. Winter hadn't been a deterrent. This year there were two more Totems and it wasn't even July yet. The body count had grown to fourteen, including the five bodies on this tribute pole.

A new record of victims meant the killer had ratcheted up the abductions and he'd gained confidence in honing a more distinctive signature, given the more detailed mutilations and dramatic posing of the bodies.

"Five this time means it's getting easier, but with the escalation, his high isn't lasting. He'll be looking for more. He won't wait. We have to monitor missing person cases to see if we can get ahead of him."

I felt my jaw tighten and my fists clenched as I stepped closer to the severed limbs. Like the other staged scenes, the flesh of the arms and legs were carved into and stripped away with an elaborate scrolling, done with a fine surgical knife. A box cutter or serrated blade would have puckered the skin. I didn't need Dr. Martinez to tell me what I could see. The bone joints were cut with precision, not jagged as I'd seen in the first victims. The UNSUB's tools had become more refined.

When I saw Dr. Martinez walking toward me, I said to my medical examiner, "He's become a true artisan with flesh and getting better at his craft."

"Like a good butcher." The man grimaced. "Similar to the last known victims, there's bruising and deep abrasions on ankles and wrists where they were bound. It appears they were abducted and held like the others."

A short man with intense dark eyes, Dr. Martinez never got rattled, even at the most heinous crime scenes. He was a good husband and father of three boys. I always wondered how he kept the demons from his door, but maybe his family kept him grounded by giving him something to go home to. Because of my dreams, I didn't let anyone get too close—for their sake and mine.

"TOD will be a challenge," the doctor said. "If these severed limbs and facial skin are like the others, they could have been frozen after death. If that's the case, rigor would've started when they were thawed. We'll have to run tests on other factors to give you an estimated time of death."

"The dead guy at the top appears to be the last killed, a work of art he wanted to flaunt," I said. "He's whole for a reason. He's our best bet to find out more about our UNSUB."

Identifying the last victim would allow my team

to back track a time line of the killer's activity to determine when the guy might've been abducted...and how.

"With any luck. As for identification of the limbs, we'll look for other aspects to help us, like an age approximation from bone joints, blood characteristics, any obvious medical conditions, scars or birthmarks, and we'll look for old bone fractures or surgical pins through x-rays. I'll put a rush on it."

"Thanks, doctor."

My ME waved a hand as he left and I got back to work. Alone with my thoughts again, I flashed on the body parts as if they were a riddle to solve. I took a knee and removed my sunglasses for a better view after I saw a pattern. With my head cocked, I glanced up at the Totem from a different angle. The move intensified the pain of my throbbing headache, but I had to do it.

As I gazed up the tree strapped with severed limbs, a pair of eyes found mine. It was an instant connection, like locking eyes with a stranger across a room, except that one of us was dead. I couldn't turn away. Whatever I felt, it was visceral and real.

My eyes burned and everything blurred around the edges as if I stared down a shadowy funnel. Any noise I had heard before faded to a muffled and distant hum. I couldn't stop my reaction. I tried to break the link, but no matter where I moved, the dead eyes followed me. That had never happened before.

I won't lie. It scared me.

Most people would question their own sanity. They'd know with certainty this wasn't normal, not even a little, but in my experience, '*weird*' had a broader definition. So the fact I wondered if this feeling came from a dead man reaching out to me—because he had something to say—didn't feel like a stretch in the bendy rules of my world.

It should have.

A dead guy staring at me should've been a warning that I was unstable and unraveling like the thread on my windbreaker, but I preferred to believe that I had a way with the dead than deal with a harsh fact.

I'd become desperate to understand what was happening to me, something I wasn't sure I could—or *should*—stop, because the big picture wasn't about me. No matter how this investigation tore into my life, fourteen families had lost a son.

The killing *had* to stop, no matter what it cost me.

Chapter Three

Snoqualmie Pass- Cascade Mountains
Outside Seattle
Ryker Townsend

The eyes of the dead man at the top of the Totem fixed on me as if he were still alive and trying to tell me something. His lifeless eyes had turned milky white and had become sweet candy to a cloud of gnats and flies, but I could've sworn his head moved.

Oh, God. What the hell?

After I heard the click of a camera, I blinked and took a deep breath. I put my sunglasses back on and Crowley's voice came next.

"At the risk of sounding like a pain in the ass, I gotta ask. Do you feel okay?" She wasn't giving it a rest. Her attention to detail was what made her good at her job, and a relentless friend when she smelled trouble.

"Yes, but I'm waving the white flag." I turned from her. "The headache has won."

This time when my eyes found the dead man's face, I'd lost my strange connection to the body. No muffled white noise. No blurry edges that made it easier to focus on those dead eyes. All of that had gone and I felt...lost. But when my gaze shifted back to Crowley, she didn't look satisfied. I knew her well enough to know I needed to distract her.

"Come here and check this out," I told her. "The Totem has a different feel from this angle."

She knelt by me and looked up to where I pointed. The symmetry of the arrangement as it silhouetted the sky took on a different feel. It struck me that the killer had designed every aspect of the array, right down to the strategic placement of the metal stakes used to tie the parts together with rope and wire.

"You're right. The structure is remarkable," she said.

"Everything is incorporated and has its place as a...thorough design element. I can almost see the online blueprint of how he conceived this."

I got the sense the killer had mapped out the sequence and balance on a computer using a software program to play with the gruesome elements until he crafted the ultimate design. Such a plan would allow assembly to be executed into a step by step 'paint by the numbers' exercise.

"The UNSUB left a metal hoist behind...to get the body up there without breaking a sweat. An elegant solution," I told Crowley.

"We'll do a search for the make and model sold in the area...or online," she said. "It could turn up something."

"Yes. Good." We both knew the search would likely come up empty, but we had to do it.

The precision and the grandeur of the showy spectacle—paired with my memory of the raven that I'd seen earlier—triggered something I'd read. I didn't believe in coincidences. Even the chance sighting of the bird meant something to a mind willing to believe everything held a purpose. Whenever my brain jumped, I trusted the leap. Crowley and the members of my team were used to my odd idiosyncrasies.

"Ever hear of the Trickster archetype in mythology, Crowley?" I asked, as she took photos of the scene.

"Don't geek out on me. All I remember about mythology I got from the Avengers movie. Thor is hot. He can hammer me anytime."

Crowley had her moments when she made me smile, even at a crime scene. I fought a grin inside, but didn't let it show.

"A Trickster gets off on disobeying normal rules of conventional behavior, often in malicious ways."

"I'd say severing bodies into Lego pieces falls into the malicious category." She stopped working long enough to listen.

"A Trickster varies its appearance to create an illusion. It uses wit and cleverness, rather than brute force, to evade trouble and it thrives on manipulation."

"You think our profile is off. I mean, really off base, don't you?"

"I don't know. After seeing this new one, it feels like smoke and mirrors to me. A grand illusion of misdirection. Our UNSUB flaunts what he does. He's organized. He thinks through every detail and plans his moves, knowing he's way ahead of us. He's holding all the cards and we're only reacting to whatever *he* does."

Any profile was a work in progress and with every crime scene, my team's view of the killer was constantly checked to make sure it was still valid, but with all the CSI shows on TV and in movies, it was too easy for criminals to know how law enforcement worked. Killers had notions of forensics or they planted evidence from another crime scene to distract the police and mislead them. Most serial killers were of average intelligence, but TK felt like an exception.

The last thing I wanted to do was underestimate him.

"He definitely has an ego." She aimed her camera toward the top of the Totem and took a photo of the last kill.

I looked up to where her camera lens pointed.

"Our guy likes playing God. He put him at the top and kept him whole to show how special he was in life. The rest of these bodies are part of an aesthetic design. They're chum in the water, second rate meat fillers compared to him. He's the main course, the real reason for all of this. He meant something."

"Meant what?"

"I don't know yet, but this has scope and depth. There's a story here and it's central to him. The meat fillers have been...foreplay."

Sometimes the callous way I declared what was in the killer's head made it seem as if those thoughts were mine. It shocked me to hear the words come out of my mouth. Sometimes even the tone of my voice sounded gruff and malevolent, as if it came from someone else.

Crowley did a double take when she heard me.

"Sorry," I said. "I say things without filter. It's my process. Sometimes I want to apologize, but I won't. Not with you."

"No, I understand. It's okay," she said. "You're scary good at your job. It's like I can hear the UNSUB...through you. What made you think about the Trickster mythology?"

"It struck me when I saw a raven in the woods on our hike in. In certain Native cultures, the raven is a Trickster."

"You should consider donating your brain to science."

"After I'm dead?"

"Whenever."

When I shot her a raised eyebrow, she smiled and asked, "You got a new theory on the Totem design?"

"Totems are used to honor the dead or tell a story or express a belief. If there's a story here, it's about our killer and his connection to the body positioned at the top. His shining star feels like a misguided attempt to pay tribute or 'out him' somehow, but there's nothing that honors the dead here. He's tossed us a morsel by giving us a corpse. He's confident and getting bolder. All the other displays that came before were only practice runs...for this one."

I raised a hand to point at each body down the line.

"After his crowning achievement, the progression of bodies diminishes their status. Their placement could be based on the timing of each kill, but more than likely it's a ranking system. Our killer targets and culls out certain victims of his choosing. He humiliates and uses them while they're still alive. After he tires of them, he harvests a body part he perceives as their strength...to show he can take it from them. That he has the power, the control."

I sank slowly into my dark world, alone. Everything around me clouded over. If Crowley had asked me any more questions, I didn't hear them. I stared up at the bloodied victims—rapt in the head of the killer—and puzzled through what TK had left me to figure out. The steady rhythm of my heart thrummed the inside of my ears as I let my eyes take in everything.

"Why here? Why leave a whole one? And why didn't you freeze him?"

I didn't expect an answer from Crowley or anyone. I only needed to keep talking.

"You ever trust someone you shouldn't have, Crowley?" I didn't wait for her answer. "These guys did. Our UNSUB knows how to be invisible and blend in without anyone taking notice. He gets them to trust him before he steals their lives."

I paced around the totem and stared up at the horror.

"Can you imagine...the fear? It's like a lingering

energy coming off these bodies. TK lulled them in and...tricked them. He got off on looking into their eyes. He had to see the moment when they knew he would take *everything* from them."

Being alone—in my forced mental exile—it helped me go where I needed to go. I puzzled through questions that led me to a reconstruction of events, the sequence and the reasons that would motivate the UNSUB. I needed to make a checklist of what the new scene revealed and compare it to my profile notes. After I stepped back to the edge of the clearing, I made a slow circle around the grim Totem.

"Overkill, ante mortem mutilations, posing. These things are part of your fantasy."

Our UNSUB embraced his signature with a flourish. He tortured his victims. I saw him as a mixed offender. He left contradictory messages at the body dump, appearing highly organized and intelligent in his MO, yet frenzied when he actually killed, selecting a knife as his weapon of choice.

Look in the mirror. What would you see?

I'd become engrossed in the mind of a psychopath and pictured a house of a thousand mirrors. Everywhere he turned his face reflected whatever he needed to, in order to stay hidden. If anyone looked at him, they only saw what he wanted them to see. Psychopaths were often charming, definitely manipulative, and they knew how to gain trust. They could mimic emotion and appear normal. Some even had families and were capable of holding onto long term relationships.

This one carefully planned out every detail, from how he hunted, how he tortured his victims, and how he disposed of the bodies. I saw his design in everything—the things he let me see—but his face was nothing more than a shadow behind the curtain in my vision. I was chasing smoke, yet I felt his taunting menace.

I would savor what I saw—to bank it for later in my dreams—but the next time I blinked, time had stuttered to a stop and I was alone. One second I'd been surrounded by investigators and evidence techs. The next I stood on the edge of a silent, depleted crime scene. My ERTs would be hauling evidence to the vehicles and Dr. Martinez would've taken responsibility for the body bags.

My team knew how I operated. They knew I needed isolation until I called it quits on my own, but something made me turn toward the mountains behind me. Still in the throes of wherever my mind had gone, I heard a whispered voice on the wind saying the words in the message.

This one is for you, Ryker Townsend...Golden Boy....

Fragments of my dream, the flashing red light and the never-ending drone of the flies magnified, until the weighty presence of a dark and faceless body drew near me. No one was around me, yet I knew what I sensed. I took off my sunglasses and squinted into the Cascade Mountains.

I didn't question the feeling that somebody watched me.

I had felt it at every scene where TK had left his bloody trail of severed limbs, but the sensation had deeper roots here—roots that I'd brought with me. Being close to Seattle, my conscience easily played its part in stirring ghosts from my past. Maybe it didn't matter what or who had instigated the feeling. All of it welled inside me—the good and the bad of a past that defined me—to provoke my paranoia.

TK stalked his victims and got off on watching law enforcement chase their tails. Now the Totem Killer had my name. I told Crowley that it wasn't a big deal, but it had been.

To me.

***

The look on Ryker Townsend's face while he read the message addressed to him had been worth every effort, every risk. From a ridge in the Cascade Mountains, the Totem Killer peered through high-tech binoculars to watch every facial flinch, every grimace, every telling nuance of the FBI agent's face. Sprawled in the dirt, the Totem Killer had stayed motionless in the growing heat of the day and kept a low profile so as not to be noticed.

It had been worth the discomfort.

In person and from a distance, the FBI agent looked taller and more physically imposing. The way he studied every last detail of the Totem had rekindled memories for each body strapped on the tree. The cries of pain, the fear in their eyes when they knew how everything would end, hit a crescendo that led to the grinding of bone, the crack of a joint, and the meaty resistance of flesh against the saw.

All of that came back with a flourish, thanks to the profiler. It was as if Ryker had relived the intimate seduction of death—a voyeur to every fleshy slice. The Totem Killer liked that. It was intoxicating. It was as empowering and blood churning as being watched while having sex.

Ryker moved with a fluid grace like a shrewd predator. The hunter. Studying every move he made around the clearing had been fascinating, but something had gripped the FBI agent when he looked up at the whole one. The perfect one. He stared at the dead man for far too long for it to be nothing. When Golden Boy shifted his gaze into the mountains behind him, looking for something—someone—that made the Totem Killer smile.

Yes, I'm here. You feel me, don't you? That's good. Real good.

Ryker had seen something, perhaps an unintended thing or maybe a subtlety only the profiler observed with his skilled eye. Whatever it had been, stirred the Totem Killer's blood like...

Foreplay.

Ryker Townsend had been intriguing—and unfortunately for him—*unforgettable*.

***

Sea-Tac Airport
Hours later
Ryker Townsend

On the ride to the airstrip with my team, I didn't have much to say. My mind had become an inventory of things I wanted to tell them before I stayed behind and my need for quiet didn't change after we'd arrived.

Some criminalists resorted to a peculiar dark humor to get them through a crime scene. Anything remotely absurd about the body, or an unusual cause of death, pushed them over a familiar line they crossed with ease. The ability to laugh in the face of death kept them grounded in a world that made more sense with rules and reasonable order.

But in the presence of bodies, I got quiet, which I'm sure pleased Crowley. I opened my mind and listened to what the bodies had to say. Victims planted their seeds in me to allow the dreams to take root. Even in body bags or on an autopsy table, I felt the phantom life force of the dead as if a part of their essence lingered for me.

I needed the silence to connect with them.

As my team loaded the bodies and the evidence onto the private jet, I thought about the eerie feeling that had touched me when I was alone at the crime scene, an inkling I couldn't talk about with the others. That sensation—and the deeply personal link it had to unfinished business in my past—made it hard to separate the insights of the objective profiler from the instincts of a guy who had lived with strange prophetic dreams his whole life.

Before I told my team what I'd decided, I called my unit chief first. Anne Reynolds answered on the second ring.

"I need a personal day. Something has...come up," I told her. "I know you thought I'd come back tonight, but..."

I explained how I would stay in touch with the latest developments of the investigation through video conferencing. I'd done it before, but my unit chief pressed me for more. My smoke screen of requesting a personal day hadn't stopped her from asking questions.

"What's up, Ryker? You don't do personal days. Talk to me."

My other reason for staying overnight was too private to disclose in confidence, even to a boss I respected.

"I'm asking for a little privacy. One night. I have...something to do here," I explained. "I'll fly back on my own. All costs on me."

My unit chief answered me with silence. It was a tactic of hers. Most people filled the gap in conversation, when it would've been in their best interest to keep their mouth shut. I had never fallen for her ploy, but the woman had a way of reading me, even over the phone.

"There's something you're not telling me. I get that you have a personal life, Ryker. Take what time you need, but what aren't you saying about that crime scene? I heard from the locals that the killer left a note with your name on it. That's new."

"He could get my name from the media. There's been plenty of coverage, but this crime scene felt...different. I can't explain it yet. We got a whole body. That has to be significant and..."

"And what?"

"I felt a stronger connection to TK, like he was...watching."

"Killers do that. They watch. They pretend to be witnesses, to insinuate themselves into an investigation. You know that."

"Yeah, but this was different." I sighed. "I'm asking for personal time. I'd like to stay over for a private matter, but it's...more than that. Call it a gut instinct."

I had a feeling that if I got on the plane, the link I had with TK would be broken. I knew how crazy that sounded, but there it was. I couldn't risk testing the theory by leaving.

"You're still holding back something from me, but I respect your privacy, Ryker. What'll you need?"

As I watched my team load the plane from inside the small terminal building on the private airstrip, I smiled. My boss had her own version of intuition.

"I'll have Crowley get me an ID on our last victim and everything we can get on him. I'll take care of my personal business and figure out my next step from there. Staying behind could turn out to be a good thing."

"Keep in touch."

"Yes, ma'am."

I ended the call and walked onto the tarmac outside the hangar to tell my team I'd be staying overnight. Crowley turned and narrowed her eyes at me as if she could read my mind. After she crossed her arms, I shrugged. Her ability to communicate with me without words had been there from the start.

The rest of my team needed a heads up on my change of plans, but not Lucinda Crowley. After I'd told my team the news I'd be staying in Seattle one more night for personal reasons, I gave them my thoughts on the crime scene.

"I'm still seeing this guy as a commuter who operates outside his body dump sites, but he's careful about picking spots where he has time and isolation to stage them," I said. "He gave us a whole body. Let's use his ego to our advantage."

The UNSUB had flawless execution and had gotten bolder. I didn't like what that meant. He wasn't going to stop. He was only getting...comfortable.

"Remember, we're dealing with three other crime scenes, not only this one. Crime scene one, he abducts them," I told them. "Scene two, he takes them somewhere else where he has time to torture them and a quiet isolated place to do it. That's where he's probably killing and freezing them until he's ready to stage their bodies. Scene three, is the truck he hauls them with. We found tire treads at this scene and the others."

"Why the remote location?" Crowley asked. "He stretched his circle into the Cascades. Why do you think he did that?"

I had my theory on why, but my thoughts ventured dangerously close to the secret I'd held back from them, about my visions and my strong use of intuition. I needed time to think, but my team deserved an answer.

"He wanted to watch us. In the open. Watch me," I said. "It's not my choice to be on his radar, but apparently I am now. With any luck, we can use it."

Cam and Hutch exchanged looks and didn't say anything. Crowley had a different reaction. She narrowed her eyes and focused on me.

"Is that why the message had your name on it?"

"No. I think you had it right the first time. This guy has seen the media coverage. He's messing with my head. More of his ego."

Lucinda was protective of her team. The UNSUB using my name riled her. I saw it in her eyes and had to defuse her by giving out assignments before she targeted me and dug deeper.

"Crowley. Input your observations and upload your photos into the ViCAP and PROFILER databases. I'll add my penny's worth when I get back. In the mean time, you're in charge. I'm only a phone call away if you need me." I fixed my eyes on her. "Call me on anything...and for any reason. Understood?"

"Yeah. Understood."

After Crowley nodded, I turned my attention to my ERTs.

"Hutch and Cam, I want you two to focus on our victimology profile. Having a body to autopsy will give us more. We need to get a handle on how he targets them and where he finds them. Our UNSUB knows how to be invisible to his victims. He blends in without them noticing. They trust him. We're missing the connection he makes with his victims."

The autopsy would be critical. I wanted the last victim to be his last kill, Wishful thinking, perhaps. I couldn't afford to indulge in it. I had to be a realist and assume the worst case scenario. Feeling the pressure of stopping this guy from killing again kept me up nights, but it also lit a fire in me to put a face and name to our UNSUB.

"One more thing."

I took a deep breath and clenched my jaw. I knew what I was about to tell them would add pressure on my team, but they had to know the stakes.

"Our UNSUB has escalated his kills. I think he has his next victim in his sights or he could already be working on him. At least, we have to assume he's got the next one."

My team looked stunned at first, but their shocked expressions were soon replaced with their usual fierce determination. Like me, they were hungry to find this guy and expose him.

"We have to know everything we can on his last victim," I said. "Nothing is too trivial. Follow your instincts. My gut is telling me that he's got his next prize and there's a missing persons report with a name we need to find. Assume the clock is ticking on someone's son or brother. We'll hit it hard when I see you tomorrow."

Taking any time off the case felt like bad timing, but I knew the autopsy would be done tomorrow and would take hours. My ME couldn't finalize his report without lab results either. I had a window of time to take care of my brief personal business in Seattle, but I had a strong feeling that I was meant to stay behind—something about this crime scene I couldn't explain to anyone.

I wasn't sure I understood it myself.

Before I left my team, Crowley caught my eye and pulled me away from the others to a quiet spot where we could talk.

"I got something you should see. It won't take a second."

She took out her camera and showed me a digital photo she'd taken earlier at the crime scene. The subject of her picture surprised me. She'd taken a photo of *me*—capturing the instant I'd first spotted the dead body staring down at me.

The haunted look in my eyes startled me. I flashed to the instant the corpse fixed on me and blinding images of rotting flesh and dead eyes hit me like a strobe light in a dark room.

My scalp prickled.

"What's your point?" I asked.

"I'm deleting the photo, but that won't fix whatever you saw." She inched closer and lowered her voice. "You've changed. Something's eating at you and you're not letting anyone in. Now you're staying in Seattle. What's the real reason?"

I could've told her of my intention to start a collection of tacky gifts. An absurd refrigerator magnet of the Space Needle would certainly be a step in the right direction. But Crowley had always been smart and although she read me better than most, that didn't give her a right to pry into my life—or pass judgment on my taste in refrigerator bling.

After I turned my back on her without an explanation, I knew she wouldn't settle for a parting shot of my deltoids. She wouldn't give up that *easy*.

"I saw the look in your eyes, Ryker. You were afraid of something. Spill it."

I should've kept walking, but I made the mistake of turning around.

"Let it go, Crowley. Pushing won't get you an answer."

Unfortunately for me, pushing was a Crowley specialty. It's what made her good at her job, but now wasn't the time for flattery. Lucinda Crowley didn't need any encouragement.

"You're a bomb that hasn't gone off, but the fuse is burning." She crossed her arms and stood between me and the hangar.

She'd been right about my burning fuse, but I held tight to my inner smart ass. Crowley was only worried about me.

"Well, when I blow, I'll think of you. Promise."

"That's not funny. Not even close."

"It wasn't meant to be, but I keep my promises.

The day I implode, you'll be on my mind. Are we done?"

She stared at me until I heard wheels cranking in her head and knew I wouldn't like what came out.

"You're a..."

"I'm a what?" I asked.

"You're a...a half-foot taller than a normal person."

"What's that supposed to mean? That I'm tall or a half-foot shy of normal?"

"Can I get back to you?"

Crowley was the only woman who ever made me want to roll my eyes. Even though I'd resisted, she'd worn me down. This time she got an eyebrow twitch. I wasn't in the mood, but when I walked by her, she wasn't done.

"How do you know the things you do...about *this* UNSUB, Ryker? Your instincts are definitely not normal."

I didn't slow down or turn. I was done enough for both of us.

"Let it go, Lucinda."

I knew Crowley would eventually hit bulls-eye if I stayed. She didn't understand that a secret was only a secret if no one else knew, but she had more than her share of tenacity and an unnerving knack for reading me. I didn't say another word. I headed to the airport hangar with the laser roast of her eyes staring holes through my back.

The fact I deserved the heat didn't change things.

Chapter Four

Seattle - Evening
Ryker Townsend

After I rented a vehicle with navigation, I plugged in a Seattle address. I followed the GPS system's audio cues over freeways until an exit and a series of side streets brought me closer to Lake Union.

A winding street took me through a popular strip of trendy restaurants and bars along the waterfront and felt like driving through a post card of the good life. Colorful lights bled across the water in shimmers as the ghost of Mount Rainier hovered on the skyline, awash in the fading pastels of sunset. Homes were nestled into the rolling hillside that surrounded the small lake and white boat masts silhouetted the dying light with well lit houseboats dotting the water's edge. I had a thing for this part of Seattle.

It was a quiet low key oasis in the middle of urban sprawl—a place I could almost forget the dark side of what I did for a living.

As GPS ticked down the distance between me and the address, I slowed my speed to a crawl until the woman with the exceedingly bossy voice told me I'd arrived. The location was not what I had expected. Vehicles were parked on the street in designated spots marked for residents. Beyond that was a locked cyclone gate that secured a wooden dock for moored houseboats. I'd have to know a code to get in or punch a button to an intercom that would announce I was waiting to be invited—an invitation I wasn't sure I would get.

I didn't need the complication.

"What now, genius?"

I shut down the engine and turned off my headlights. Second thoughts closed in as I sat in the dark, but I'd come this far. I peered through deepening shadows to look for the address without much luck. Gripping the steering wheel too hard, I stared at the ribbons of light that stretched across the still lake and debated my next move.

"Don't think. Just do it."

I got out of the vehicle and took a deep breath. The cool night air was ripe with the aromas of grilled steak and seafood coming from the restaurants down the street. I would've listened to my growling stomach more if I wasn't about to confront my past.

The locked gate was an obstacle I wasn't getting around, but a walkway along the lakefront would keep me close enough to see houseboat numbers. Seven boat slips down I found the one I'd come looking for. Lights were on inside. The boxy green and tan painted houseboat had round nautical windows with the drapes open. Toward the rear I saw a dark haired man cooking in the kitchen and heard a muffled song. It proved to be a challenge not to judge his taste in music.

Air Supply...really?

After I slipped into the darkness, my eyes wouldn't settle as I searched for Sarah.

When I didn't see her inside, an urgent sense of guilt took hold of me. Did she live here anymore? Had she gotten a divorce? The fact that I didn't know the answer to even basic questions about her life struck me as pathetic. She had made the decision to never see or talk to me again. Even though I'd respected her choice and kept my distance, I didn't like not being a part of her life. Hated it, in fact.

I'd never been to my sister Sarah's home and never met the man she'd married a year after the funeral of our parents five years ago. I didn't get a wedding invitation, even though Sarah had my mailing address at the University of Maryland. I had to hear about her news from family friends.

The day I'd heard about her getting married put me in a spiral. One minute I had a family and my future prospects looked bright—the next, my parents had died and something dark in me had been triggered. I was alone and plagued by escalating nightmares I didn't understand and I had no one to talk to about it. My mother was the only one who understood and accepted me. Not a day went by that I didn't miss her.

I honestly didn't know what my unit chief had seen in me during my final year at UMD that she wanted to recruit, but the fact she wanted me— *someone* needed me—made the job offer an easier decision to make when I had nothing of my old life to leave behind.

"Damn it, Sarah. Where are you?"

My one and only search for my sister had been a cursory paper trail, without 'eyes on' photographs. I only wanted to know she was alive and well. I hadn't asked for her to be stalked. I'd done a discreet background check through a private investigator and found that Sarah and Jake had settled in Seattle after becoming Mr. and Mrs. Jake Fuller—far away from me. She had gotten her real estate license with Jake financially supporting her efforts as a business developer and architect.

After that I never intruded on her privacy again. I respected her wishes to cut me out of her life. It was how she dealt with the accident that killed our parents—a tragedy she found easier to blame on me. I accepted how she felt after the funeral, but the wall between us had gone up brick by brick over time. The accident only sealed the deal.

If I could have changed things, I would have.

Hindsight sucked.

The way my parents died drove a bigger wedge between me and Sarah. I became an easy target. I didn't understand my sister's need to hate me. I let it happen for her sake, but by that time, my dreams had turned into nightmares and grown worse. My mother's death had pushed me over a line, because I had no one left to tell, no one who wouldn't judge me. I quit talking about how I dreamed. That part of my life got buried—deep.

My nightmares became my payback for being the center—and the reason—for my fragmented family. I thought my sister would reach out to me in time, but as the years went by, I'd lost hope that would ever happen.

"Sarah," I whispered in the dark.

When I didn't see her inside the houseboat, I felt a hollow in the pit of my belly. It was as if I'd lost something important that I didn't even know was missing.

She could've moved and left the state for all I knew. In that moment of doubt, I'd been thrust back to my darkest days after our parents had died, after I'd lost everything that mattered to me. A sudden rush of memories hit me hard—bad ones that slashed at me like fresh wounds. I shut my eyes and winced when I heard my sister's voice in my head—the yelling and the arguments we used to have—the accusations that could never be taken back.

Because Sarah looked like our mother, seeing anger and hatred in her eyes killed me.

"Stop it, Ryker. Quit being the self-appointed poster child of dismal."

I fought the flood of memories. What did I expect? I'd gone looking for my sister and a past I didn't want to relive. I wasn't ready. I turned to leave, but stopped when I heard the clank of a metal gate, followed by the hollow thud of heels on the wood pier and a voice I recognized.

Sarah's voice. She spoke to a child she held in her arms.

It only took one glimpse of the dark haired woman dressed in a business suit for me to know. I'd found Sarah and she had a child who looked to be three or four years old. They were talking and touching, the way a mother spoke to and held a child. Even though I was too far away to hear what they said, there was no mistaking it. The likeness was too strong.

My sister had a little girl.

"Sarah," I whispered.

I had a niece—and I didn't even know her name. *Oh, God.*

I had every intention of walking away, but my sister caught my movement in the shadows. The khaki in my FBI gear didn't exactly make me camouflaged. I'd been a moron, but what else was new?

"Hey. Stop right there."

"Who's that, mommy?" Her little girl pointed toward me. Before I could step out of the dark, my sister deflated me.

"No one, honey," she said. "Go inside and help daddy. I'll be in lickity split."

With my jaw clenched, I stepped into the light, with a cyclone fence between us. I hadn't missed the irony that a barrier separated us.

"Ryker?" She stared at me in disbelief with her arms crossed, until her expression hardened. "Why are you here? What do you want?"

I couldn't find the words. Despite her abrupt cold response to seeing me after all these years, I honestly didn't know why I'd come. Nothing had changed.

"I'm working a case. I thought..."

She didn't let me finish.

"You thought you'd stop by for a chat, catch up on old times? How did you get my address?"

She treated me like a stranger. A stalker. I should've turned and walked away, but an ember burned hot in my belly. I didn't deserve this, not from her.

"I thought time would...help, but I can see you'll never change. You're always gonna blame me for what happened. Well, take a look in the mirror, Sarah. For once in your life, own up to your part."

My words hung in the air like a caustic cloud. I never should've said it. I'd lost my temper and crossed a line I swore I never would. I'd hurt her. It showed in the stunned expression on her face and her eyes welled with tears.

"I'm sorry. I never should've come." I turned and stepped into the shadows and didn't look back, not until she called to me.

"Ryker. Wait."

Hearing her voice gave me hope, but when I faced her, I knew I'd been wrong to believe anything would change between us.

"Don't make me live with this," she said. "I just...can't."

She acted as if I were the one torturing her with our past, like it was all on me.

"But you make *me* live with it, every day," I told her. "You've cut me out of your life. Why? You're all the family I have, Sarah."

"I can't let you in, Ryker. I told my husband you died in the car crash that killed my parents. He doesn't know you exist. Please try to understand," she said. "The day our parents died, you came to me with your crazy dream, telling me how it would happen. It scared me, but I hated how connected you were to mom. I thought you only wanted her attention...again. You were the special one, not me. She loved you...so much."

Tears streaked her face and Sarah sobbed.

"Yeah, you saw how they would die and you told me, but they were only driving to church. Ten minutes away. I never thought..." She broke down. "You're right, I made the choice not to warn them...and I'll have to live with that for the rest of my life. But that's why I haven't told my husband and daughter about you."

"What? I don't understand."

"I don't want you in our lives. If you have another vision about something happening to them..." She stopped and wiped her face. "I couldn't go through that again. I won't. There are things a person shouldn't know. You'd be forced to tell me and I...would be living in constant fear. I'm sorry, Ryker. I'm not as strong as you. I don't know how you live with what you see."

"That's just it, Sarah. Sometimes I c-can't." I couldn't stop the catch in my voice. I prayed she hadn't heard it. "Sometimes it would be nice to have a sister to talk to, someone I don't have to keep secrets from."

What I saw on the day my parents died had triggered my escalating nightmares when it came to violent death. Nothing was simple after that. I'd become an FBI profiler to put my sorry ass misery to good use. Now the dead tell me their story and my mind interprets their message and I fret over missing something—over not doing enough. Because of what happened to my parents, I couldn't stop from pulling back the curtain in my dreams. I knew whatever I saw would be terrible, but I forced my eyes to look.

I *always* looked. No matter how ugly things were, I had to see it—*feel* it—and dream about it. It was my process. My burden. My gift. I don't know what I expected from my sister. I'd cut open a vein and stood bleeding in front of her, but she only shook her head and a tear slid down her cheek. She headed for the door to her houseboat, but turned to me one last time.

"Don't come here again, Ryker. *Please*. I'm begging you."

She closed the door and a profound emptiness squeezed my chest and made it hard to breathe. I struggled with how to feel about Sarah. I wanted to remember the childhood we shared, the happier times that had gotten buried along with our parents. Maybe one day the good stuff would come back, but all I felt now was sad. Sarah had turned into unfinished business. Regret and penance, she was a heavy medicine ball of guilt I carried and a gaping chasm in my life that will never be filled, because she kept clawing away from me as if I were the enemy.

Yeah, that pretty much described Sarah. Our blood line made her a reluctant hostage tied to me. She reminded me how fragile the bond of my family had always been from the start—thanks to me.

In the dark my head filled with flashes of severed limbs. The case implored me to remain faithful, but I resisted the morbid distraction. My sister had put a face on blame for our parent's death—a face I saw everyday in the mirror. She expected me to carry that burden for the two of us.

In a cruel blow, I'd invited my headache back.

"This day continues to bear gifts."

I watched as my sister went inside, picked up her small daughter, and cradled the child in her arms. My gaze followed them from window to window as they moved through the houseboat. Sarah kissed the man cooking in the kitchen. I thought I'd seen the worst my sister could hurt me.

I'd been wrong.

She'd made a life in Seattle—one that didn't include me—and I knew I'd never see her again. I'd seen enough. It had been a mistake to come. Sarah was afraid of me. I wasn't her brother anymore. I'd become a freak show circus and threatened everything she valued. She had a normal life and a family she loved. I wanted to be happy for her. One day I hoped that would come, but not today.

Definitely not today.

***

Belltown, Seattle
After dark

Ben Stevens carried a large takeout bag as he left the front entrance to the Palace Kitchen at the corner of Lenora Street and 5th Avenue in Belltown. The neon yellow and red sign over the door cast its hue on the sidewalk and made his body a shadow on the cement. He grabbed his cell phone from his jeans pocket and took a selfie shot of him standing under the iconic neon sign, holding the handle of his takeout order in his teeth. He'd post the picture on Facebook later with the caption, *Gonna eat 'til I have a food baby.*

A cute girl sitting by a window inside the restaurant saw the goofy face he made for the picture and she smiled and gave him 'the look,' the expression any guy wanted to see. Ben's face heated up and he shrugged back. She looked real sweet, but she was with another guy and he had somewhere else to be.

He stashed his cell back into his pocket and hoofed it to his car. The popular restaurant had customer parking on the street and around back, but with the usual crowd, the place was packed. He'd left his Subaru a block down on Lenora Street behind a closed office building.

After his morning shift at Pike's Market, he'd been at Seattle University's Garrand building in the clinical performance lab most of the afternoon and had binged on Red Bulls and Cheetos while he studied. He could use real food. The smell of chicken made his stomach grind.

"Oh, shit. Promised to call."

He had a not-so-surprise "surprise" for his mother. After he crossed the street, he pulled out his cell phone again. His mom answered on the fifth ring. He had to be patient. It took her time to get to the phone.

"Hey, Mom. I'm on my way home. Should be there in ten."

"You didn't need to spend your money on dinner, honey. I would've made your favorite. My homemade spaghetti and meatballs."

"Not on your birthday, Mom. You better be hungry."

Today his mother turned forty-eight.

"Hungry for what?"

"I thought you liked a good mystery." He grinned. "I'll see you soon. Love you."

"Love you more, honey."

He ended the call, still smiling. She always pretended to be surprised when he brought home her favorites from the Palace Kitchen. The rotisserie chicken was killer and the coconut crème pie may as well have been crack. He craved it as much as she did.

In his backpack in the car, he had another package stashed with his textbooks. He'd wrapped a gift to make her laugh—a kid's bicycle bell for her wheelchair. Ben couldn't wait for her to see it. She'd never use anything as rude as a bell in public, but at home she'd make an exception to see him laugh.

Since she'd been diagnosed with multiple

sclerosis seven years ago, they had to work harder to find something funny to keep their spirits up as she struggle with the ebb and flow of her incurable disease. It was only the two of them. Taking care of his mother had steered him into SU's College of Nursing graduate program. He had a year to go and she'd gotten him through it, despite what was happening to her.

He owed her everything.

Ben had his mind on his mom as he approached his Subaru and noticed an old truck with a canopy parked next to his vehicle. Someone was working under the hood. Car trouble.

"You need any help? I got a cell phone...and jumper cables."

Ben wanted to get home while the food was still hot, but he wouldn't leave if the guy could use his help. When the man didn't answer, he stepped closer and tried again.

"Did you hear me, mister?"

Ben saw the guy move too late. The shock of being hit across the face with something hard bombarded him with blinding stars. He cried out and collapsed as he dropped the bag of food and everything went black.

***

After the driver secured the hood and locked the tailgate of the truck—with another perfect one drugged and tied up inside—the smell of food filled the air. The contents of the takeout bag were on the asphalt, but the containers hadn't spilled.

No sense wasting good food.

Sitting in the shadowy cab of the truck, the Totem Killer ate the chicken and pie. This one had come with a meal.

***

Two hours later
Ryker Townsend

I found a no frills motel room near Sea-Tac, the Seattle-Tacoma International Airport. After the trip to Sarah's houseboat, putrid slime from the pit of hell would've carried more cheer and made better company than me.

My sister had been my tipping point. Guess I wasn't as evolved as I thought. It had been too easy to get mired in a brooding funk, reliving the worst of my childhood. Whenever I thought I'd moved on and had made a life of my own—using my gift in a way my mother would've been proud of—it only took one glimpse of Sarah and her daughter to dropkick me.

I had to let those feelings go. Obviously I didn't know how.

"Desperate times. Desperate measures."

Beer. A cold one. Something spicy.

I wasn't hungry, but I needed a diversion of insanely hot food chilled by the mellow comfort of a cold brew. After I'd taken a long hot shower and changed into fresh clothes, I made a call for takeout to be delivered and forced myself to eat.

Vegetarian Pad Thai with extra tofu and a chaser of Singha beer.

After a particularly rough crime scene, I usually ate vegetarian for days after, but when the words of Jeffrey Dahmer—*I've got to start eating at home more*—refused to leave my head, I thought of meat as I ate. Weird.

Nothing had gone as planned, but being consumed by the TK case would distract me from the sister who'd written me off. At least, that was the idea. Lucinda Crowley hadn't wasted any time. She knew I'd want a rush on identifying the last victim, so she'd scanned the body's fingerprints before she departed Seattle, and texted me about it. She transmitted them to Sinead Royce to run through a series of databases, to search for a hit on ID while they were in the air.

Before my team had returned to Quantico, I had a video call from Royce, who'd worked overtime to get me what I needed. The word *unconventional* didn't begin to describe the fifth member of my team.

She'd graduated from high school at sixteen, finished her undergrad degree two years later, and received a Master's in Computer Science with a specialty in Security last year, before she turned twenty-one. The way her mind worked, if Sinead had an inclination to walk on the dark side, she would've made a genius hacker.

When I punched up her video call, I got a surprise.

"Hey there, Ryker. How's the Grunge capital?" Sinead Royce's eyeball filled my display screen when I answered the call. "I got new contacts. What do you think?"

When she pulled away from the video cam lens, I got a better look. Sinead had an addiction to weird eyewear that she donned when she worked after hours. She had a collection of peculiar eyeglasses at home and at her office, but her assortment of contact lenses were her pride and joy. The one she wore now made her eyes look like black pits with shark teeth on the edges. When she blinked, it looked like a remake of 'Jaws.'

"Your best yet," I said. "Real subtle."

No matter what kind of day I had, Sinead always made me smile. Her dark hair and eyes and delicate facial features made her appear younger than she was. Sinead looked like Ellen Page in oversized black glasses. She had the actress's intelligent wit and wry cynical humor, but there were days she channeled Zooey Deschanel's quirky weirdness. Either way she was a refreshing oddity within the disciplined structure of the FBI.

"You think? I got a shark week marathon party coming up. We're having sushi to balance things out." While she popped out her contacts, she kept talking. "Got a hit on those prints Lucinda sent. You ready?"

"Yeah. Shoot." I grabbed a motel notepad and pen.

"His name is...was Nathan Applewhite. It made me sad to see his face on DMV. He was a hot guy with a body like a lumberjack. He also had a little boy. Tanner, five years old. Nathan was only twenty-seven, Ryker."

Sinead felt everything and it showed on her face. Her emotion and passion were strengths that made her good at her job, but I knew every case took a toll on her. She gave me the run down on the last victim. Applewhite was a young guy who worked as an outdoor guide for several lodges and charter services near his home. He had an ex-wife and a kid he'd never see again. He had taken root in me and the more I learned about him, the more I hated what happened to him.

"The weird thing is, he lived and worked on the Prince of Wales Island in Alaska, but I couldn't find a residence for him in the Seattle area or a flight itinerary," Sinead said. "So how did his body end up tied to that tree, Ryker?"

If she knew about the tree, she'd seen the images Crowley had taken at the scene. Sinead didn't have to look at them, but she often did to appreciate the stakes and be part of the team. I respected that.

"Good question. Give me his address." I took down the information. A post office box. "He had to have a connection to Seattle...a reason to come here. Most killers hunt in the general proximity to where they live. It's a comfort zone because it's familiar. Applewhite had to cross this guy's path somehow. What about social media? Did he have a Facebook page?"

"Yeah, he did, but he wasn't very active. He hadn't posted anything for months. Nothing to indicate why he'd traveled to Seattle, but I'll keep looking. Maybe an older wall post, or reading what his friends wrote, will give us a lead on any connection he had to Seattle."

"Good idea." I made a note. "Maybe he used an online dating service? I hear the ratio of men to women in Alaska is four to one."

"Sounds like a place I should visit. A girl's got to test drive her eyewear."

I smiled.

"Oh, and check to see if he had a pilot's license or owned a plane. Living on an island, being a pilot would come in handy for weekend getaways."

"Will do. Anything else?"

Sinead's simple question stopped me. *Anything else?*

Yeah, there was something else—a missing piece that made me think of the grisly photo I'd taken with my cell phone of Nathan's dead body and his terrorized face—with his dead eyes, gray lifeless skin, and gaping mouth. That image had been a far cry from Applewhite's DMV photo where he'd grinned.

How, where and why had the guy crossed paths with a killer? Something in his life made that happen. It struck me that I had to dig into Applewhite if I wanted an answer. I had to make a deeper connection with a dead man.

"Gimme a sec." I turned away from the lens to shut my eyes and focus.

Don't go there.

No, I have to.

I forced my mind to imagine what he'd seen through those dead eyes in his final seconds. Applewhite's eyes had been portals for the evil that had hunted him and his brain still held the terror of being butchered—dark memories cruelly fed to him by all his senses as it was happening.

I felt it...*all of it.*

It was never difficult for me to imagine the atrocity. My mind had become fertile ground over the years, but picturing the gruesome photos triggered the sensation I had at the crime scene when I was alone yet felt a presence over my shoulder.

That odd feeling of being watched and my deep connection to Applewhite hadn't happened before. *Why this guy? Why now?* I'd stayed behind in Seattle—alone—for personal reasons. I'd preached to my team they should follow their gut.

How could I do anything less?

"Hey Ryker, are you feeling okay? You look...tired, like you're coming off a weekend bender," she said. "Don't take this the wrong way, but you look like something they use to grow mushrooms."

I sighed and dropped my chin to my chest.

"Thanks for the visual, Royce. Gimme a sec."

I stood and found a mirror. Apparently, dropping in on my sister, cold, hadn't been enough self-abuse. Under fluorescent lights, my skin looked pale and I had dark bruising under my eyes. I looked like a booking photo.

"Truly wretched." I grimaced. "Dylan Avery would disavow knowing me."

Dylan was my roommate in college. He relished his hours in front of a mirror and spent more on hair products than he did on textbooks. His priorities were quite clear. When he was satisfied with the way he looked, he'd indulge in one more spin by the mirror and say, 'Yeah, I'd screw me.' Only one good thing came from my time of living in the shadow of Dylan's ego. He'd cured me of clocking face time in front of a mirror. I splashed cold water on my face and toweled off.

After I got back with Sinead, she furrowed her brow and opened her mouth to speak before I interrupted her. I'd made up my mind.

"Let Crowley and the others know I'm booking a flight to Alaska, to search Applewhite's home. I'm following a hunch."

"Okay. Whatever you need, Ryker, I'm on it."

Sinead signed off, leaving me to feel the weight of my decision to stay. I'd asked my unit chief for a personal day in Seattle to go looking for my sister, but maybe my intuition had shown me a better reason for my change in plans. The case. My decision to stay had been about doing something unprecedented to stop this guy and unexpected minutia often broke a tough investigation. I couldn't ignore the feeling.

My mother had taught me to accept my dreams as part of who I was. She didn't live long enough to know how I'd use my ability as a profiler, but her strength filled me now as I shook off the hurt of seeing Sarah.

I had a new plan that felt right, as if I really didn't have a choice. If our UNSUB thought our vic was important enough to leave whole, I had to look into Applewhite's life to find out why. Getting to know the last victim—and the reason the dead man plagued my dreams—had to be the key to finding the Totem Killer before he killed again.

I was sure of my choice to stay—and sensed a clock ticking down—even though I had no clue why I was so certain.

***

Spots of intense light broke through the darkness. His head ached with the stabs of light that slashed at him like a razor. The right side of his head throbbed with pain. Once Ben Stevens cracked his eyes open, he saw pinpoints radiate their glow in blurry colorful rings. The colors bled into the darkness to leave a ghost image on his mind, even after he couldn't hold his eyes open anymore. When he tried to feel his arms and legs, he couldn't. They were numb and his body was ice cold.

He couldn't shake the stupor of being drugged.

In the distance, he heard a steady drone that made him want to sleep, but when a hard jolt made it feel as if the ground pulled from beneath him, his mind seized on the idea that the shake had been air turbulence and the drone was an aircraft engine. He blinked and forced his brain to think. Nighttime. In the shadows of a dark fuselage, he glimpsed the cargo hold of a small plane and saw the movement of the pilot, a silhouette awash in lights off the control panel.

Who are you? Why are you doing this?

He wanted to cry out, but couldn't make his mouth work. Ben wracked his brain to recall what happened. The last thing he remembered was being in Seattle—his home—but as the gaps to his memory filled in, he knew he'd been abducted by force.

Ben's heart hammered and a surge of adrenaline punched through his body as he battled the effects of the drug he'd been given to subdue him. Details came back to him—faster now—but too late to do anything about it. The face of his poor mother came to him. Picturing her brought tears to his eyes.

Mom.

Her face was the last thing Ben saw before the shadows swallowed him.

Chapter Five

Seattle - Next morning
Ryker Townsend

I hadn't slept well and blamed it on a lousy pillow, but my disdain for the torture of down feathers was the least of my worries. My last phone call of the night had been to my unit chief, Reynolds. She hadn't given me any flack over my side trip to a remote island in Alaska to investigate the life of Nathan Applewhite. In fact she commended me on my thoroughness, but after she pressed me for my thoughts on the latest crime scene, I'd been purposefully vague and she knew it. Although I'd chalked it up to a long day and she let it go, I didn't like misleading her.

Keeping secrets had become second nature to me, an aptitude I'd never expected to refine out of necessity. I justified my behavior by thinking that if I came back with something solid, it would make me feel better, but it did nothing for my sleep. My mind wouldn't rest.

When a rain storm had rumbled across Seattle during the night, I'd awakened in the throes of another dream. This time I'd sensed Nathan Applewhite behind the curtain, but I couldn't make myself draw back the drape. I didn't know why. Maybe seeing Nathan dead would've severed my tie to the dream and put finality to his life. I wasn't ready for that. Something of him still lived in my dreams and I wasn't ready to let him go.

Instead of getting up to shake off the dream, I shut my eyes and listened to the rain in the dark until the alarm woke me. I showered, dressed, packed, and checked out of the motel in a merciful mind fog.

On my drive to Sea-Tac Airport in my rental car, the gray skies of Seattle shed a heavy drizzle over the city. The streets glistened with the steady sluice of rain. The somber overcast morning suited my mood and wrapped me in its muggy arms, but not in a nurturing way. Within hours I'd leave the urban landscape behind for America's last wilderness frontier. Only one case had ever brought me to Alaska, but that trip had been to Anchorage, nothing as remote as the Prince of Wales Island in the southeastern part of the state.

Once I dropped off my rental and got to the terminal, I placed a courtesy call to the Alaska State Troopers who had jurisdiction for the island. The troopers assured me they'd have a representative meet my charter at Point Baker, someone who could take me to Nathan Applewhite's home and knew the island and its residents.

Applewhite lived in a very remote part of the island—Point Baker— the most northern part of the island, in a place little more than a village with a slim population, outside of peak tourist season. Wherever he actually lived, he collected his mail in Point Baker. It was a starting point.

Seeing where he lived on a map, I wondered how Nathan Applewhite had been lured from his isolated home in Alaska and ended up strapped to a tree in the middle of the Cascade Mountains atop a brutal masterpiece of human depravity.

I was convinced, more than ever, that I'd made the right decision to learn more about him.

Although I had a long day of travel ahead, I took comfort that I'd have help on the island.

The first leg of my trip was a commercial flight to Ketchikan, where I had my longest layover. I had to allow enough time for the seaplane service to pick me up from the main airport and take me to a departure location at Harbor Point. By the time I checked in for the final part of my trip, it was late afternoon. I traveled plenty, but I'd never become good at it.

I saw my gear loaded into the cargo hold of a de Havilland Beaver before I stepped off the dock onto the seaplane's float pontoon. I had to duck under the overhead wings to get into the plane and I folded like a human accordion. After that picture invaded my brain, polka music became my 'ear worm' and I couldn't make it stop playing in my head. It would be a tedious flight.

With my long legs, the interior was a tight fit, but it could accommodate up to six people. The only other passengers onboard were three older Native women. None of them made eye contact. I took comfort in my cloak of invisibility. I would've reveled in quiet reflection, except for the musical instrument bellowing in my head. There was only one way to tolerate an accordion—ending the blasted song.

As the aircraft taxied across the harbor, I felt its uneasy buoyancy as it skittered along the surface of the water, jetting a rooster's tail of spray as the plane built speed. The loud mind-numbing drone of the single-engine, propeller-driven aircraft didn't allow for much conversation with the pilot or the other passengers. That suited me fine.

The plane lifted off and leveled out, making the visibility better. I couldn't take my eyes off the abundant terrain dotted with evergreen trees and scattered lakes that mirrored the sky. Steep forested mountains had snow still nestled deep into ravines and a family of white Dall sheep leaped through jagged rocks without effort.

The sheep were a beautiful remedy to my raging case of ear worm. The polka music died to a low *oompah* thump.

After a long hour, the pilot made an

announcement he'd be landing soon. He'd have to rely on instrumentation and keen eyesight. There was no control tower in such a remote locale. When I saw the pilot search for other planes in his flight path and look below for a safe place to land—where he wouldn't settle on top of another pilot—I couldn't help but do the same.

Ass preservation. It had always been a good motivator for me.

Crosscurrents tossed the plane and whipped it sidelong as the pilot made his final approach to Point Baker. My stomach had to catch up with the rest of my body as the fuselage dipped and plunged. Within minutes the aircraft made its watery landing and pulled next to a wooden pier for offloading.

The Native women deplaned in a hurry and disappeared before I had a chance to dazzle them with my charm. After I claimed my one bag, I followed the instructions I'd been given by the Alaska State Troopers, to wait for the local contact. I found a place to stand near the Point Baker Community Building with its makeshift U.S. Post Office. At this hour, the place was closed, but Applewhite's mailbox would probably be inside. The red-stained wood, with large letters painted in white, made the building an easy spot to notice me, but I had a feeling I'd stand out anywhere in Point Baker.

I pulled out my cell phone to check for messages, but before I thumbed through my calls, I heard a sound that flashed me back to the Cascade Mountains. The loud throaty caw of a bird forced me to look up. In an evergreen tree near me, a large black bird eyed me and cocked its tufted iridescent head to get a better look.

A raven.

I would've dismissed the scavenger, but I found it hard to look away until the purple tinged Trickster took off with an ear-piercing shriek. It screamed its passage as it lifted off the branch with ease, a creature of the wind. Massive velvet wings beat and caught air currents to defy gravity in a powerful, explosive exit. I watched the bird fly toward the nearest mountain until it disappeared.

Not a coincidence.

Although I couldn't see the raven anymore, I felt the wake of its presence and my never-ending tether to a crime scene that I couldn't shake. To distract my mind from my raven conspiracy, I checked my voice mail messages that had stacked up while I was in the air. Most of the calls were from Lucinda Crowley. Her last message summed it up.

Something's got you spooked and you're shutting me out. Man, normally you're fearless. Kind of spooky cool under fire actually, but something's up that you're not telling me. I heard her sigh over the phone recording, but before she ended the call, she said, *Watch your ass, Ryker.*

I sighed.

"Sorry, Luce. It's hard to watch my ass when I'm fondly attached to it. It's a matter of perspective."

I had to admit. A part of me had been unraveling since the start of this case. My escalating dreams were only a bad sign things were getting worse. If the job had become too much for me to handle, I didn't know if I could face everyone knowing it. Some things a man had to deal with alone.

My job defined me. It was part of who I'd become, by choice. If I couldn't do it anymore, I didn't know what that would make me—except a misfit, prone to insomnia with social skills in dire need of a makeover.

After I deleted her messages, I got a chance to look around and saw Point Baker wasn't complicated. I'd seen pictures and researched what I could online last night. The village's main economy came from commercial trolling and gillnetters. Although the setting was breathtaking, only a handful of cabins, docks, and public buildings gave any indication people actually lived here year round.

The utter silence took me completely by surprise. No city noise. No traffic.

With the sun hanging low in a cloudy evening sky, the dank smell of the cove mixed with the stench of decaying fish carcasses and brackish seawater. I closed my eyes to listen to the lapping waves against the shore until I heard the screech of a bald eagle. The impressive predator made graceful circles in the sky. Held aloft by its ample wingspan, the eagle foraged for a meal in the fading hours of the day as deepening shadows stretched along the steep craggy bluffs surrounding Point Baker.

It would be dark soon and I'd need a place to stay and something to eat. In the interest of full disclosure, I had to hit the head, too. Even though I had crossed the line into Nathan's world—a place radically different from anything I'd ever experienced—I felt an undeniable bond with an island I'd never been.

The cold slap of déjà vu made me realize. What I sensed had come through the eyes of a dead man.

**

Hearing about the FBI's Ryker Townsend coming to the island and Point Baker had been a shock at first. It hadn't been easy operating under the radar of law enforcement and doubts over getting caught were natural. The Totem Killer had made the initial assumption that the investigation had turned up a clue that pointed an accusing finger. It had taken guts to stick it out and not run—but that element of danger had turned into an irresistible thrill. To stay ahead of the FBI and operate under the noses of the state troopers had turned into a deadly game.

In hindsight, Nathan Applewhite had been the perfect bait to lure Townsend. It all felt like part of the plan now.

Residents on the island had been talking about dead Nate and the FBI coming to investigate. After the initial uncertainty, the profiler's unexpected visit seemed like a stroke of fate now, one that would play nicely into the hands of the Totem Killer. Any encounter would be risky, of course. The Alaska State Troopers were in the mix, since the profiler had contacted them for help, but that only made things more fun.

Seeing Ryker up close fueled an adrenaline rush of excitement. The federal agent stood outside the Point Baker post office with a stern expression on his face as he thumbed through his cell phone, checking messages and killing time.

Killing time. They had *that* in common.

Ryker looked bored. If he'd come to the island for excitement, he'd come to the right place. Having the FBI's lead investigator at Point Baker made it feel like the moth flitting perilously close to a warm flickering death, but who was the flame—and who would play the part of the oblivious insect?

The Totem Killer smiled.

***

Minutes later
Ryker Townsend

When a vehicle rumbled to a stop behind me, I glanced over my shoulder to see a white Ford Explorer with the blue and gold Alaska State Trooper logo on the door. The words *Loyalty, Integrity,*

Courage were painted on the rear panel. I locked eyes with the trooper and nudged my chin in greeting before I grabbed my bag. By the time I reached the truck, the driver had boots on the ground and showed me an ID badge.

"Alaska State Trooper, Sergeant Peterson. Justine." She grasped my hand. "Are you Special Agent Townsend?"

"Supervisory Special Agent, yes. Ryker. Thanks for meeting me." I fished out my credentials and showed her.

Even off-duty and out of full uniform, Trooper Justine Peterson was clearly law enforcement. She carried a holstered weapon on her duty belt and had on jeans, well-worn hiking boots, and a navy polo with the Trooper's emblem on it. Her windbreaker and cap bore the official logo, too. Clothes and weapon aside, the tall blonde had a no nonsense attitude and a slender body, lean with muscle. She had a penetrating stare that had sized me up.

If I were a fish in Alaskan waters, she might've tossed me back.

"I'm here to search the residence of Nathan Applewhite. Deceased. We positively identified his body yesterday outside Seattle in the Cascade Mountains. He's a victim of a serial killer my team's been after."

The trooper's expression turned harsh and unyielding.

"It's been on the news. Everyone on the island is talking about it. Word even got out about you coming here," she said. "I was the one who notified his ex-wife. Too bad you didn't stop whoever did it before he got to Nate."

The woman glared at me, without backing down. Although I hadn't expected a show of hostility from someone in law enforcement, I didn't take it personally. Hearing about a murder made it easy for those who knew the victim to lash out in frustration.

Justine had to know Applewhite. She'd called him Nate.

"The body count is fourteen. That's why I'm here. This killer has to be stopped." Since I needed her cooperation, I let her show of attitude slide. "Applewhite had a post office box for his mail, but I'm assuming he lives near here. How far is his place?"

The woman let her eyes drift down my body and back to my eyes again. It had been a long time since a woman made me feel like a porterhouse steak.

"His cabin is a trek. You look fit enough, but when was the last time you slept? You look...rough."

"Just try me."

"Don't get your male hackles up. It takes effort to get to Nate's cabin, especially without the right gear for a proper stay. Besides, I had to be sure you could handle it. City Fed like you." She looked at my one bag. "Is that all you brought?"

"Yes."

I wanted to tell her that size shouldn't matter. The most impressive thing about a man's luggage was in how he packed it. I was tired enough to say that—with a raised eyebrow and a stern chin jut—but I opted for a modicum of restraint. Her face twitched with an odd smile after she sized me up.

Apparently I came up short. *Again.*

"I got extra gear you can borrow until you leave," she said. "I take it you'll be staying at Nate's while you search his cabin. It doesn't make sense to overnight in Point Baker while you're working. I'll make sure you'll have what you need when I take you up there."

"Up there?"

"Yeah, I can't exactly drive you to his door." After

she heaved a sigh, her expression softened. "Nate's cabin is in the mountains. It's real nice. He kept it well-stocked, but I haven't been there in a while."

She got quiet and avoided looking at me.

"If you've been to his cabin, you must've known him. Sorry for your loss."

"Yeah, I knew him." She didn't say anything more, but she did give me the critical once over. I wanted to tell her I wasn't that complicated, but she'd figure that out soon.

"I got some good news and some bad. What do you want first?" she asked.

I grimaced. I'd had about as much bad news as I could handle.

"Tell me something good."

"The local motel doesn't have anything open for tonight. They're renovating before peak season. No vacancies."

"That's *good* news?"

"Yeah, it is. Trust me."

"What's the bad news?"

"You'll have to settle for *my* place. You're staying with me tonight. I got dinner waiting. Come on."

I didn't know if her bad news referred to my accommodations—or her cooking—but I was about to find out. She climbed into the truck and started the engine as I got in.

"Your family won't mind?" I asked.

"No. In fact you'll be lucky to keep them off you."

She smiled as if there was an inside joke. I didn't ask. Justine Peterson struck me as a woman who appreciated her privacy. I'd find out what she meant soon enough.

***

Justine had a small cabin not far from Point

Baker. She must've had a thing for seclusion. I wanted to keep an open mind, but for me, the isolation would've worn thin. Her closest neighbor was nothing more than an open gate and a gravel road with acres between them. The outside of her home looked more like a working hunting lodge. It appealed to me. A couple of hanging baskets of purple flowers was as close to homey as she got.

A canoe was in plain sight under a deck and she had an axe and stump for chopping wood at the side of her house, with a bench and table near her front door that looked more like a work station. She looked like a no-frills, practical woman. I heard dogs yelping out back and saw the fencing of a dog run toward the rear.

"You've got a nice place. Daniel Boone would've found it welcoming."

I grabbed my bag from the front seat and shut the passenger door. Justine was already walking inside. She hadn't locked her front door. I'd never lived in a place where locks weren't necessary. The island was growing on me.

"Thanks. It suits me."

"What's with the dogs? Sounds like you have a pack."

"I foster wounded animals and strays. They're the family I told you about." She waved her hand to invite me into her home. "Put your bag anywhere. You'll be sleeping on the couch."

"Thanks."

While Justine took off her weapon and placed it in a drawer, a short brown mutt barked and kept his distance until I knelt down and let the dog sniff his way to a deep abiding friendship. A big yellow tabby squinted at me until it turned and flashed its butt. Not being a cat expert, I didn't feel qualified to make a determination if that was a good or bad sign. I'd leave that for the professionals. I stashed my bag near the sofa.

"The mutt is named Sancho and the tabby is Pinot Grigio. Whatever they do, don't take it personally. We don't get many houseguests."

"Thanks for the warning." I glanced down at the mutt and pointed. "If I ever need a wingman to thwart giant windmills, I know who to call."

Justine stopped and stared at me with a questioning look.

"It's interesting you made the leap to Sancho Panza. Not many people make the literary connection I intended. You probably saw the Broadway musical Don Quixote on stage, like most people," she said. "Is that how you're familiar with the name?"

"No. I read the book, the work of Don Miguel de Cervantes Saavedra. The Old Castilian from the early sixteen hundreds is the medieval form of the Spanish language. It was a challenge at first, but once I got into it, it was a sumptuous feast for the soul. After the book, a stage play in English for the masses wouldn't cut it."

"Impressive." She cocked her head.

"No pictures even." Beyond Crowley, not many got my humor. "If reading old Castilian makes me sound like a pompous ass, I occasionally indulge in comic books. I'm a fan of Marvel. They have better women."

"Be still my heart."

I had no idea if I had impressed her. Her facial expression gave nothing away. She had trumped my straight-faced restraint with her own, which made it hard to read her. I rather liked the challenge.

After Justine left the room, I took a look around. The inside of her home was different than the hunting lodge look of the outside. I liked the casual warm feel to it. Her living room had a sofa and two chairs with quilts and pillows that added a feminine touch. A pot belly stove had a fire burning and the aroma of something good came from the kitchen. She had Native art and prints on the walls. One large wall-mounted wood carving stood out, an elaborate depiction of a whale with colorful beads hanging beneath it.

"This is a nice piece."

"The Tlingit tribe. It's my favorite." She seemed glad that I noticed. "Can I get you a mug of Swamp Tea?"

"No, thanks. I'm good. Trying to cut down on my intake of intestinal parasites."

She laughed.

"I know Swamp Tea doesn't sound appealing. Natives refer to it by that name, but you might have heard it called *Hudson Bay Tea* or a *Labrador Tea and Spruce Toddy*. I have it simmering on my stove. I was preparing some for myself."

"Then I guess...when in Rome. I'll try it."

She told me the tea was a staple with Natives and island residents. It was rich in Vitamin C, had medicinal properties, and was made from the Labrador tea plant, plentiful on the Prince of Wales Island. I thought of the first person who ever made the plant into tea. What made anyone grab what looked like a weed, boil it, and take that first sip? If they were smart, they would've gotten someone else to drink it—very much like Justine was trying to get me to do.

After I took my first sip and I told her I liked it, she said, "It's only slightly poisonous."

"Ah, good to know. Thanks for the heads up."

I played it safe and waited for her to take another sip before I did.

"Keeps moths and mice away, if that's a problem," she said.

I narrowed my eyes at her. Now she was definitely trying to get a rise out of me.

"Is serving poisonous tea your idea of rolling out the welcome wagon?" I asked. "What's for dinner...whale blubber with a side of baby seal?"

"Just testing your sense of humor. That's all."

"Did I pass?"

"Too soon to tell."

Knowing Justine was a state trooper gave me a solid feel about her, even though she was still a stranger, but I hadn't expected to be sharing her home, especially with her being a single woman. Maybe with me being a Fed, she was okay with inviting an outsider she hadn't met to stay on her couch overnight—that, and the fact she carried a weapon.

A loaded gun was a great equalizer.

"Can I help with dinner?" I asked. "I know my way around a kitchen and dirty dishes don't stand a chance."

"I got everything under control. If you want to freshen up, there's only one bathroom. Have at it."

After I hit the head and washed my hands, I took off my weapon and placed it in my overnight bag. Justine already had the table set with two steaming bowls of stew. It smelled incredible, and not because I was on the verge of starvation.

"It's venison. A 'go to' meal for me."

"Looks great," I said as I sat down.

"Good looks can get you into trouble." Her lips curved into a suggestive smile. "If you want to experience something truly satisfying, you gotta take a risk and venture out of your comfort zone."

She held my gaze until I had to look away. Her eyes looked at me square and without flinching. I wasn't sure she was talking about the stew. The woman had a way of saying unexpected things that carried the weight of more than one meaning, but I didn't know her well enough to be sure.

"Looks good and it tastes great," I told her after my first bite. "Thank you."

She told me the ingredients were homegrown on the island. She had a freezer full of deer meat and fish, and she grew her own vegetables and herbs for seasoning. Grocery supplies were limited, but residents knew how to fend for themselves. The island was known for its trophy sized Sitka black-tailed deer, large black bears, and salmon and halibut fishing, depending on the season.

The venison was fork tender and melted in my mouth. It didn't take me long to finish one bowl and she ladled out a second serving, without my even asking.

"I like pleasing a man, especially one who knows how to eat," she said. "Save room for my salmonberry cobbler. I picked the berries myself."

"I always have room for homemade cobbler."

Justine smiled, but got quiet. For the first time, I heard the steady tick of a clock and paid attention to it. It counted down every second of silence between us. Unit Chief Reynolds had the same tactic of using silence to get me to say something. I didn't mind the quiet, something Trooper Peterson would soon understand.

"How close are you to finding who killed Nate...and the others?" she asked. She fixed her gaze on me and put down her spoon.

"I can't talk about an ongoing investigation."

"Throw me a bone, Fed. I'm taking you to Nate's place. I'll stay with you as long as you need me. I even took personal time off from work to help. Give me something. I'm law enforcement. I know how to keep my mouth shut about a case."

Her eyes carried an edge of intensity that was

hard to read. Nate had been important to her, beyond being a fellow resident on the island. I sensed she had an agenda for inviting me to her home and I wondered how far she would've gone to arrange it.

"Was the motel really full up, or did you ask me to stay here to see what you could get out of me?"

Chapter Six

Prince of Wales Island, Alaska
Evening
Ryker Townsend

What I'd said to Justine came out harsher than I had intended, but I didn't apologize. She didn't strike me as a wilting flower. I expected her to balk. When she didn't, I pushed my dish away and slouched back in my chair with my arms crossed. I waited her out and let the silence work in my favor.

I'd inherited my mother's stubborn gene and my dad's quiet patience.

"I didn't lie to you about the motel being closed." She lowered her gaze to my lips. "But I get it. You need to trust me. I can be patient."

Justine had come at me head on, looking for insider information on the investigation. When she didn't get any, she let the subject drop, but I knew she wouldn't give up. She didn't strike me as a quitter.

"Trust must be earned and I don't *ever* give it freely," I said. "Fair warning."

"Are you talking about work...or personal?"

I wiped my mouth with a napkin and tossed it on the table.

"My reluctance to confide has nothing to do with you. Consider me an equal opportunity prick. Others do."

Her eyes held mine, unaffected by her faint smile. I refused to give in and look away, but the woman had stirred something in me that I had yet to name.

"Understood," she said. "Dessert?"

"Please."

I hoped the promise of homemade cobbler and

casual conversation would follow. Justine made sure I wasn't disappointed. She dropped the touchy subject of Nate's investigation and carried on. I should've been relieved, but I wasn't. Justine had a deliberate intention with me and I had yet to uncover it.

I helped her clean up and clear the table as she washed dishes in the sink. We got into a rhythm without the distraction of conversation. She thanked me in other ways with unexpected smiles and times when I caught her staring at me, but she never broached the subject of Nate's case. I would need her cooperation, when I was ready to ask questions about Applewhite, but agents asked questions. They seldom answered them. Justine would've known that from her law enforcement training.

"Beautiful view out of every window," I said. "I can see the attraction to living here."

I gazed out the window over her sink as I stood next to her and wiped a pot dry. The sun had gone down, but with the trees backlit and a hush closing in, I was mesmerized by the peace and quiet. I saw a glimpse of water and a jetty through the trees. Her property backed up to a private cove where she had a dock, a good place to launch a canoe or watch the sun go down with a cold beer.

The island calmed me in a way I'd never felt, as if I had come home to a place I'd never been.

"Does it get lonely? You're a young woman, living alone and doing a tough job. That can't be easy."

She looked up and smiled. The suddenness of the gesture surprised me. It made me stare at her too long. The way she brushed against my hip and thigh, I should've moved away, but I didn't want to. I hadn't been touched like that in a long time. I liked it.

"It can be a challenge. Some days are harder than others, but I grew up in Alaska. I wouldn't live anywhere else."

I handed her a pot lid, but when something in the trees caught my eye, I turned to see a shadow move. It took me a moment to realize I hadn't imagined it. A man stood in the trees. I couldn't see a face. The guy was big and the fading light caught strands of his long blond hair and beard. But the minute I noticed him, he vanished into the deepening shade. It happened so fast, I thought I'd imagined it.

I leaned toward the window and craned my neck to look for where the man went, but I lost him.

"What's the matter?" she asked. "Did you see something? We get moose and other wildlife through town."

"I saw a guy. Blond hair and beard. He stood in those trees to the right, staring at us."

Justine looked out her window and dried her hands.

"That's my neighbor, Josh. We share the jetty behind my place. He helped me build it...and the kennels. He feeds and takes care of the rescue animals for me. That's why the cages are between both of our properties. Most of the dogs are strays, but a couple are his." She hung the damp towel on a hook to dry. "He's an acquired taste...doesn't like strangers, but he's harmless. Sometimes he gets curious when I have men over. Nothing to worry about. He looks out after me."

I shot her a questioning look. Any other place, the neighbor would get reported as a stalker or a Peeping Tom. He hadn't been down by the shared jetty. He'd stared into the windows of her house. A woman living alone should be more cautious, but Justine didn't seem worried.

"Here on the island, we take care of each other," she said. "To people from the city, Josh might look like a pervert, but I don't mind that he takes an interest in who comes here. I like knowing he's out there."

"You want me to make sure it's Josh...to be on the safe side?"

"I'm a Trooper, Ryker. I carry a weapon and I'm used to living alone." She touched my arm. "Thanks, but I can take care of myself."

The intimacy of her touch sent a mixed message. It stirred my need to protect her, but when I looked in her eyes, she clearly didn't want or need my help. Her strong reaction took me off guard.

Most women I knew liked it both ways. They liked being independent, but if a guy played the white knight once in awhile, it was a gesture they appreciated for different reasons. Sometimes it paid for a man to be a mind reader, but I didn't know Justine well enough to call it either way.

"Okay. I understand."

After we finished straightening the kitchen, she poured two mugs of Swamp Tea and doctored them with drizzled honey and a stiff shot of bourbon before she handed me one.

"Come with me. You've done enough work."

She took my elbow and walked me outside to her back porch, where she had two wooden rocking chairs. A sudden feeling of déjà vu hit me as if we'd done this before and the sense of home swept over me again—stronger this time.

Justine sat with me for a few minutes and sipped her tea before she looked at her watch and got up again. She wasn't one to sit still.

"I've got a sick one that needs my attention before I get to bed. It's time for his medicine. If I don't give it to him, he'll cry all night."

"I thought your buddy Josh took care of the dogs."

"Not the meds. I do that. He only has access on

the rare occasion I give it to him."

"You need any help?"

"No, thanks. Just sit and unwind. Enjoy the view...and the quiet."

"You do all the nursing yourself? What if an animal needs a vet?"

"I work with someone in Ketchikan. They hook me up with anything I need. Life on an island, you've got to improvise and cut corners." She shrugged. "This won't take long. I'll be back in a few."

"Will you be okay alone?"

"I told you. I'm sure that was Josh. He's harmless. I'm fine, but thanks."

Justine slipped inside her cabin before she returned to disappear into the darkness and head for the makeshift kennels that bordered her property, cages she shared with her neighbor. I heard her boots on the wooden pier I'd seen earlier. Her footfalls faded once the animals started yelping. After she gave her foster dogs attention and meds to the ailing one, she settled her charges for the night and things grew quiet again.

I heard the sound of Justine's soft voice. She must've been talking to the hurt pup, but when another voice cut through the stillness, I stood and peered through the shadows.

I thought I heard the deeper voice of a man.

"Are you okay?" I called out to her from the porch and headed down the steps, but when she called to me, I stopped.

"Yeah, I'm done. Relax, city boy. Be there in a second."

I kept my eyes alert and strained to hear the man's voice, but after nothing came, I went back to my rocker. The way noise carried on the wind and through the trees on the island, I could've imagined the second voice—a seed that had been planted after

I'd seen a guy in the woods staring at us. I let it go.

"Will your charge sleep through the night?" I called out as Justine's faint silhouette came into view.

"Yes. I hope so."

She slid into the rocking chair next to me and grabbed her tea. With things quiet again, her dog Sancho had curled up at my feet and her yellow tabby had claimed my lap. Justine smiled when she saw I didn't object.

"My lap had a vacancy. Your tabby saw an opportunity and seized it."

"I noticed."

I took a deep breath and drank my tea. Except for the rampant carnage coming from the mosquito zapper, I was once again struck by a sense of tranquil bliss. Exhaustion from a long day of travel made me drowsy and settled. I felt a connection to this place, as if I'd been to the island before, even though I knew I hadn't. Maybe that feeling came through Nathan. The closer I got to Nate's life and his past, the more I felt a tightening bond with his killer, like we'd all walked the same ground—victim, death dealer, and man hunter.

A chill touched my skin that not even a fat tabby could change.

With the sun buried beneath the horizon, a wash of bluish gray filtered through the thick stand of evergreens behind her home. The night sky already showed signs of a dense canopy of stars. Without city lights to dilute the dazzle, I would have a front row seat to the show. While I waited for darkness to close in, I had questions.

"How well did you know Nathan? I don't mean to pry."

"I see that the questions come one way and on your terms." She hadn't said it with anger. "Actually, I understand. I'm giving you a hard time. Sorry."

"I need a feel for the kind of man he was. Insight from you could help."

A sad expression swept across her face. She didn't hide it.

"Nate reported a poacher last year. I responded to the call."

"So that's how you met. Purely professional. A one-time incident." I fixed my gaze on her, but when she didn't return the favor, I pushed. "Anything beyond that?"

She drew a deep breath and hid her face behind her tea mug before she answered.

"We saw each other for awhile. By 'seeing each other,' I mean sex."

Justine had a plain unvarnished honesty about her, but from the look on her face, I knew she hadn't shared the whole truth. Something in her eyes told me her physical relationship with Nate had been about more than satisfying her sexual urges. She let me see her vulnerability and I liked how she wore it. Perhaps I liked it too much.

"Both of us were beyond playing games," she said. "Living remote like this, that's how it is sometimes. You take what you need, when you can get it."

"I can see that. You won't get any judgment from me."

I truly did understand the need for physical intimacy without the burden of strings attached, but in my experience, it never stayed that way. Someone always got hurt. After I took a gulp of tea, I looked up to find her staring at me and sensed a potent sexual energy from her. Her sensuality was clear and unmistakable. At the risk of seeming egotistical, I made a daring assumption that her attentions were targeted at me, considering no one else was here.

"You remind me of him," she said. "He was like

lake water—still on the surface—but teeming with life and hope and possibility underneath. I haven't figured out what *you* have underneath, but it's...something."

"You give me too much credit. I'm no man of mystery. What you see? That's all there is. I'm an open book."

"That sounds like something Nate would say, too. The day we first met, he became shy when things turned personal, but eventually he let me in. I miss him."

Her gaze held mine for a beat too long. I hadn't been around a woman as direct as Justine. A part of me wanted more. Another part pulled at me to change the subject to get it off me. My instincts for isolation and secrecy won out.

"You *loved* him." The words were out before I filtered them. "Sorry. That's none of my business."

After a long strained moment, she finally spoke.

"I never told him, something I'll *always* regret. I never said anything, because his life was all about Tanner, his little boy. He told me he'd made a mistake marrying his ex, but Tanner balanced things out and made that mistake go away. Everything he earned, he socked away for his boy. I understood his feelings, but he had a life that satisfied him. I didn't see my part in it."

Realizing how close Justine had been to Nate, I thought about how difficult it would've been for her to break the bad news of his murder. Carrying heartbreaking news to a victim's family was never easy, but having a vested interest made it far worse.

"Notifying his ex-wife must've been tough."

"It didn't have to be me, but I did it...because of Nate. His ex never knew about us. Not many people did."

Through Justine's relationship with Nate, I got a

better feel for the guy, but no closer to finding an answer as to how his body ended up in the Cascades. Living on the island, Applewhite's life would have been simple, but something had made him a target in Seattle.

"From everything you told me, his life was here. What might've drawn him out of Alaska?"

"I don't know. I've been wracking my brain about that, but we stopped seeing each other weeks ago." She wiped a hand over her face and eyes. "I can't tell you much about where he went and who he saw. I wanted more than he was willing to give, so I had to walk."

"Do you know of any connection he had to Seattle...someone he may have known down there?"

"Alaskans go through Seattle when they fly on business, or take vacations, or shop for goods they can't get here, but Nate wasn't into those things. He saved his money to spend on his kid."

"Did he ever say that he felt someone...watching him?"

"Like a stalker?" she asked. "No, but I guess most guys on the island wouldn't think about reporting that. I mean, living here, a guy might handle it on his own. Everyone carries a weapon. Nate had a shotgun and rifles for hunting and protection. Do you think someone stalked him?" Before I could answer, she shook her head and said, "I still don't understand how he ended up in Seattle."

"We're hoping he had a laptop or an iPad that'll tell us more. That's why I came to search his cabin. He had a Facebook page that he didn't update much. With his home in the mountains, do you know how he connected to the Internet?"

"There are Wi-Fi hotspots in Point Baker. I can't say what he did, for sure. I never saw that he had his own laptop, but if he didn't have service at his cabin,

I think he could've used the Internet at the various outfitters he worked for. They book business online and it wouldn't have cost him a dime."

"That makes sense. Do you know who he stayed in touch with online?"

"Sorry. Can't help you. Talking wasn't exactly our strong suit. That worked for both of us."

When the conversation came back around to her physical relationship with Applewhite, I found her staring at me. The way she held my gaze reminded me that we were strangers—a man and a woman—alone together in a house where I would spend the night. Her invitation to stay didn't have to mean anything beyond hospitality, but her eyes sent a message that was hard to mistake.

"How early should I get up tomorrow?" I asked.

"That...depends."

Another awkward silence filled with sexual innuendo.

"You said something about taking gear," I said. "What did you mean?"

"Stand up for me."

"What?"

"Come on. Humor me."

When I did as she asked, the tabby didn't appreciate the interruption. The cat scurried under the deck as I stood. Justine finished the last of her tea and ran her fingertips over my shoulders. After she had me turn around, I felt her hands along my back and down my arms. I hadn't expected her touching me. Before she said anything more, Justine left me standing alone on her back deck. I heard the sounds of her rummaging inside.

If I lost sleep tonight, I imagined it would be for an entirely different reason.

Justine had a sensuality that came easily for her. I had no trouble imagining Nate with a gravitational pull toward an attractive woman who didn't play games, knew what she wanted, and took it when it suited her. Life in Point Baker would've left Nate few options when it came to willing females who'd settle for what he had to give, but a woman like Justine would stand out anywhere.

If she had cut Nate off, because she needed more from him, maybe the guy felt the void strongly enough to go looking for gratification outside the fishbowl of Point Baker.

"Here, try these on. They should fit you." When she returned, she tossed me some work shirts and pants that looked better suited for cool nights in the mountains than what I'd brought. I wanted to ask if the clothes were Nate's, but I didn't.

"I got a backpack, a sleeping bag, and other gear you can borrow, too." She smiled when she held up a shirt across my shoulders and saw it would fit. "When you asked about what time we'd get up in the morning and I said 'that depends,' you actually blushed. I like you, Ryker Townsend. You're okay...for a Fed."

I blushed again and didn't know what to say. She'd baited me on purpose and my mind went exactly where she thought I'd go. Utterly predictable, I'd been played.

"We'll get up early, but we'll have to pack gear and food. That's why I hedged on our departure time. 'That depends...on *you*. No breakfast. We'll eat on the way."

"What about your animals?"

"I've already made arrangements with my neighbor, Josh. He takes care of them anyway. He knows where I'll be, so I'm good to go. If I have to get up in the middle of the night to take care of my sick one, I'll try not to wake you." She grabbed our tea mugs and said, "You hit the bathroom first. Good night, Ryker."

When I came into the house, she'd disappeared into her bedroom. I yawned, barely able to keep my eyes open. A soft glow came from under her closed door, but she'd left me fresh linens, a pillow, and a blanket on the sofa.

I definitely felt Justine's connection to Nate and grasped the mutual attraction. I'd had my share of physical relationships, but with my nightmares, I'd grown used to leaving afterwards. No one got too close. Doing what I did for a living, it was easier to live alone. But after spending one evening with Justine, I understood why *any* man would've been drawn to her as a lover—and how empty Nate's life might've become without her.

She was a straight forward woman who tapped into a man's need, without going the long way around to get there.

***

Cold. A foul stench. Bleary shadows wavered in and out of focus.

Ben Stevens woke on his knees with his arms tied above his head, not knowing where he was. The weight of his body tightened the rope that cut into his wrists. As he lifted his head, he felt sick with the taste of bile in his throat. The smell of vomit was thick in the air—his vomit—but a more disgusting odor came from something else.

Something putrid and dead.

"Help...m-me."

He didn't know if he actually said the words or if anyone would hear him. Ben fought to stay awake. He took deep breaths and pulled at his restraints, but his ankles and legs were strapped down. As his eyes cleared, he glimpsed the walls around him and felt a chill in the tight space. An exposed red light bulb burned outside and its light cut through the wood slats of a small door. The rope that bound his hands hung from a metal ring bolted into the roof of a compartment too small to stand in.

Faraway, he heard the footsteps of someone coming. He didn't know if he should cry for help or stay quiet. Something deep inside him kept him still. He clenched at the ropes that held him and felt his lips quiver.

God, please help me.

Ben held his breath as the footsteps stopped outside and a shadow crossed the red light. When the door opened, he squinted into the intense light. He couldn't see a face. He only caught a glimpse of torn Carhartt work coveralls that he remembered guys wore in Alaska, worn work gloves, and a dirty ball cap. The guy crawled in fast and blinded him with a hood over his head.

"Who...are you? Why are you—?"

Ben never got to finish. He felt the stinging cut of a blade at his throat and he choked on a gasp. This time his whole body shook as the knife inched down his chest. Piece by piece, the blade ripped through his clothes to strip him naked. Ben froze and let the man do what he came to do. Goosebumps raged over his chest and legs and a chill chased the warmth of his body away when the night air hit his skin.

Fear gripped him hard when a hand ran the length of his naked body.

"Please. Don't do...this."

Every word tore from him in tremors until something jabbed him and he cringed. The hot sting of an injection burned the flesh of his neck.

This time Ben welcomed the dark.

***

Prince of Wales Island, Alaska
Hours later
Ryker Townsend

A punch to my ribs jolted me awake and I choked a gasp.

In a fevered sweat, I opened my eyes and saw only shapes until something moved. A tall shadow leaned over me. My mind flashed on the man I'd seen out the window as a hand grabbed my chest and I reacted. I yanked my attacker off balance and wrestled my arm around a throat and squeezed. Nails dug into the skin of my arm and I heard a voice in the dark, one I didn't recognize.

"Let me go."

I didn't let up. I held the body firm against me.

"Stop it. You're hurting me."

I took a shot to the ribs, but I didn't let up until a stern voice got my attention.

"Ryker. You're having a bad dream. Can you hear me?"

I stopped thrashing long enough to gaze around the room. The dim outline of a wood carving of a whale hung on the wall and I took a deep breath to slow my heart. Hair brushed against my face and I smelled a subtle fragrance I remembered—Justine.

"I'm sorry. What happened?"

After I let go, she went to a lamp and flipped the switch. A pale wash lit the room. She wore a blue nightshirt, thin enough for me to see her nipples. Her blond hair hung across her face in a tumble.

"You were having a nightmare. I heard you call out Nate's name. It sounded bad."

She went to the kitchen and brought back a glass of water. Without a word, she handed it to me and I drank.

"Bad dreams come with the job," I said. "Sorry if

I scared you."

When I sat up and saw I only wore my boxers and a T-shirt, I pulled a blanket over my bare legs. My clothes were soaked in sweat and I needed another shower.

"Do you remember the dream?" she asked. "Maybe if you talked about it..."

I didn't let her finish.

"No. Nothing stays with me. Probably a good thing."

I'd lied and from the look in her eyes, she knew it.

In the dream, Nate didn't stay hidden behind the curtain. This time I'd been the one kneeling over him and driving a butcher knife into his heart. *Me!* The shock of it still gripped me hard.

I remembered the buck of his body when I shoved the blade into him and the force it took to drive it into his heart. God, what was wrong with me? I'd pushed down with both hands and had even felt a warm gush of blood. The cruel smell of it had lingered in my nostrils.

But I'd never tell *her* that. I wouldn't tell *anyone*.

"What time is it?" I asked.

She glanced over her shoulder to a clock in the room.

"Almost three. Sun will be up soon, this time of year."

She touched my shoulder, but because of what I'd done to Nate in my dream, I didn't feel right about her comforting me. I pulled away.

"You want me to put on some coffee?" she asked.

"Yeah, if it's not too much trouble."

Justine went to her kitchen and started a pot of coffee as I sat alone on the sofa, stunned by the intensity of the dream. The smell of it had grown thick and smothering. Sounds were still in my head.

Nate's skin had been carved and bloodied raw. I pictured his eyes. They condemned me as he gasped for air, dying. Even the blade rocked in my hands, mirroring the final beats of his heart.

Damn. I rubbed my face with both hands, unable to shake the dream. On the island, the stark vividness of my strange yet undeniable bond with Nathan Applewhite had grown stronger and made me feel closer to something vile. The evil I sensed hadn't come from merely being here.

Whatever was happening, it came from *inside* me. I'd brought it with me and it was getting worse.

Chapter Seven

BAU headquarters
Quantico, Virginia
Morning

With Ryker in Alaska, Lucinda Crowley took lead in the investigation and pushed as hard as he would've done. Wired, she hadn't slept much. A demanding internal time piece ticked down in her head and had her up before dawn. Five bodies at the last crime scene meant the killer had sped up his timetable.

Like Ryker said, the bloodlust high had worn off fast.

The UNSUB needed more bodies to fan the flame and would start hunting again soon, if he didn't already have his next victim. Because Ryker seemed sure that he did, she wanted to report progress on her next call to him, something that might help him sleep better—and her, too. Maybe distance from the investigation had been a good call for Ryker. Everyone dealt with the stark realities of their work in different ways.

She was no one to judge. He'd been at it longer than she had.

The first time she'd met Ryker Townsend as her new boss, she had to suppress the immediate attraction she had for him. Most women would've considered it a bonus to work with someone who looked like Ryker, but for Lucinda, it became an uphill challenge with no end in sight. Although he was only a year older than she was, he'd been recruited earlier, received legendary test scores, and earned rank. His quiet intensity made him seem older.

For her, Ryker had it all—looks, brains, and a wry sense of humor that she loved prying out of him. He was brilliant, yet clueless when it came to social cues. He picked up on the most obscure details at a crime scene, yet missed when any woman flirted with him, charmingly oblivious to his effect on the opposite sex. Ryker always looked good, had great taste in clothes, and never appeared to try hard.

A guy like him was rare—an endangered species, in fact.

Ryker got her jokes, although sometimes it was hard to tell. She'd catch him fighting a grin, after she'd launched into her best material. That was a good thing. The few times he laughed aloud or flashed a full-on smile, it was pure torture to pretend it didn't mean much, when she couldn't take her eyes off of him.

He had a stare with equal parts intelligence, curiosity and passion. His eyes reminded her of the sweet richness of Chai coffee—the dark and unstirred bottom half of the glass—tinged with a warm drizzle of honey. Ryker had an amazing mind, but there was an intuitive side to his nature that blew her away. To hear him delve into the psyche of the killers they hunted—as if he could connect to them or understood how they hunted their victims—his low voice often gave her chills. Her respect for him had grown over the years and her attraction had only grown stronger, but Ryker had never given her an opening and she didn't know if she could handle it if he did.

The guy had complex layers and secrets. She knew it, but he was also a one-way trip of the heart.

Although she'd deleted the photo she'd taken of him at the crime scene, she had the picture of his face in her mind. She hadn't misread him. She only knew he didn't want to talk about whatever it was. She had to respect that, but the mystery of him plagued her even more. She had it bad.

"Let it go." She mumbled the words Ryker had told her on the tarmac and she didn't like hearing it a second time either.

Lucinda sighed and set aside her thoughts of Ryker. She had a full day ahead of her and Dr. Martinez would be on duty early. When she stepped into the bright lights of the autopsy room, she saw her team already hard at work, prepping for the day. Devin Hutchison and Camilla Devore, had the last victim's body and the severed limbs on five stainless steel tables. Seeing the bodies in the stark light shocked her. They looked like butchered meat.

If she ever became numb to such brutality, she'd quit.

Several enlarged photos of the intact Totem were positioned in an eerie display along one wall, giving a full view of the entire tree, front to back. Similar to other crime scenes, they would use the poster-sized images to number the body parts as they identified the victims and confirmed ID. The ghastly image— enlarged and in color—only galvanized the memory of a crime scene she'd never forget.

"I bring you the gift of caffeine. Nectar of the Gods," she said, as the automatic glass doors closed behind her.

Lucinda had her hands full. She'd made a coffee run and brought back everyone's usual orders, along with scones for those with the stomach for food before an autopsy. Hutch and Cam usually did.

"I smell something good," Hutch said. "Did you bring treats?"

"Whatever's in the bag, I smell blueberries. Yum." Cam grinned.

Twenty-five years old, Devin Hutchison was tall and lanky and looked like a lazy Sunday morning spent in bed. He wore his dark hair long and resembled a professor with glasses balanced on the end of his nose. He usually wore vintage clothing that looked as if they'd come from a theatre costume trunk—tweed vests, odd neck scarves, and an assortment of hats. Camilla Devore was his polar opposite and two years his senior. She had a sense of style that made anything she wore look trendy and chic. With auburn hair and green eyes, she had a way of attracting male attention, no matter what she had on.

Cam and Hutch were inseparable.

"Only you two could smell scones in an autopsy room."

"You act like that's a bad thing," Hutch said.

"Yeah, good point."

Justine set the coffees and bag of pastries on a side table, away from where they'd work. Dr. Martinez, Hutch, and Cam were already dressed in protective gear—surgical gowns and caps with face masks hanging around their necks, and shoe covers. When they were ready, they'd add face shields to catch spatter from the procedures.

"I'll be geared up in two shakes."

After she got dressed in proper attire, Lucinda joined the others.

Dr. Martinez voice recorded his autopsies to help him complete the final paperwork. Since they'd already identified the body of Nathan Applewhite through fingerprints and Ryker had wanted a rush put on the procedure, they started with the last victim. Hutch and Cam helped the ME measure, weigh, x-ray, and photograph the body. Every scar, birthmark, tattoo, and distinguishing feature had to be recorded before Applewhite's body would be cut open.

In his usual calm demeanor, Dr. Martinez spoke in a steady voice as he chronicled the mutilation and murder of a twenty-seven year old man. Lucinda already had a pretty good idea what had killed him. From what she'd seen of the body, Applewhite would've bled out after a lethal stab wound to the heart, but she'd have to wait for the official ruling from the doctor.

There was trace evidence collected off the body, a fine powder found near his genitals, as well as sperm and an oily substance discovered on his penis and in his pubic hair. When the doctor recorded the discovery of anal tearing, it was a significant finding. Having a whole body to examine, for the first time, gave them insight into what the killer did to his victims.

Lucinda clenched her jaw. Nathan Applewhite had suffered degradation and torture at the hands of a merciless killer. He'd endured the abuse for days. She could see that the carvings on his skin were done while he was alive. Some of the older wounds were healing and had scabbed over.

TK had taken his time with this one. He hadn't been cut into pieces. Why had Nathan Applewhite been so special?

Lucinda had seen enough. She slipped off the face shield and removed her latex gloves to get a cup of coffee as she watched her team.

The Applewhite autopsy would take most of the morning, but the official report would take time to finalize until the lab results were in. After the Y-incision, the heart and lungs would be removed. Blood would be typed, DNA analyzed, and toxicology tested. Organs would be weighed, stomach contents examined, and the brain would get a closer look.

She gauged the time these procedures would take, trying to decide when to call Ryker. He'd need an update and she wanted to know what she could do to support him.

Besides the Applewhite autopsy, her team would have a full afternoon of trying to identify the severed limbs. They'd run fingerprints on the hands first. If they didn't get a hit on ID, they'd look for blood characteristics, scars, birthmarks, or other distinctive markings. If necessary, they'd do an age approximation from an exam of the bone joints, and they could x-ray for old bone fractures or evidence of previous surgical procedures.

She decided to make a call to Ryker by the end of their day. The time difference between D.C. and Alaska would buy her a few more hours to gather as much information as possible. She had a plan. As she sipped her coffee, Lucinda stared at the enlarged images of the grisly Totem she'd seen in person only a day ago. She focused on the dead body of Nathan Applewhite, trying to reconcile the image of his corpse to his DMV photo. In life, he'd been a good-looking guy with warm eyes and the father of a five-year old son.

Why you, Nathan? She chewed the inside corner of her lip as she watched the ME weigh Applewhite's heart on a digital scale.

"It's gotta stop here," she whispered.

Lucinda made a vow she desperately wanted to believe.

***

Prince of Wales Island, Alaska
Midday
Ryker Townsend

Point Baker was hours behind us and I had no idea where we were. Justine led the way and I followed her on a worn path along a ridge that skirted a gorge cut by a rushing river. The swirling waters below were an odd color of bluish green that looked like a gemstone. I'd worked up a good sweat, hiking the vertical climb and carrying the weight of my backpack, filled with gear and enough food and supplies for a few days. The exercise and the mountain air gave me a rush.

When I looked through a stand of trees, I caught a glimpse of a mountain through a break in the clouds. The snow covered peaks loomed on the horizon as if they were suspended in the blue sky, looking more like a ghostly image than a formation of rock and stone.

"What's that mountain?"

She turned and I pointed in the distance.

"That's Calder." She spelled it for me. "We're lucky to see it. The top is usually socked in. A sighting is good luck."

Yeah, well, I didn't feel lucky and Nathan Applewhite had been anything but a fortunate man. After Justine stopped for a rest to hydrate, I did the same. She handed me a plastic bag of a nut and raisin mixture and I ate in silence as I gazed across the valley toward Calder Mountain, filling my lungs with the crisp cool air.

Justine finished her snack and wiped her hands on her pants before she said, "You sure don't talk much. Or maybe it's me."

"Sorry. It's not you. I'm doing you a favor. Feel free to thank me whenever the impulse strikes you."

"I'd rather tell you to shut up, but you're not giving me the chance."

"With an enticement like that, how can I refuse?"

"But you will...and I still would like to know why you're channeling Clint Eastwood."

"Actually I was going for John Wayne, but I get your analogy."

I fixed my eyes on her, unsure what to say. A regular guy might've opened up to her to pass the time, but I usually had disturbing things stirring in my head once an investigation took over my life. With my team, I'd grown used to letting my thoughts leave my lips, uncensored. It helped my process, but there'd been times when even those I worked with were shocked as I let my mind 'free associate' into empathizing with a killer.

The skills of my trade were always with me, even off the job. Whenever I thought about getting to know an interesting woman, my random brain would latch onto a quote from Edmund Kemper, the Co-Ed Killer. *One side of me says, I'd like to talk to her, date her. The other side of me says, I wonder what her head would look like on a stick.* Outside of my work, knowing that line might be construed as peculiar. Although my mind leaps could definitely be described as ice breakers, their social results often rivaled the success of the Titanic's maiden voyage.

I wouldn't expose Justine to that. If I did, she might use me for target practice.

"Most people don't have the stomach to hear what I'm thinking," I said. "Trust me."

"I'm not like most people. The nightmare you had, it was about Nate." She brought up the dream and said it plain, as if it were a fact and not a question. "Is that how it is for you...each case brings its share of demons? Do the faces of the dead go away when the case is over?"

I wasn't sure how to answer her questions. The truth was that I never talked about my work with anyone outside of my team and my Unit Chief. If I told her the truth—that the dead never left me—it only sounded like a solid way to get me fitted for a straitjacket.

"Every case is different."

Tight-lipped. Stoic. Macho. John Wayne would've been proud.

"But Nate is definitely with you now, right? He is with me." She fixed her gaze on me as if she saw through my bullshit. "I haven't been able to get him out of my head. Maybe that's why I sense him in you."

"I don't know what you're saying. It would appear you have an active imagination and you loved the guy. You miss him. There's no room for me in that equation."

I didn't like talking about my cases, but the subject grew even more uncomfortable after Justine had hit the mark when it came to my odd link to Nate. After she caught me in the grips of a nightmare last night, I couldn't deny how much cases affected me.

She'd seen a glimpse of my secret—something no one outside of my family had witnessed—and she didn't make a big deal about it. I couldn't help feeling closer to her. She'd been curious about my dream, yet she didn't make me out to be a pitiable nut bag in need of medication.

Still, I had no intention of granting her a full all-access tour of the inside of my head. That wasn't in the cards. I didn't talk about this stuff for a reason. It was private. I could lose my job. I could lose everything.

I turned to go, but she grabbed my arm.

"Give me something. You don't have to confirm or deny, but if I'm in the ballpark, don't say anything. I have to know."

I heaved a sigh, unsure where she'd go, but I didn't stop her.

"This case has gotten to you, hasn't it? That's why you're here alone and not with your team. It's Nate. There's something about Nathan's case that's got its hooks in you, hasn't it?"

When I couldn't look her in the eye and kept my

silence, she nodded and said, "I knew it. Thank you...for that much."

I knew firsthand what it felt like to see through the eyes of a dead man. There were things in this world and beyond that no one could explain through pure science. The human mind used only a fraction of its capability.

If Justine had a close relationship with Nate, maybe she did sense him. She was the closest I'd come to knowing anyone who shared my sensitivity to the dead...or maybe believing she had a gift helped me not to feel like a freak.

"Some people think that when a person dies a violent death, their retinas are imprinted with the last image they saw. Do you think that's possible?" I asked.

Justine narrowed her eyes and looked surprised.

"Considering how Nate died, I hope not...for *your* sake."

If I'd been vague on my nightmare being linked to Nate, Justine had her own way of distancing her feelings. She'd admitted to loving the guy, but I had a notion she understood the subtlety of the understatement. She cared more than she'd told me, especially if Nate haunted her memory and she had an open mind to what that meant.

The woman intrigued me. She treasured her secrets and her privacy, like I did, yet I could imagine her falling in love, hard. Justine was an independent and strong woman, doing a tough job under challenging conditions. She had been blessed with finding someone to love and had that taken away from her, but she was dealing with it.

"How much farther?" I asked.

Justine smiled. She knew I'd changed the subject on purpose.

"Not far," she said. "Let's go."

***

An hour later

I'd let my body get into a rhythm as I pushed up the mountain. The muscles in my legs burned with the exertion as if I were on a long punishing run. I liked the challenge. Justine walked ahead and led the way to an isolated cabin she knew well. I got the sense she had pressed harder to test me. I caught her looking over her shoulder and saw her amusement. Her subtle smirk only made me stick tighter to her heels.

It's what John Wayne would've done.

There were a lot worse places for a guy to be than staying close to Justine. At the last stop, she'd stripped off her windbreaker and tied it to her pack. She wore a blue tank over khaki shorts. Her arms were toned and tanned and her long legs were hard to ignore.

If Lucinda Crowley had been with me, she would've noticed my interest in the trooper and given me flack over my idea of subtlety. I didn't have much of a life outside the Bureau and Crowley knew it. Sometimes she made fun of the way I acted around women, her idea of encouragement. I considered it a priceless gift to have people in my life who never hesitated to tell me I was full of bat guano.

Crowley was the gift that kept on giving.

When my cell phone rang for the first time on the island, I smiled and reached back to pull the phone from a zippered compartment in my pack.

"I've gotta take this call."

Justine stopped and turned with a surprised look on her face. "How are you getting reception? It's usually hit or miss up here. Mostly miss."

"It's a smart phone with satellite capability. I get

global reception in remote areas because the phone doesn't need a cell tower signal."

Sinead had picked a global service provider that integrated with any smart phone device and app—using orbiting satellite signals instead of cell towers—to provide reliable service in remote areas all over the world. Our new SAT capable phones were encrypted for privacy and could also be tracked using Doppler shift calculations, between the satellite picking up the signal and the phone location, the way cell towers triangulated GPS positions. Given the remote areas we traveled to investigate crime scenes, we were testing the usage based on Sinead's recommendation.

"This won't take long."

I backed down the trail and headed for a boulder that overlooked a valley. Justine was a state trooper, but I considered her an outsider to the investigation. I put distance between us out of habit and answered the call, without my usual greeting.

"Tell Sinead thank you. SAT phones were a stellar idea."

"You're welcome, but was that a pun? Ryker, you made a funny." Sinead said. "Just remember your extreme gratitude come review time."

"Done."

"We're all together in a conference room." Lucinda's voice came over the line. "Everyone's here. We have a prelim on the Applewhite autopsy, but what are you doing? Where are you...exactly?"

"I'm on a mountain, earning macho points on my man card." I looked out over the valley. "Have Sinead track my location coordinates, if it'll help you sleep nights. She could use the practice. We're almost to Applewhite's cabin. Talk about off the grid. If he left the Prince of Wales Island for Seattle, he had to have a damned good reason. I'll call if I find a laptop or anything else interesting."

"You said, 'we.' Who's with you?"

"Sergeant Justine Peterson. She's a State Trooper and lives on the island. She knew our vic and she's taking me to his cabin."

There'd been a long enough pause to make me wonder if the call had been dropped, but eventually Crowley came on the line.

"You got time for an update from our end?"

"Yes. Shoot."

"Lab work isn't final," she said. "No toxicology or DNA yet either, and we're still working on the identities of the others, but I wanted to update you on the autopsy of Nathan Applewhite. Doctor?"

Dr. Julian Martinez came on next and briefed me on the preliminary findings of the autopsy. The ME went through a litany of observations, as if he were mentally filling out his official report, until he got down to the core of his initial conclusions.

"We found a trace of powder residue on the body. The residue is consistent with the powder found on the inside of latex gloves, the same as the others. Nothing new there, but here's where things got interesting."

The sound of papers rustling came over the line until Dr. Martinez went on.

"The carvings on the skin were done over time. Some cuts had even started to heal. Lucinda is sending you digitals. Prior to Nathan Applewhite, I haven't seen this in other victims. Applewhite was held and tortured for days longer."

I heard my phone signal that I'd received a message. I punched up key images of the autopsy as the ME continued.

"Something else. There was evidence of anal tearing and blood, but what we didn't find might be more telling."

"What was that?"

"There was no pubic hair, other than from our victim. No epithelial traces and no evidence of condom use. We found traces of sperm and a lubricant on his genitals, but nothing inside the anal cavity."

"We'll have to revise our profile for the sexual assault. We could be dealing with a sadist," I said. "The kill and dismemberment aren't the only things that get him off."

"Already done," Lucinda agreed.

The most inventive, vicious, and elusive serial offenders were ritualistic sexual sadists. They were cunning predators, like the Great White shark, and the biggest challenge for law enforcement. Stunningly brutal, they were meticulous planners. The carvings on the bodies and the evidence of prolonged torture, coupled with the autopsy findings on Applewhite, had changed my thinking on our UNSUB. We had to stay open to the possibility he was a sexual sadist.

That would mean he could spend countless hours in his own head, perfecting his fantasies. Many rehearsed their crimes with great patience. I had no doubt that this one had indeed created a schematic of how to construct his Totem for aesthetics and ease of assembly. Sexual sadists didn't like surprises and they hated failure, especially after obsessing over the details.

"Our killer has been careful about leaving evidence. He's meticulous. Odds are that the sperm will be from Applewhite. The blood too, but I see your point." I didn't wait for the ME to confirm. "The body wasn't wiped down to remove trace evidence, because there wasn't anything to get rid of that wasn't from Applewhite."

"Exactly. Tissue damage might've been caused by a foreign object inserted into the body. No trace of lubricant."

The sexual assault wasn't about physical gratification. The killer tortured his victims for other reasons and had found another way to get off or punish them. The violence itself could be a turn on.

When I heard about the sexual aspects of our case, a random flash hit me. I thought of Gary Ridgeway, the Green River Killer, convicted of killing forty nine women and girls, confessed to seventy one deaths, but law enforcement speculated he had severely underestimated his body count. The words of Gary Ridgeway came from a dark corner of my mind when he said, *I'm a murderer, not a rapist.*

Apparently even serial killers had standards.

"TK wanted to humiliate him, and he wanted it to hurt, before he took away everything that mattered to him," I said.

"Everything that mattered? You mean his life?" Crowley asked.

"No. He cared about something more. The trooper I've got with me, she knew Applewhite. She said his son meant everything to him. The killer stole his life and degraded him. With a knife shoved into his heart and the days of torture, this feels personal. The killer wanted to see his face—look into his eyes—when he took everything from him...a future with his kid. Applewhite is the key. He's important to our killer, in a way that none of the others were. He could even be the reason for all of this."

"We came to the same conclusion, but I've got a question for you, Ryker," Lucinda's voice cracked. "You made the call to stay behind two days ago. How did you *know*?"

"I didn't know anything. Call it a gut feeling, but that last crime scene felt...different to me. I had a feeling about Applewhite being special and I went with it. Let's hope it pans out."

The call lasted another few minutes with

promises made for updates. I hated being apart from my team. I liked the energy of our dynamics and missed it, but my instincts to follow the Applewhite lead to the island felt solid.

After I ended the call, I heard the sound of boots behind me as I returned the cell to the zippered compartment in my pack. Justine had followed me. She looked worried...and unapologetic.

"I didn't mean to eavesdrop, but I couldn't help it. I had to hear what you found out...about how Nate died."

A tear drained down her cheek.

"We're gonna catch this guy," I said. "I promise you."

She surprised me with a sudden flash of anger, softened by fresh tears welling in her eyes.

"We both know you can't promise that. Nate was number fourteen. If the FBI has met its match, with all its resources and fancy phones, what makes you think you can stop this guy?"

Justine didn't say anything more. She wiped the tears off her face and walked away, leaving me alone with the start of another headache.

Chapter Eight

Prince of Wales Island, Alaska
Forty minutes later
Ryker Townsend

Under a dense cover of trees, I left the river gorge behind and followed Justine through a meandering and worn path. The forest floor had a thick layer of decaying pine needles and fallen leaves that gave a pungent rich smell to the soil. The path buckled under my weight as if I were treading on a mattress. The sensation was unsettling at first, but knowing the cushy feel had been caused by years of decay, layer upon layer built up over centuries, I felt lucky to be walking on it. It was like treading on history.

After the sun broke through the clouds and made a brief appearance, a microcosm of insect life had been drawn and suspended in the sun's rays. Spears of light filtered through green leaves and daylight dappled the ground in colors that reminded me of light shining through the stained glass of a church.

The solitude and the quiet touched me in a way I'd never expected.

With half-lidded eyes I relaxed into the moment and dropped my gaze to Justine's boots as she walked ahead. I listened to the hypnotic sounds of the forest and let the subtle noises close in. A light breeze jostled the treetops and birds flitted in the branches over my head. My boots made soft thuds on the decomposing sod under my feet. Nature had a palpable and soothing rhythm.

Nathan Applewhite had been where I stood now and I knew why he would've chosen to make his home on the island. There was a soul quenching refuge I sensed in my bones. I knew Applewhite must've felt the same. Perhaps like Henry David Thoreau, Nathan had sought the nurturing solitude of the woods *because he wished to live deliberately* and get the most of his life.

Nate had chosen a quiet, simple life. The fact he was dead now—after being tortured and murdered— struck a harsh blow in me. It was an odd feeling to miss someone I'd never met, but the more I saw of Nate's life, the greater I sensed the wake of his absence. Violent death was never fair. The haunting words of David Richard Berkowitz, Son of Sam, seeped from my brain. *I didn't want to hurt them. I only wanted to kill them.*

Making sense of those words would be unfathomable for most people, but it was my job to try. No, I had to do more than try. I had to crawl into the heads of killers like Berkowitz. If I didn't, other people would die and I couldn't live with that.

The UNSUB had picked Nate and killed him. It hadn't been random, but when a guy's number was up, apparently there wasn't a place to hide. Not even in the secluded mountains surrounding Point Baker.

As Justine crested a hill in front of me, she pointed.

"That's it. Nate's place."

A rustic log cabin was nestled in a clearing below. A small creek cut through the trees and made the setting complete. Justine didn't move. She clutched the shoulder straps of her backpack and stared at the home where Nate had lived. Knowing she'd shared nights with him here, I realized that her decision to come with me had not been an easy one to make.

"You okay?" I asked her.

She took a deep breath and let it out. Her eyes were fixed on the cabin as if she expected to see him there.

"Yeah, I will be. Come on. Last push, city boy."

***

As we neared the log home, Justine held out a hand and ducked fast. Her quick move took me by surprise. She gave me a tactical hand signal to stop and I reacted on instinct. It didn't take long for me to understand why she'd gone silent.

Noise came from the cabin. The front door was open wide. Someone was rummaging inside and tearing up Nate's place. A metal pot hit a wall and dropped hard to the floor and something heavy got shoved with a loud angry grunt.

No telling how many guys were in there.

Justine slipped off her pack and retrieved her service weapon in steely silence. By the time she racked the slide of her Glock and chambered a round, I had followed her lead. With weapon in hand, free of my gear, I crouched low beside her.

"My turf. My play. Understood?" she whispered.

I nodded, without a word.

Justine signaled her plan. She had me cover the back, but she wanted me to keep her in sight, in case she had to move fast. To do that, I'd have to take a position that would put me at a distance. I'd have ground to cover if she needed me, but if the guy inside bolted, she knew the cabin layout and the points of egress. I had to trust her instincts as if they were mine.

After I nodded once, she stood with her weapon in a two-fisted grip and shuffled toward the front of the cabin. Treading lightly on the wood porch, she kept her back to the wall and crept toward the open door.

Whoever had done damage inside hadn't

stopped. They cursed and created enough noise to mask any sound Justine made as she approached. She made eye contact and gave another signal for me to back her up.

"Alaska State Troopers," she cried out, in a stern voice. "Inside the cabin. Come out with your hands up."

The noise stopped. Dead silence. I tensed as Justine raised her Glock and aimed at the open door.

"Alaska State Troopers. Come out. Hands up. *Now!*" she yelled.

"I told you what would happen, bitch." A man's voice came from inside. "Death set him free. What was his, is mine now."

Justine braced her body when she heard the man and cocked her head, listening.

"Grady Matson? Is that you?"

The scuff of boots on a wood floor forced Justine to take a step back.

"I won't go to jail for protecting what's mine," the man said. "Back off!"

"Can't do that, Grady. Come out with your hands up. We can talk."

When the man gave her nothing, Justine glanced toward me, but a loud bellow erupted inside and we both braced for a fight. The heavy thud of boots echoed to break the stillness of the standoff. A big man shoved through the door—yelling like a lunatic—and didn't stop. He headed for the tree line and shoved through the thick brush. I saw the flashing glimpse of a red plaid shirt, dark bushy hair, and a full beard. Over six-feet tall, the guy had to tip the scales toward a meaty three-hundred pounds.

Justine didn't hesitate. She took off after the man who'd ransacked Nate's cabin.

"Damn." I backed her up, without question.

The man had crashed through the trees and

became a hulking shadow. All I saw was Justine's back as she raced after him. She cut through bushes without stopping. Branches slashed her bare skin, but she didn't slow.

She picked up speed.

When the trail split, I slowed, unsure what she'd do or where the guy had gone, but Justine didn't stop. Over her shoulder, she called out to me.

"We can cut him off, but you gotta move." She shouted and waved a hand. "You go that way. Our paths will cross. *Go!*"

I did as she told me. Up ahead I heard the man trampling through the quiet of the forest. Every crack of wood and heavy thump of boots echoed off the trees and made it hard to tell where the noise came from. Justine had said our paths would cross if I moved fast. Drenched in sweat, I pushed to catch up. I followed the sounds of a foot chase on a trail I didn't know.

I heard Justine in pursuit to my left, but couldn't see her. She wasn't far. If she got to the guy first, she'd be alone. I ran harder. I spotted a clearing ahead. With the level ground, I could make up time. I hurtled a fallen log and hit the clearing to pick up my pace.

When one of my boots hit something hard, my ankle twisted. A sharp pain shot up my leg and a crushing vise cut deep into my skin. I heard the heavy snap of clamping steel that held me firm and wouldn't budge.

I cried out and slammed to the ground, landing face first. My head hit hard, enough to see stars. In excruciating pain, I lay belly down on the ground. I struggled to stay conscious and smelled blood as a burning agony shot up my calf. With sweat pouring off me, I lay panting in the dirt, unsure I could move. I felt nauseous and couldn't focus. Everything spun in a blur.

Stay awake. Shake it off.

When I looked down at my ankle, I saw a steel trap had cut its teeth into my leg. Blood saturated my jeans. The bone could be busted. Without help, I wasn't going anywhere. Every move I made, the trap cut deeper into my flesh and closer to the bone.

Barely able to keep my eyes open, I fought the shadows that edged in. I pictured the night sky, the one I'd seen from Justine's back porch, except the stars were spinning and falling to the earth.

Justine.

She was alone and chasing after a man who'd been desperate enough to run from the law. She'd counted on me to back her up, but that wouldn't happen. When I heard the distant crack of gunfire, the muffled sound carried through the trees. I couldn't tell from which direction. Numb and in pain, I closed my eyes and let my body sink into the growing darkness.

Chapter Nine

Prince of Wales Island, Alaska
Ryker Townsend

I felt hands on my body. I wanted to open my eyes, but I couldn't. Someone brushed fingers through my hair and ran a hand over my chest. The touches drifted down my legs. I was content to tread the line between consciousness and a restless sleep until a worsening pain gouged deeper into me.

"Ryker. Can you hear me?" A woman's voice.

I heard a distant moan. It took me awhile before I realized the sound had come from me.

"Wake up," she said.

Fingers patted my face. I cracked my eyes open and a bright light blinded me. I squinted and held up a hand, but when I moved, the agonizing pain shot through my body. I cried out and a hand touched my thigh and held on.

"Don't move. Stay still. That's it."

Fingers trailed down my cheek. Cool velvet. *Don't move. Yes, I can do that.* I saw a misty puzzle in flesh tones spiral in front of me. A face. It looked like colored fragments shifting in a kaleidoscope.

"Stay with me. I gotta get you out of here. It's not safe."

The pieces pulled together and the face of Justine Peterson stared down at me. She looked worried.

"What...h-happened?" I asked.

"The guy I chased got away, but I know who he is. He's the poacher I told you about. Grady Lee Matson, the bastard who had it out for Nate."

"Slow down. Your lips are moving, but the words need time to catch up."

"Yeah. You got it." After she took a deep breath, she poured water into her palm and cooled my face with it. "You landed in one of his illegal bear traps. I don't think you broke a bone, but I can't be sure. Your leg is hamburger."

I winced with a strained laugh.

"Don't sugarcoat it. Give it to me straight."

"Sorry. I call it like I see it." She put her hand on my shoulder. "I did the best I could with your leg until I get you back to the cabin. Can you sit up?"

"I don't know. Upright is overrated."

Justine fended off my sarcasm like a pro and helped me off my back. My jeans were spattered in blood, but the wound was covered with a makeshift bandage. In the clearing, an animal trap was snapped closed near my feet and marred with blood and chunks of fresh skin. *Mine.* I hadn't seen it before because it had been buried in pine needles and debris until I stepped in it.

She told me she'd pried open the steel hinge using a sturdy branch to free my leg. The metal teeth had cut deep into my calf and raked down the flesh to my ankle, but she'd staunched the bleeding by using an improvised tourniquet and wrapped my wounds with a clean cotton shirt from her pack. Her dressing on the fly would have to do until I could get medical help.

"He got away, you said?" I asked. "You think he'll be back?"

"The guy's crazy mean. Guess we can't rule that out. Is your bad luck contagious?"

"Let's hope not, for your sake."

In that moment I flashed on Franklin Roosevelt and his take on good fortune. He believed too many people talked about the good luck of the early bird, when the hard luck of the early worm had its own side of the story.

"You talked about Nate having a stalker," she said. "I can see Matson being that kind of guy, now that I've had time to think about him. He used to work at the same hunting lodge as Nate, before the poaching incident, but the guy got fired. He wasn't very reliable and the lodge got complaints from clients. Nate took on the extra work and essentially replaced him."

"Did he blame Nate for him getting fired?" I asked. "There doesn't have to be a real connection. A guy like Matson doesn't need much of a catalyst. If he did blame Nate, the poaching could've been his way of targeting him. Matson hunting illegally in his backyard may not have been a coincidence."

"Could he be the one who killed Nate?" Justine had a hard time looking me in the eye.

"Revenge is a powerful motive. If Matson has a connection to Seattle, he'd be a suspect. Our killer operates out of that area. If Matson lives in Alaska, Seattle could be his body dumping ground so he can keep suspicion off him. He wouldn't crap where he eats. Do you know if he has a plane or a pilot's license?"

"I don't know. I'd have to check, but since he works with hunting lodges, it's very likely. Alaska has six times as many pilots than any other state in the Lower 48."

"Do you know if Matson is working somewhere now?"

"Not in Point Baker, but I heard he might have something out of Klawock, a town just south of here. After the poaching incident, I thought he was out of Nate's hair when he moved away, but if he's got traps here, I was wrong. *Really* wrong. He must've come back to old hunting grounds so no one in Klawock would know about his poaching."

She looked down at my ankle and touched my

thigh.

"Can you move?" she asked. "I have to get you to Nate's place. With Matson in the wind, I'd rather have walls around us. We can make a call for help using that fancy FBI phone you have."

"Yeah, good. At the risk of tarnishing my John Wayne bravado, I need your help to stand."

Justine held out her hand and braced her body for my weight. When she pulled me up, I winced and stifled a yell. With my leg on fire, I almost passed out when I got to my feet. Everything spun until I took a deep breath and held on to Justine.

"You okay?" she asked. "You're not gonna nod off again, are you?"

I groaned and shook my head. *Liar.*

"Take it slow." Justine grabbed my arm and pulled it around her shoulders. "Lean on me. I can take your weight."

No part of my inner smart ass had a voice. I let her help me and didn't bother regaling her with my keen affection for the absurd. Even my teeth hurt. She pulled me into her body and held on. One of her hands was tight on my wrist while the other took hold of my hip to keep me steady. I felt her strength and drew from it.

Every step I took felt like the stab of a knife and the return trip to Nate's cabin was arduous and slow. With the sun gone from the horizon, the night air carried a chill. I wanted to believe my shivers came from the dropping temperature, but behind my eyes, I felt the heat of a fever.

As we approached the cabin, it didn't look as welcoming as it had in the daylight. Murky shadows made me wary, but I breathed a sigh of relief that I didn't have to keep walking. I only wanted to lie down and sleep, until I saw my clothes strewn on the ground near my pack and my adrenaline kicked in.

Justine's gear had been rifled through, too. Her backpack looked as if it had exploded.

"Ah, hell. He must've doubled back. I tell you, that bastard is messed up." Justine helped me to the porch and made sure I could stand on my own before she pulled her weapon and checked the inside of the cabin for intruders.

"All clear, but the place is a wreck." She holstered her gun and headed for her gear.

I felt lightheaded from blood loss and nauseous as I leaned against the threshold of the front door, watching Justine. Crouched on the ground, she went through her stuff first and crammed things back into her pack.

"He took a little food, but I don't see anything else missing," she said. "You want me to check yours? Anything valuable you want me to search for?"

The instant Justine looked at me, I felt as if I'd been cold cocked. My badge and gun were with me. Beyond that, I had only one thing I cared about.

"My phone. Bottom right zipper pocket."

Justine's eyes grew wide. She knew what I thought the minute I'd asked her to look for my cell. I couldn't take my eyes off her as she searched. When she came up empty, Justine shook her head and heaved a sigh. Her shoulders slumped.

"Damn." I leaned my head against the log cabin and shut my eyes. "My bad luck would appear to be a malignancy. Let's hope it's not terminal."

The mountain of my misfortune weighed heavy on me—made worse by what I suspected. If Matson had risked doubling back and rifled through our gear—taking our lifeline for help—it could only mean one thing.

Grady Lee Matson wasn't done with us. He'd be watching and waiting to make his next move.

***

BAU headquarters
Quantico, Virginia
After dark

In a dimly lit room Special Agent Devin Hutchison sat at his desk huddled over his keyboard. He'd softened the overhead lights in his office to make it easier to see the screen and his fingers tapped out commands that retrieved online records. He read through another missing person report filed in the Seattle area as he ate a stale blueberry scone.

"Sanforth, John. You don't fit the victimology, Elvis. Righteous sideburns though." After he clicked on another profile image, he winced. "Oh, dude. Seriously? The eighties called. They want their mullet back."

When he worked alone, after hours, Hutch often talked to himself to help him focus. He liked hearing a voice in the quiet, even if it was his. He glanced over his shoulder at another computer screen that ran his fingerprint scans against other databases using software he'd created to save him time in the cross reference process. His program had a certain amount of acceptable redundancy since fingerprint records were shared across resources, but if his secondary query scored a hit, he didn't care if his program search criteria appeared inelegant. All that mattered was getting results.

He had to resort to a derivative search after his first pass had been a bust on the FBI's Integrated Automated Fingerprint Identification System. With IAFIS being the largest biometric database in the world, the odds of him finding a match elsewhere was statistically a long shot, but he refused to accept that. Local, state, and other federal law enforcement agencies voluntarily shared fingerprints and criminal histories with IAFIS, but when he didn't get a hit, he'd been forced to cross check for prints that may have fallen through the crack of such a massive system and look for matches in more obscure resources.

He hadn't gotten a first hit yet, but he wanted to be in his office when he did. Every positive ID they made bettered the odds of getting another lead.

"Gotta have faith, baby," he said with a yawn. "And a shot of Red Bull."

Hutch's eyes were strained from a long day. He took off his glasses and shut his eyes for a break and pinched the bridge of his nose to stave off a tension headache. He stretched his arms and rolled his head to ease the tight muscles in his neck and shoulders. He'd been sitting too long.

When he heard the sound of a buzzer coming from a secured door down the hall and the echo of footsteps, he knew it would be his ERT partner, Camilla Devore.

"Good timing, Cam," he whispered as he keyed up another report.

"You look exhausted." She smiled as she came up behind him and worked her fingers deep into his neck muscles to give him a massage. "Lucky for you, I find tired boys very sexy. Sleepy eyes make me think of a hot bath and bed...for two."

"Oh, God, you're not playing fair." He shut his eyes and gave in to her. Hutch dropped his chin into his chest and let Cam's fingers work their magic. "Ahh, that feels...amazing.

"I'm only getting started, love." She trailed her hands down his chest and slipped one under his shirt. The warmth of her touch gave him a second wind. He leaned his body into her and let Cam have whatever she wanted.

During work hours, she kept their relationship

professional. She'd shoot him a wink, text him, or catch his eye across a conference room table to let him know she thought of him, but after hours when they were alone together, things were different.

He never knew what Cam saw in him. She was a couple years older than him and hot as hell. She could have any man she wanted, but when she'd hit on him first—seriously—how could he refuse? Dating was an epic fail for him, but with Cam, he flew his geek flag with pride and never worried what she thought.

They kept a low profile on the job and had separate apartments. Since they didn't want to jeopardize working together, neither of them broached the subject of moving in. Whatever they had, it worked. Lucinda Crowley and Sinead Royce suspected he had something going on with Cam, but they never made a big deal about it.

"No hit on IDs yet?" she asked, nibbling his ear.

"Not yet." He sighed. "I'm running prints and searching missing person reports, looking for anything to tie these body parts with a name. I don't want to miss anything. Did I mess you up for dinner?"

Cam had offered to cook at her place. She'd gone home to start dinner, but when he didn't show, she called to say she would head back to help him and dinner would wait. Cam was cool like that. Nothing riled her and she understood how he lost track of time when he was on a tough case. They were both like that.

"In case you haven't noticed, I'm not exactly hungry for food, Devin." She nuzzled kisses down his neck. "I'll help you now...if you make it up to me later. And trust me. You're gonna pay. Deal?"

"If that means you're gonna spank me, 'cause I've been a bad boy—deal." He stood and pulled her into his arms. Hutch held her face in both hands and kissed her long and slow.

"Seriously, thanks. I'll make it up to you," he whispered.

"Yes, you will." Cam settled into a chair and got to work, sifting through online records to cut his time in half.

Thirty minutes in, one of the database alerts sounded and Hutch did a fist pump and yelled, "Yes!" He raced over to the computer to grab the mouse and pull up the file.

"Ha. I knew you'd bring me luck. We got our first hit." He grinned. "Fingerprints off one of the severed arms. Brian Dunkirk. See if you can pull up DMV on him."

"On it," Cam said as she hit the keyboard on another computer. In minutes, she had more on their first body identified. "Dunkirk lives outside Seattle in Redmond. Good job, Boy Wonder. Check him out."

Cam had pulled up a DMV photo and had it displayed on the screen. The young man looked eerily similar in appearance to Nathan Applewhite, the dead guy at the top of the Totem.

"You know, when TK started killing, the earlier victims didn't look like this, but I'm beginning to see a more defined pattern," Hutch said, not taking his eyes off the computer. "It's like he's zeroing in on a type and not hiding his preference now."

"You channeling Ryker?" Cam asked. "Because you just gave me goose bumps. I think you're right. You know what else this means, Hutch?"

He shrugged and shook his head, too tired to play twenty questions.

Cam smiled and said, "You're getting so laid tonight."

***

Prince of Wales Island, Alaska
Ryker Townsend

I listened to the eerie stillness as I stood outside Nate's remote mountain cabin with Justine. Birds and other animals were noticeably quiet. In the distance I heard the sound of a rushing river and the night's chill settled onto my skin through my clothes as a breeze rustled through the evergreens in an unsettled whisper.

I shut my eyes to listen to it all.

I had a sense Matson had eyes on me. That's what I'd be doing if our situations were reversed, but the macabre feeling of being watched hadn't left me since the Cascades. That could be paranoia, but after the connection I'd made from the last crime scene, I hadn't experienced anything like it before. If the hair on my neck stood at attention, my primal instincts had a good reason to flare.

The sensation of being watched had followed me here. It was with me now. I couldn't break free of it.

TK's here. I can feel it.

The sun had gone down, but this time of year in Alaska—when the days were getting longer—it never got totally pitch black. A bluish haze shed enough light to see under the night sky, but inside the cabin, things were impossibly dark.

"Wait here until I find one of Nate's lanterns," she said. "I don't want you tripping over anything in there."

"Good call. If there's anything to trip me in there, I would find it."

Justine disappeared into the cabin as I leaned against the front doorjamb, feeling utterly useless and wincing in pain.

A faint glow lit the small dwelling enough for me to see the damage. Grady Lee Matson had torn it apart in what looked like a blind rage. Pots and pans were strewn on the floor and cupboards were open with shards of broken dishes scattered. Nate's mattress had gaping tears through it like Matson had bludgeoned it with a knife. The rage it took to wreak such havoc meant Matson had a personal grudge or a vendetta against Applewhite that made him want to wipe out his very existence, even after he was dead.

Killers often targeted surrogates to murder, substitutes for the violence and hatred they felt for someone else. A practice run they could repeat over and over. I didn't know if that was the case with Nate, but the destruction in the cabin looked out of control.

"This guy has anger issues." I gazed around the shadowy room and looked for something I'd expected to see. "Did Nate have weapons? Knives, hunting rifles, ammo? We'll need 'em."

"Yeah. He hid them. They'd be locked away. I'll check his cache when I've got you settled."

With Justine's help, I hobbled into the shambles of Nathan Applewhite's cabin.

Before Matson got to it, Nate's place must've been well-stocked and homey. He had heavy quilts on the bed, utensils for cooking, and a small pantry. The stone fireplace had seen plenty of use with a loaded bin of firewood outside, as if Nate would be home any minute. Framed photos of him and his boy had been smashed to the floor and his son's water color pictures had been trashed and torn off the pins that must've held them on a wall.

I didn't know what Nate had done to become a target for such hatred.

"Matson is a real piece of work." Justine sighed as she gazed over what remained of Nate's home.

"Yeah."

She helped me to the bed and scavenged for blankets to keep me warm. Justine made me lie down before she hoisted my leg and elevated it onto pillows to slow down the bleeding. On my back the dizziness had returned, but it felt good to lie down and take the weight off my ankle.

"Do you think he was looking for something?" I asked. "Why would he rip things up like this? Stealing I can understand, but this is...rage."

"The guy's deranged. He fixated on Nate after he reported him. I told Nate I didn't like him living alone and isolated. I wanted him to stay with a friend until I figured out Matson's deal, but he refused. He said he wouldn't let the guy intimidate him, not even after he found the butchered animals."

"What animals? Tell me."

"We could never pin anything on Matson, but after the confrontation with him, Nate found animal carcasses strung from trees on his property, around his cabin. The smell was bad enough, but the scent of blood brought the bears in, foraging for food. That was a dangerous thing to do."

"How were the dead animals strung up? Any details could help."

"The smaller ones were strung with fishing line, but the bigger carcasses were hung with rope and staked into the tree trunks," she told me. "Nate never heard him do it. They would just appear and got closer and closer to his home. He dealt with bears for months, but he knew it was Matson."

"Forgive what I'm about to ask." I hesitated. I had a hard time focusing and knew I had a fever now. My thoughts were muddled.

"Go ahead." She stopped picking up the pieces of Nate's life and sat on the edge of the bed. "Say it."

"Do you think Matson's obsession with Nate was...sexual? Our ME found evidence of...rape." When I saw the shock on Justine's face, I sighed. "Sorry. I didn't know how else to say it."

Her eyes filled with tears.

"I don't know how far Matson would've gone to hurt him." A tear spilled down her cheek. "That kind of degradation and torture would have terrified Nate, but to take away any future he had with his son would've been worse. Whoever did this to Nate had to know him well enough to find the one thing that would devastate him. Matson would've known about his boy, Tanner. Nate talked about him all the time. That's all I can say with any certainty. Sorry I can't be of more help."

Hearing her talk about her regrets with Nate, I thought about the happiness they may have squandered because of bad timing, different ambitions, whatever the excuse. I didn't know if it would've been a good thing for them to be together. I only knew they quit before they found out and Justine would always wonder.

Nate had died, but at least he had his son, Tanner, to be his legacy. My one thing that would devastate me, if I didn't have it, was my job. It was important to me and to those unnamed souls whose lives I saved because I stopped someone from killing, but I still felt like I've been missing something.

I carried the weight of a hard to describe emptiness. A void I wasn't sure how to fill. I thought about the choices I'd made—and what the unopened boxes sitting in my living room said about me. All of it made me sad and feeling bad didn't help my sullen mood.

"No. It's okay. I understand." My eyes were getting droopy and I couldn't focus. I was getting sucked into '*what ifs*' and the only thing that would buy me was a one-way ticket on the pity train. I didn't like it. "It can't be easy for you to talk about Nate, not like this."

"No, it hasn't been. No one knows about my

feelings for him, but it's been good to share things, especially with you." She touched my forehead and brushed back my hair. "You don't look good. Your skin is hot and clammy. I think you have a fever. I've got something in my gear for that."

She left me to haul our stuff inside and search her pack and Nate's supplies for anything she could use as first aid. After she found what she wanted, she came back to me.

"Here, take this." She had a few white tablets in one hand. In the other, she had a tin cup of water.

"What is it?"

"I had meds in my Trooper first-aid kit. A couple of aspirins for your fever and a pain reliever for your ankle."

"No pain med. Only aspirin. I want a clear head if Matson shows."

Justine grimaced.

"Okay, but say the word if the pain gets bad."

She picked out two pills and handed them to me. After I tossed the tablets in my mouth, she held the cup of water for me to wash them down.

"I've got fresh bandages, but I'll wait until the aspirin kicks in before I dress your wound. That's gonna hurt like hell, I'm afraid," she said. "No more talking until I get this place in shape. I got work to do and you need to rest."

I nodded. Through half-lidded eyes, I watched her clean up the cabin. I'd closed my eyes and lost track of time until I woke to the sound and the warmth of a crackling fire in the stone hearth. Gazing into the blaze, I drifted in and out of consciousness as I listened to the scuffs and thumps of Justine's boots on the wood floor. The throbbing burn of my ankle had gone numb as long as I didn't move.

"You ready to see the damage?" Justine looked ready to hurt me.

"Yeah, I guess."

She cut away the soaked shirt she'd used to bind my ankle and stem the bleeding and sliced open my pant leg. With the wound exposed, I got my first look at the injury that had me flat on my back. The metal teeth of the trap had slit the skin of my calf in gashes, down to the bone in spots. After I'd hit the trap and it held me, my momentum from running had done the worst damage and caused jagged steel to rake down my leg.

"This needs to be cleaned. I can't just cover it up. Infection can set in too fast."

"Okay. Do it."

With meticulous care, she rinsed my wound in water and cleared dirt and debris from the gaping trenches before she applied an antibiotic ointment and fresh bandages. It hurt like hell, as promised.

"We'll have to change the dressing daily and be careful not to disturb the clotting, or else you'll start bleeding again."

I winced and nodded after she was done and settled into the covers she tossed back over me. I stared into the red burning embers of a dying fire in the hearth, mesmerized by the glow that flickered in the dark until I closed my eyes and gave in to the numbness crawling through my body.

When I felt the mattress jostle, I saw the shadow of Justine climbing into bed with me. The intimacy shocked me. We were still strangers, even though we were on the fast track to changing that. I don't know what I'd expected. Guess I thought she'd be more wary of me and choose the privacy of her own sleeping bag, but that didn't happen.

Justine nestled close to me with her clothes on and a blanket over her. Although her move to join me had surprised me, I had to admit. I liked having her in bed with me. I closed my eyes and listened to her breaths with the warmth of her body next to me.

***

Hours later

A red light throbbed like a steady pulse. A heartbeat in the dark. Masking the rhythm was the raspy and frantic gasp of someone running and the buzzing undercurrent of flies. In the distance I heard the caw of a raven and the frantic flap of wings that set me on edge. The erratic and unsettling sights and sounds made me sicker. Sweat poured from me and trickled down my body until the wetness pooled. Water swirled up my skin and inched toward my chest and chin. I craned my neck to keep above the swell, but something held me down.

Can't breathe. Help me.

I felt a weight crushing my chest and I couldn't move. I had my eyes open, but everywhere I looked, I only saw the pulsing red light cutting through the darkness. I reached out my hands to feel my way through an endless void—tumbling weightless, end over end—but something cut into my wrists and tethered me to a growing danger. As the tether got shorter, I was tugged toward a place I didn't want to go.

Something warm and sticky drained down my arms. I smelled the stench of blood—and a far worse odor—and I fought harder to pull away. Flies clung to my skin, feeding off me.

No! Get off me.

The more I thrashed, the more frantic I became. A raging fever churned under my skin as the weight on my chest took shape. Someone was on top of me.

I can't breathe.

With the red glow casting its eerie light across a chasm, it took time for my night vision to adjust to

132

the murky depth. It felt as if I'd been blinded by the light and could see what lay beyond it. I wasn't alone. A dark faceless silhouette stared down at me as I lay helpless underneath the dead weight of the body straddling my chest.

You...

I heard the sound of another's voice, as if someone spoke through me, and all I could do was watch...and do nothing.

The dark face disturbed me. With my heart pounding through my throat and ears, I couldn't take my eyes off the black shadowy skin that puckered and undulated as if every cell were alive. The shriek of the raven and the drone of flies got louder.

The shadow shifted and raised its arms. In the red throb of light, I saw the glint of a knife hovering over me.

Oh, God. No! I jerked under the weight, but couldn't get away.

The blade plunged into my chest. I cried out in agony, drowning in the blood filling my lungs. The face of my killer broke apart into hundreds of flies and writhing maggots slithered down. The winged insects swarmed over me and fragmented the body that had held me down. I was free of the burden, but it was too late.

In shock, I gasped as I stared at the blade protruding from my heart.

No! No!

***

"No! No!" I yelled and shoved at the hands holding me down. I felt sick. I wanted to throw up.

"You're having a bad dream, Ryker. Another one. It's the fever this time. You need more aspirins."

Justine's voice cut through the haze. "Please...take the pain meds. You need 'em. You're making your ankle worse. You have to stay still, or you'll start bleeding again."

I shook my head, but Justine put something in my mouth and made me swallow water from a cup.

"I know...what happened to...Nate," I mumbled. "I know what he saw...when he died."

"No. You're hallucinating. You couldn't have seen it. It's the fever talking."

Justine washed my forehead and neck with a wet cloth to cool me, but stopped when she realized what I'd said.

"What exactly did you see, Ryker?" She held my face and forced me to look at her. "How can you *know* what Nate saw? That's...*crazy*. You're scaring me."

Caught in the vise of my nightmare, I forced the haunting images from my mind. I stared at Justine until I let my gaze drift through the shadows of the cabin to ground me in reality. I was wounded and sick and stranded unless I could make my way down the mountain.

A dead guy had led me here, possibly straight to his killer, a skilled and angry hunter who looked to be out for more blood. That was *my* reality. I slowed my heart by taking deep breaths and waited for the meds to take hold.

Get a grip. Let it go.

What I'd told Justine made no sense, yet it still felt true. Even before I'd gotten the call to investigate the crime scene in the Cascade Mountains, the dream had started in DC. It was as if I were channeling Nate through a strange vision at the worst torturous moment of the guy's life—the instant of his death. I didn't understand any of it.

How could I trust my nightmares—and who

would believe me if I could?

Chapter Ten

Prince of Wales Island, Alaska
The next day
Ryker Townsend

An abrasive metal sound jolted me awake from a dead sleep. I cried out as I thrashed free of my bed sheets, stunned. It took me time to realize where I was and what I had heard—the scrape and clack of a spoon on a skillet.

I felt like an idiot.

"Ah, hell." I collapsed onto the mattress, gasping.

My heart pounded my ribs and the sudden rush to sit up left me dizzy. My body was on a collision course I couldn't stop and I hated not being in control. Some people knew how to behave when they were sick. I wasn't one of them. I fought every symptom, like my defiance would make a difference.

"I didn't mean to wake you."

"No. Sorry. It's all me."

With the things I see in my job, it wasn't hard to hear the rasp of metal and not flash on a knife grating flesh from bone. Justine's culinary skills had nothing to do with my mental state and she didn't look as if she'd taken offense.

"I'm making us breakfast. How are you feeling?" She had a fire in the hearth and stood cooking over a camp stove. "You look..."

"Look like what?"

I really didn't want to know.

"You don't wanna know."

She'd read me, admittedly not much of a challenge. It sounded like she'd teased me, but the worried look on her face told me she wasn't joking.

"I don't think I can eat," I said. "I feel...sick."

The smell of food made me queasy. I knew that wasn't a good sign. What the hell was *wrong* with me?

"Maybe you've got a concussion. From the bump on your head, you must've hit the ground hard."

I hadn't been thinking clearly and this morning I felt worse, but I didn't want to worry her.

"We gotta talk. Make a plan." I propped a pillow under my head and winced with every move.

Justine took the skillet off the stove and sat close enough for me to see her with my bad eyes. The light coming in from the windows blinded me and every squint made my head pound. My misery would be compounded by having to actually think. If I could've found a way around the strain of mulling over my situation, I would've done it, but that would require more mulling. The irony made my head hurt and I was back to square one. We needed a plan.

"I came to see if Nate had a laptop here," I said. "...and search his place for any connection he might've had to the Seattle area. I'd appreciate your help."

"Yes, of course. Anything I can do." She furrowed her brow and watched me with laser focus. "That's why I came. It hasn't been easy being here, but if there's anything I can do to get you one step closer to Nate's killer, that's why I'm here."

"Being at his cabin again, it's been hard on you, hasn't it?"

"Yeah, you have no idea, but I had to come. I had no choice." The vulnerability had returned to her eyes. "I'm worried about you. We have to consider going back...and when to do it."

I couldn't shake my bleary eyesight. The muddled edges of my vision forced me to see everything through a foggy tunnel. It was as if I were trapped in one of my dreams, unable to tell what was real.

Justine wanted to talk about going down the mountain, but if we got ambushed, I wouldn't do her much good in my condition. I could make everything worse. I couldn't think or see straight. Maybe I *did* have a concussion.

"I'm not sure how safe that would be with Matson out there. If you're dealing with me, he could take both of us out easy. We'd be in the open." I hated putting her in more danger, because of me. "You could leave me here and try it on your own. You'd move faster without me and besides, I'd have my gun and whatever Nate left here for weapons. I could hold out until you got help."

I listened to my voice as if someone else were speaking. Muffled sounds made it feel like my ears were stuffed with cotton. I was getting worse, but I struggled not to let my growing list of warning signs show. Justine was worried enough.

"You're too messed up to stay here alone, Ryker. Matson could slit your throat in your sleep. You were delirious last night and if your fever gets worse..." She didn't finish. Didn't have to. She only shook her head and said, "Besides, if Matson got to me on the trail, you'd never know it. You'd be waiting for help that would never come."

"What do you propose?"

"I think we should stay together...here. You need me to take care of you. If I can stabilize you in a day or two, it would be easier to make the trek down."

"And if you can't, what then?"

Justine only shrugged and avoided my eyes. We both knew what would happen if I got sicker. Her option sounded overly optimistic.

"What about Matson?" I asked. "He'd still be out there, whether we stay or not."

Justine got quiet with a grave look on her face.

"I could hunt him. He wouldn't be expecting that. If he still has your phone, I can get it back. We could call for help and get you a doctor. With him out of the picture, we'd have options without looking over our shoulders." She clenched her jaw and took a deep breath. "I wouldn't have to leave you for long...and you'd have your gun. He may not even know you're hurt."

"Come on. He's a hunter. He has to know I'm wounded. I left enough blood on the trail and his trap is full of my hide." I winced at my aggravated headache. "If my team can't reach me by my SAT phone, they'll know something is up. They'll track me. My cell can be located by satellite. Matson may not realize that. If he leaves the phone on, it'll be like a beacon."

"Oh, yeah? Good to know." Justine sighed. "Well, I'm not leaving you. End of argument. Since my head is clearer than yours—which is not a high bar, by the way—you're gonna have to trust my judgment. You good with that?"

I had no choice. She would beat me hands down if it came to an arm wrestle or a rigorous game of rock, paper, scissors. After I nodded, Justine got back to work and made breakfast. The food smell tortured me, but after she'd brought me a plate, I ate what I could. I had to keep my strength up...and the food down.

She'd made a skillet of potatoes, onions, sausage and cheese from items she'd brought in her backpack. In a plastic tub, she'd brought her leftover salmonberry cobbler and served it cold. If I felt better, the hearty breakfast would have tasted good, but I had to force every bite.

We ate in silence with Justine keeping her eyes on me. She could play poker with the best of them. I had trouble reading her. After she took away my plate and cleaned up, she was the first one to break the stillness as she sat at the table, working.

"While you were sleeping last night, I got up and searched the place for a laptop and didn't find one. Didn't expect to. He was familiar with computers and being online. More than me, but if I had to guess, I'd say he used a computer at the lodges he worked out of."

She told me once tourist season started and the lodges got busy, Nate would come down from the mountain and stay put with the hunting or fishing parties he would serve as guide. He'd work long stretches of time with booked parties, but get time off where he could score downtime at his cabin between work shifts.

"Seeing how remote his cabin is, that makes sense. He had the best of both worlds. He worked hard when he was on, but his downtime was his own." I nudged my chin at her. "I see you've been busy. You found his stash of weapons."

Justine had a few knives in leather sheaths on the table, as well as a twelve-gauge shotgun, and she prepared to clean a couple of hunting rifles.

"Yeah, he used a .300 Remington Ultra Mag for bears and a .243 Winchester for black tail deer season," she said. "I'll load the shotgun and one of the rifles and put them by you when I'm done cleaning them."

I blinked to clear my vision as I sat in bed. My condition hadn't changed much. A rifle with a scope seemed like a waste for me—given the shape I was in—but I might need the long range weapon to keep Matson at a distance.

"I'll be out for a while," she said. "I'm taking the Remington and my handgun."

I didn't like what I heard and it must've shown on my face. Justine stopped what she was doing and came to my bed. She sat on the edge of the mattress and ran a hand across my brow and down my cheek. She had a reason to touch me to check my temperature, but the sympathy on her face made it more personal.

"Your ankle has stopped bleeding, but you haven't shaken the fever. I won't be gone long. Stay alert if you can. I don't want Matson getting close to you, not in the shape you're in. You think you can stay awake?"

"Yeah, I'll try," I said. "Don't make any risky moves. I don't like you being out there without back up."

"Welcome to my world, Ryker. Troopers in Alaska cover a lot of ground alone. I work in isolation all the time. Back up isn't always possible. Solo comes with the job."

I didn't like Justine hunting Matson alone, but in my condition I wouldn't do her any good. She didn't need an albatross like me hanging around her neck.

"To be clear, by hunting him, you mean take him alive, right?" I asked her. "If he doesn't give you a choice, you have to defend yourself, but we need to question him."

"So you *do* believe he killed Nate and the others." She touched my arm. "I got a feeling about him, too."

"I'm not rushing to judgment. There's too much we don't know yet. We have to question him. If he's our guy, we have too many families without closure. We need to ID every one of those bodies. We need him alive, no matter which way this goes."

"Yes, of course. I understand." She nodded. "I'm leaving you with a canteen of water. Stay hydrated. I also made you a crutch if you have to get up, but I wouldn't advise it unless it's necessary."

"Yeah...thanks."

She fixed her gaze on me and said, "This is

important. When I come back, I'll call out to you before I hit the porch. Don't shoot me."

"You'd have to be pretty close for me to hit you. My eyesight...it's not good."

"Maybe I should stay." She touched my cheek with an affection that surprised me.

The shadow of her hand crossed over my eyes and I flinched. The sudden move. My disconnected brain. I don't know what triggered my reaction, but it happened. The minute I shied away, I regretted it. She looked hurt, but the damage was already done.

I felt like an ass.

"Sorry. I just didn't expect it. That's all."

"If I had to guess, I'd say you don't have anyone special in your life. You're not used to the intimacy of a woman's touch. Nate was like that too, at first. When you live alone too long, it's easy to forget what it feels like to be touched."

"He must've gotten over that pretty quick...if you were lovers." After her expression changed and she avoided looking me in the eye, I said, "Sorry, I didn't mean to pry."

"I opened the door. You had a right to walk through it."

"No, you're right. I've lived alone for years and I'm afraid it shows."

"The thing is about living alone, there's no one there to...*stop* you."

I wanted to ask, *stop you from doing what...exactly?* But the pathetic part was that I didn't need to. I had no one to answer to, no one to debate the countless ways I sabotaged my personal life—and did so with impunity.

"The truth is that I miss him in my life. I miss what we had. He made me want...*more.* I guess since you remind me of Nate, my touching you could be part of that. If it bothers you, I'll stop...except for when I have to change your dressing."

I forced a smile.

"No, it's okay, really. I'm not thinking straight. It's not you. It's me." I took a deep breath before I fixed my gaze on her. "You should go. I don't like you out there solo, but I see your point. If you find Matson and take him into custody, getting my phone back could make all the difference. Do what you have to. Find him."

"I'll do my best."

Before Justine left the cabin, she set me up with everything I would need by my bed. She had my canteen of water, aspirins, and the twelve-gauge loaded. I sat up, with pillows behind my back and the shotgun across my lap.

I popped pills in my mouth and washed them down with a long pull on the canteen. By the time Justine headed out, my fever had come back with a vengeance—something I hadn't told her.

***

BAU headquarters
Quantico, Virginia
Noon

ERTs Devin Hutchison and Camilla Devore came into the conference room where Lucinda Crowley had asked them to meet her at noon. She wanted a briefing of their progress in identifying the latest bodies. Cam set up the visuals they'd need and Hutch handed Lucinda hard copy file folders.

"Don't forget that..." Hutch said to Camilla.

Before he finished, she answered him.

"Yeah, got it."

Her ERTs had their game faces on, but as they worked side by side preparing for their meeting, Lucinda fought a smile. Outwardly, her evidence recovery techs were polar opposites in nearly every way.

Hutch dressed with all the subtlety of a rock star. Today he wore a plaid scarf draped around his neck, a cotton shirt with pulled up sleeves, an unbuttoned vest, jeans, and ankle boots. When he'd come in earlier, Lucinda noticed he had on a black porkpie hat. The guy had eclectic taste and always looked like he'd taken a dive in a theatre trunk. He reminded her of a quirky Johnny Depp in the movie, *Benny & Joon.*

Camilla was petite and had the body and the graceful movements of a ballet dancer. All business, she wore a tan pencil skirt with a subtle animal print blouse and nosebleed heels. Her jewelry, suit jacket and accessories were always tasteful and sharp. She dressed as if she'd come off a runway.

Hutch and Cam were definitely different in appearance, but their personalities worked and made them a good team. They were intuitive with each other. They'd even taken to short talk with one another, almost in a code only the two of them understood.

"Cam and I were able to ID two victims. Here's what we have," Hutch began.

Hutch and Cam had identified two of the severed arms from the Cascade Mountains crime scene using fingerprints they'd run through a series of databases and had compiled solid background information on both victims. Brian Dunkirk and Michael Wesson had corresponding missing person reports and lived in the Seattle area. Dunkirk had been twenty-five when he died and Wesson, twenty-six.

"You two must've worked late last night." Lucinda sipped on her fourth cup of coffee and looked over the files they'd created on the two young men. "The others will be harder. We may never know their names."

It would be tougher to ID the other body parts. Unless the victims had distinguishing tattoos, scars, or joint damage that could be backed up with a medical file, they'd have a harder time with associating a name. The severed butt cheeks and penises would likely not be positively identified unless they got a hit on DNA, which would be long odds if the victims didn't have a criminal history or didn't have another reason to be in a DNA database.

"I'll keep looking," Hutch said. "I can cross reference missing persons to likely victims, based on their DMV photos. I believe that TK has evolved what he's looking for in a target. Searching for his new 'type' would be another way to come at this."

"A change in victimology?" Lucinda cocked her head. "Explain."

"Show her, Cam."

Camilla grabbed the remote control in front of her and clicked a button. She pulled up the DMV photos of Brian Dunkirk and Nathan Applewhite.

"Hutch recognized a similarity between Dunkirk and Nathan Applewhite. The resemblance is uncanny and his theory fits Wesson, too. Look." Cam brought up another slide that had an array of three DMV photos. "Here are all three men. I think Hutch is on to something."

"I see what you mean," Lucinda said. "Good eye, Hutch. It'll take longer to sort through missing persons to search for the specific victimology, but you could narrow the field. That would definitely help."

She stared at the DMV photos and focused on every feature of these men. Something bothered her, but she couldn't put her finger on it. Hutch looked troubled, too.

"One thing concerns me about this new victimology theory," he said.

"What's that?"

"Applewhite was special enough that we got a whole body and our UNSUB took great pains to give him a place of honor on his Totem. If our killer is targeting guys who look like Applewhite, now that he's dead, what's next? Who's next?"

Lucinda nodded, not taking her eyes off the photos.

"I see your point. We have to figure out what these victims have in common. How does he pick them? And if our UNSUB's targets evolved into Applewhite lookalikes, when did that happen? What triggered the change in his victimology? If we can figure that out, we might stand a chance at getting ahead of him."

After a plan took shape in Lucinda's mind, she pointed at Devin Hutchison.

"I agree with how you're thinking about this. Run with it. Cross check missing persons with DMV. Pull any that fit the profile of TK's victim, Applewhite. This new approach could help us ID the bodies we have no names for."

"I'm on it," Hutch said.

"And Cam, you look at what we know of previous victims. Let's see if we can isolate when and why our UNSUB changed his victim profile. You'll be looking for anything that links our victims, from places they work, where they live, service providers they share, anything where our UNSUB might've crossed their paths."

"Yeah, got it," Cam said.

"We'll regroup in three hours."

Camilla took down the slide images off the screen, but she left the hard copy files. After Lucinda hit the break room refrigerator and grabbed her sack lunch, she returned to her office and laid out the file folders across her desk. She stared at the faces of the dead men as she ate yogurt and slices of apple.

What did the Totem Killer see in these men? Why had they been targeted...and why had Applewhite been special? Something in the eyes of these men gripped her once again. She couldn't put her finger on it, but when she felt a strong urge to talk to Ryker, she tried his cell.

No answer. No voice mail. She got a signal that meant his SAT phone wasn't in service.

"That's strange."

She tried several more times, but when she couldn't reach him, she called Sinead. After two rings, Lucinda looked at her watch and realized it was still the lunch hour. She almost hung up, but before her call rolled into voice mail, Sinead answered.

"Royce."

"Hey Sinead. It's Crowley. Sorry if I disturbed your lunch."

"No worries. I'm here. What can I do for you?"

"I've been trying to reach Ryker, but he's not answering. Can you help me figure out if there's a service problem or if the trouble is with his phone?"

"Yeah. Definitely. I'll hit you back in a few."

A 'few' turned out to be twenty minutes later.

"The problem isn't the service. I confirmed that. The service provider says his phone is off, but it gets worse." Sinead sounded worried.

"Worse?"

"Yeah, they lost him on their network grid. His phone is offline. He'd have no reason to do that, Lucinda. Not unless his phone is damaged. We can't track his coordinates. It's like he's fallen off the planet."

Ryker's SAT phone should have worked in the mountains. The higher elevations would've given him a clearer shot at a satellite to ping his signal off, but Sinead was right. There'd be no reason Ryker would have turned off his phone. His phone would be crippled and they'd have no way to track him.

"Give me the last coordinates you had on him ASAP. I want to see it on a map and get a satellite view, too." She swallowed, hard. "Keep trying to reach him. If his service resumes, I want to be the first to know. Leave him a message to call me if his cell rolls to voice mail."

"Yeah, got it."

Sinead ended the call and left Lucinda alone with her dark 'what if' scenarios. Ryker's phone could have been damaged like Sinead had said. He could have dropped it off a cliff or in a rushing river. He was in a remote location and on a hike up a mountain, but Lucinda had a bad feeling the explanation wouldn't be that simple.

She should never have let him go to Alaska alone. *Yeah, right*—as if he'd given her a choice.

***

Prince of Wales Island, Alaska
Hours later
Ryker Townsend

In my condition, time wasn't merciful. Each second piled on to minutes that turned into hours and moved like a thick sludge of oil. I was mired in it. It crawled through my body and threatened to suffocate me with fever and doubts and guilt. My skin was on fire, my head ached, and seeing daylight actually hurt. I had to quit wiping my watery eyes. The skin around them had turned raw. The aspirins quit working and nothing made me feel better.

The canteen had become my new best friend. I slugged down more water and wiped my mouth with the back of my hand. Hydration was important, but I did it to keep moving. To stay awake. My tunnel vision had gotten worse and I had a hard time

149

keeping my head up. I sat on the bed with the shotgun on my lap, groggy and sick.

I'm not a guy who likes staying still. Being stuck in one spot makes it too easy for my mind to tear down the walls I'd built with care and good reason. The shape I was in made it hard to stay in the moment. For Justine's sake, I had to try.

The more I thought about what she had said, about me having a concussion, it made sense. Head trauma. When I played football in high school, I'd been hospitalized and put under observation overnight with close medical attention. I remembered enough to realize I had many of the same symptoms. *Headache. Pressure in the head. Confusion. Dizziness. Nausea. Fatigue. Sensitivity to light, to noise. Memory loss.*

I couldn't remember the warning signs of a concussion when the condition shifted from bad to worse and I would need a hospital. Probably a good thing. I had to find a way to ride it out. Nothing else I could do. My thought process, my reasoning, I'd been injured there, too. I had to rely on Justine now. I didn't have a choice.

After I took a deep breath, I drank more water, desperate to stay alert. Whenever I nodded off, noises jerked me awake and I'd grab my twelve-gauge. In my tormented naps, I pictured Matson beside me as if the man could walk through walls, but not even the adrenaline rush from the scare kept me awake. I imagined strange things with every sound as my mind conspired against me.

To sidestep the mind clutter, I got up and stretched my back. When my gaze landed on the photos of Nate's family and the water color drawings his son had made, I hobbled over to the stack Justine had left on a wooden bookshelf near my bed.

Nate's boy looked the spitting image of him.

With every photograph I saw the love and pride of a father for his young son. I recognized the background in some of the shots. Many of the photos had been taken at the cabin or in Point Baker.

Piecing together the life of a victim, after seeing their marred bodies in death, always stayed with me long after the case closed. The sadness and sense of loss lingered, at least it had for me after I lost both my parents in that sudden unexpected way. A '*not so harmless*' drive to church had changed everything.

Nate's boy would have to grow up without his father, because Applewhite had crossed paths with the wrong guy. Violent death was like a ripple across still water. It spread to touch anyone in its wake, even the investigators who worked the case.

As I flipped through the pages of water color, one caught my eye. The kid had drawn a small craft airplane, similar to the one I'd flown to Point Baker. Maybe the boy had watched float planes land near the lodge where his father worked, but it could also mean Nate might have been the pilot or had been working toward getting his license.

I was grasping at straws. A kid in Alaska probably saw plenty of float planes, but given Applewhite was a sports guide, he had to know pilots. Maybe one of his co-workers at the lodge would know if he had a connection to Seattle. When I got back to Point Baker, I'd have to talk to the lodge owner.

Being hurt, I felt useless and stuck where I was.

Lucinda, don't let me down. I knew it would be only a matter of time for my team to notice they couldn't reach me, but waiting for *that* to happen—and for Justine to get back—was driving me stir crazy. I tossed the stack of drawings on the mattress and slumped back on the bed.

Justine had been gone a long time. If she'd gotten into trouble with Matson, I wouldn't know it unless I heard gunfire. Noise made me jumpy, but waiting without knowing anything had been far worse.

Enough. I gotta get fresh air.

I reached for the crutch Justine had made me from a sturdy tree limb. She'd put padding in a crook of the branch using a couple of Nate's shirts that she'd tied together. With the cushion of the fabric, I could put my weight on it, without the rough bark hurting me. After great effort I stood and wedged the crutch under my arm as I held the shotgun. I shuffled for the front door with my wounded ankle raised. Every step hurt like hell and I felt dizzy and hot.

When a shadow eclipsed the light coming from a window, I jerked my head up and stopped dead still.

"You. How did you...?"

I raised my shotgun and nearly fell when my crutch dropped from under my arm.

"I'm FBI. SSA Townsend." I panted. "Don't come any closer."

A tall scruffy man with long hair and a beard stood in front of me, dressed in a red plaid shirt. Grady Lee Matson. How had he gotten into the cabin without me knowing it? When the man didn't say anything, I blinked to get a better look with my eyes watering. Daylight coming from the window turned Matson into a blur.

"What did you do with Trooper Peterson?"

The man's eyes flared in anger. His matted dark hair and beard had dirt and leaves encrusted into the tangles and his clothes were disheveled as if he'd been in a fight. I braced for the man to charge me, but when Matson's face distorted, his eyes and mouth drooped like water colors bleeding in the rain.

"What the hell?"

The face of the man in red plaid faded and morphed into a more familiar one. I recognized the white filmy eyes, gray mottled skin, and the gaping mouth of Nathan Applewhite. Grady Lee Matson was gone. A dead man stood naked before me, with his skin carved bloodied and raw. The stench of death filled the cabin.

"Oh, God."

My heart pounded and I couldn't stop staring at the horror. Dead eyes fixed on me as they had at the crime scene in the Cascades. When I stumbled back, the corpse of Nathan Applewhite turned its head and its haunted gaze followed me.

There's no light without the dark. My mother's words came to me. I wielded them like a protective mantra to rationalize what I saw. Even inside the cabin, flies hovered over the grotesque body and a cloud of gnats swarmed its eyes. The dead man didn't blink. Not once. Even Nate's hair drifted as if every strand were stirred by a preternatural wind.

I sensed the strong presence of evil. Nate had brought it with him. A criminal malevolence shadowed his spirit. Palpable and strong.

"You can't be real. Why are you doing this to me?" I limped back and raised my shotgun. Every move hurt.

Nate dropped his jaw open as if to answer me and his trembling lips mouthed a message, but no sound came out.

"This can't be happening. I'm not sleeping. I'm *not.*"

There's no light without the dark.

Panic gripped me hard. I felt wide awake. If I wasn't asleep, I had to be hallucinating, yet I sensed the same link to Nate that I had in my nightmares. I couldn't catch my breath and the ache in my head throbbed hard like an adrenaline fueled artery.

"Stop talking to the dead guy, Townsend. What the hell's wrong with you?"

When Applewhite drifted toward me—without the corpse's feet touching the floor—that's when I lost it. I couldn't take another second of a vision that had crossed over from my tortured sleep into my waking consciousness. The room spun with Nate Applewhite coming closer.

"No. Stay there. Don't!"

I smelled death. The air was thick with the stench. Sweat trickled down my brow. I couldn't fill my lungs as I backed away and raised a hand to the nightmare standing in front of me.

"Don't come any closer...or I'll shoot."

I don't know why I said it. Threatening to shoot a dead guy?

"There's no light without the dark."

I said my mother's words aloud as if they'd ward off whatever was happening to me. I wanted to picture her face and feel her arms around me, but I couldn't.

None of this made sense. Every instinct in my gut screamed that the dead body had brought evil to my door. First Matson. Now Applewhite. I had to stop it. I raised the twelve-gauge and took aim. I had to shoot. It was all I had left. Without hesitating I pulled the trigger. The blast made me cringe and everything in my head went numb.

Applewhite broke apart in front of my eyes. Every fragment coiled into a thick cloud of flies. I couldn't hear the buzz of their wings. The shotgun blast had destroyed my hearing, but I watched the swarm of insects slip under the threshold and I followed them.

I flung open the door and aimed the shotgun.

"Stop! Don't shoot! It's me." Someone stood in the clearing outside the log cabin and aimed a weapon at my chest and yelled, "What's *wrong* with you?"

It took too long for me to recognize Justine's face. She stared at me, wide-eyed, and held her handgun on me. *Oh, God. No.* I lowered the shotgun and collapsed against the doorframe, panting and shaking.

How could I tell her what I'd seen? How could I tell *anyone*?

"I don't know." I shook my head and winced. "I really...don't know."

I lowered my head to my chest and shut my eyes. I could have shot Justine. *I'm losing it. What the hell's wrong with me?*

Seeing Nathan Applewhite in my dreams—and calling it a vision—was one thing. But when a dead man haunted my waking mind with delusions that invaded my reality, I had to wonder about my sanity. This was new. It scared me beyond my worst nightmares. It felt like the walls I'd carefully erected in my mind had burst open and bled a lifetime of horrors over me. After I'd seen Matson, I knew I couldn't blame all my hallucinations on my delirium from a fever or a head injury from a fall.

I had one unrelenting fear that had been plaguing me ever since my visions had gotten worse. Being a profiler demanded I become a voyeur into the dark minds of prolific killers. Lately I questioned the way I separated my work from my personal life.

I compartmentalized the horrors I saw on the job by erecting barriers around them in my mind, but what if those walls I'd built to protect myself were fragile? If my dreams brought those walls crashing down, I could easily imagine my nightmarish visions seeping into my waking reality.

If that happened, how would I hold on to who I was? How would I know the difference between insanity and what it meant to be me?

As I stared at a stunned Justine, I saw fear in her

eyes—and I couldn't blame her. I was scared, too.

Chapter Eleven

Prince of Wales Island, Alaska
Ryker Townsend

"You could've shot me. What happened? Was it Matson? Was he here?"

Justine confronted me in wide-eyed outrage. She expected an answer, but I didn't know what to say. I stood on the threshold of the cabin, barely able to stand. My mind reeled with what might've happened.

I could've *killed* her.

"I...don't know, exactly."

"How could you not know?"

Justine took a deep breath and inched closer, looking unsure of me. Hell, I was uncertain too. I must've looked like a crazy man. What had happened? Eventually she reached out a hand and touched my cheek with trembling fingers. Her sudden change of heart surprised me.

I hadn't realized how much I needed her touch. Her acceptance.

"Something is happening to you, isn't it? Something you're not saying. What is it?"

She leaned into my body and pressed into me. Her lips, her eyes, the smell of her skin hit my senses and I lowered my chin and shut down, giving in to her comfort. Her touch and the feel of her body reminded me I wasn't alone.

We were strangers, but that was changing fast. I needed my connection to her. I wanted her understanding. The weight of being alone—of shouldering the accountability for a *gift* I wasn't sure I could carry on my own anymore—had left me tired.

"Trust me, Ryker. Please."

She kissed my cheek and a part of my steely stoic

manhood melted on the edges. Her lips felt good on my skin and I let it happen.

"I'm risking my neck here," she said. "We're in this together. Talk to me."

I shut my eyes tight and breathed her in. I'd kept my secret for so long, but the burden had caught up to me. On the island I was wounded and exhausted and the hunt for the Totem Killer had drained me, especially since my worsening visions had kept me from sleeping.

Justine was right. I had to trust her. After I'd almost shot her, I owed her an explanation. I stared into her eyes and raised a hand to brush my fingers through her hair.

"You're right. Something *is* happening to me, but I'm not sure I understand it."

"Let me help you inside," she said. "You can tell me everything."

Justine hugged my chest and nuzzled her shoulder under mine. She touched my belly and held me in ways that were meant more as affection, rather than her being my crutch. I liked it. I endured the pain as I hobbled across the cabin to the bed. After Justine helped prop my leg up on pillows, she sat on the edge of the mattress and held the canteen to my lips for me to drink.

"Thanks. I—"

Before I thanked her, Justine lowered her lips to mine and kissed me. I braced my body and resisted at first, but I eventually gave in. I pulled her into my arms, caressed her face, and returned her kiss—long, slow, and deep.

When it was over, I was confused. I'd been attracted to Justine and had connected to her strong sensual nature from the first night I'd met her, but I was sick. I wouldn't have kissed her if she hadn't made the first move. I needed her in a different way, at least for now. I was hurting. Romance shouldn't have been on my radar, yet my lips and my tongue had gone rogue.

"That was...nice." I touched her cheek and smiled. "Unexpected, but nice."

"I did it again, didn't I?"

For the first time since I'd met her, Justine looked shy and she blushed. Her fragile smile gave me a glimpse of the little girl she used to be.

"I pushed you to kiss me," she said. "You remind me so much of Nate. I'm sorry. I didn't mean to..."

Nate again. I reminded Justine of her dead lover. Whatever she felt toward me, it was for someone else. Not me. Her displays of affection were ways she had for grieving over Nate. I had to remember our predicament, and Nate's death, had instigated a rush of emotion for both of us. I wasn't sure how much I should believe, from either of us.

Perhaps I was nothing more than a pound pup in need of a home and a good chew toy.

"It's okay. Really. I kissed you back because I wanted to," I said. "But there's something I have to tell you. I *do* have a connection to Nate. Maybe that's what you're feeling."

"What are you talking about?" She pulled from my arms with a worried look on her face. "You're scaring me."

Yeah. Get in line.

Lately I'd been living in fear. With each case, my abilities had grown stronger. A good profiler had to rely on a certain amount of intuition when it came to drawing insight into the psyche of mass murderers. Excelling at understanding the deviant mind carried a risk that I'd lose sight of normal. But after years on the job, I'd honed my gut instinct and had learned to trust it, until I realized what I'd tapped into was more than my gut.

The more I used my natural ability, the more I'd come to think of it as a '*gift*' I couldn't explain. My dreams often linked to the cases I investigated—symbolic glimpses my mind had to interpret. I didn't examine a crime scene and make deductions solely by observation. It was more than that. Intuition and my experiences within my dreams played a part. I had *second sight* and my penchant for oddly connected insights had become keener and undeniably valuable.

When I realized my mind craved the high of solving the puzzle, my freak side made me an addict in want of a fix. My hunt for the Totem Killer had stirred darker visions that had led me to Nathan Applewhite—and now Grady Lee Matson. I didn't know where to begin to explain all this to Justine, but things had gotten out of hand and I had to tell her everything.

She had a right to know.

"Even before I got the call about Nate's body being found outside Seattle, I had a dream about him. I've since come to believe it was more of a vision."

"A vision? About Nate?"

"It's not the first time it's happened to me. I dream and the things I see, sometimes they happen. But this time I think Nate reached out to me. At the crime scene, his eyes, they…"

God, this sounded crazy, even to me. I stopped. I couldn't look at her. Was this it…my psychotic break? With every word out of my mouth, I saw doubt building in Justine.

I couldn't blame her for not believing me—for fearing me.

"What *about* his eyes? Tell me." She clutched a hand tight to my shirt and held on. Tears welled in her eyes.

I didn't know how much of her pain came from her grief over losing Nate or her being afraid of me.

The cost of my need to open up to someone was in Justine's eyes. She hadn't deserved any of this.

"His eyes followed me, as if he watched me, like he tried to tell me something. I was awake, but it happened." I shook my head. "I know how this must sound. I've never told anyone about this, not even the members of my team, but after I almost shot you, I figured you had a right to know."

"Are you psychic?" she asked. "Wait. You're a profiler with the FBI. How is this possible? If they knew, you'd be under psych eval. People might think the stress of the job is getting to you, wouldn't they?"

I grabbed for the canteen and took another long pull of water to stall my answer. The room closed in on me and I felt lightheaded again. I was about to cross a line that would change things forever. To let someone in on my very private life—and trust a virtual stranger with my darkest secret—it could cost me my job and my future and everything I was or could become.

"I've never told anyone this before. That's why I don't talk about it. You're right. I'm not sure the FBI would understand what's happening to me. They could sideline me."

"There's more, isn't there? Come on. You can trust me, Ryker. Talk to me."

I tensed my jaw and heaved a deep sigh.

"I have the gift of second sight. I've used it to solve cases before and I've never told anyone on my team because...they wouldn't understand, but ever since the Cascade Mountains and the way Nate...looked at me, my visions have been different."

"Different? In what way?"

"I think Nate is showing me the last thing he saw...when he died. Some people believe those who die at the hands of violence, their retinas get imprinted with the last thing they see."

Justine pushed off the bed and glared at me. She didn't say a word. I'd lost her. She shook her head and paced the room, stealing glances at me as I tried to explain.

"I know it sounds crazy. That's why I haven't told anyone, but that's what happened today. My visions have turned into hallucinations. I saw Matson—here in the cabin—but he...turned into Nate. Nate's dead body was here. I saw it. I smelled the stench. His eyes followed me like they had in the Cascades. I tell you, he was *here*."

I was nearly through the worst of it. There was no going back anyway. I had to make her see.

"Did he talk to you? Say anything? Maybe he knew his killer." Justine ran a hand through her hair and choked down a laugh. "I can't believe this. You're seeing a ghost and I'm asking if it talked to you. Unreal."

It was more than seeing a ghost or having visions. I had to tell her everything. She needed to know—or maybe I needed the freedom of breaking through my own barrier.

"No. He didn't say anything, but there's more," I said.

"Oh, this I gotta hear." She crossed her arms.

"My hallucinations have been worse since I linked to Nate and came to this island. I'm seeing things whether I'm sleeping or not."

"Wait a minute. Do you know how insane that sounds?"

"Yeah, believe me, I do."

I took another gulp of water from the canteen and heaved a hefty breath. I only saw Justine. Everything else in the room closed tight around me in a vague haze. My tunnel vision had become worse.

"It's my greatest fear," I said. "I think these hallucinations aren't coming from my psychic abilities."

"What are you saying?" She stepped closer and sat next to me, touching my arm. "What's happening to you?"

"I nearly shot you because I couldn't tell what was real. Who I am is slowly slipping away and I can't stop it. I'm unstable. My visions only compound the depravity I see. I never get a break from them. I'm losing control and it feels as if my own mind is attacking me. Even in my sleep I'm forced to sit on the bench and watch the carnage over and over, like it's a punishment."

"Punishment? For what?"

"For being powerless. For not stopping it. I wake up in cold sweats, paralyzed with fear. Bodies are falling because I can't figure out a vision fast enough and someone innocent pays the price." I shook my aching head. "I'm not sure I can do this job anymore, and I certainly can't be trusted to have your back the way I am."

Justine touched a hand to my chin and trailed a thumb across my lower lip.

"You lost someone close to you, like I did. Didn't you? Someone you loved. Someone you connected to with your ability," she said. "Please...tell me what happened. Maybe talking about it will help."

I'd never told anyone about what happened the day my parents died. Even Sarah was in denial and dealt with that day in the only way she knew how. Because she didn't believe me when I told her what I saw, she let it play out and neither of us will ever know if we could've saved them. Now my sister had written me off because I scared her, like I was an immoral oddity she had to protect her family from.

Justine wanted me to open the baggage I'd been carrying all these years. She'd made it easy for me to talk to her, but I couldn't tell her the whole truth.

"My parents. I had a...vision. I could've saved them if I'd made different choices, but..." I shut my eyes, unsure I could finish. "...they died anyway. I can't let that happen again. I mean, what good is it to have these terrible visions and be powerless to stop the slaughter? If that happened again and someone died because of what I did—or couldn't figure out—it would *kill* me."

"Death is powerful. Maybe once someone is marked, no one can stop it, not even you with your incredible gift, Ryker." She stroked my cheek. "How did Nate get targeted? You have any theories?"

I didn't talk about my cases, but Justine had broken down my barriers. I needed to talk as much as she wanted to listen.

"This killer gets off on taking everything from his victims. That means he crossed Nate's path and knew how he felt about his son." I closed my eyes to connect to the killer. "He uses a knife to get in close and watch them die, knowing he's taken everything that matters. With Nate, it would've been a future with his boy."

"Matson knew how Nate loved his son." Tears welled in her eyes. "Maybe poaching on Nate's property had been Matson's way of riling him. Nate thought he knew Matson and would've wanted to protect his boy from him. His son made him vulnerable."

"You mean Nate might've forced a showdown without thinking...because he had something at stake?"

"Yeah. He would've seen Matson as a threat to his son and the life he'd built."

"He wouldn't have been wrong," I said.

Justine narrowed her eyes and stared at me.

"What?" I shrugged.

"Sounds like you see your job as being the voice

of the dead, like it's your calling," she said. "You watch over them, but who watches over you?"

When I gritted my teeth and didn't answer, she sighed.

"It took a lot of guts to tell me, but I'm getting you out in one piece. I know you want to protect *me*, but *you're* the one who needs help now." She kissed my cheek. "Thanks for the trust. Your secret is safe with me. I promise. We're getting off this mountain, you and me."

I wanted to believe her. Her words were only promises she had no control over, but they made me feel better. She gave me hope, something I needed in a bad way. I leaned my head back as the growing pain of a headache burrowed its roots deeper in my skull.

"Did you find Matson?" I asked.

"I found a campsite that could've been his. It had the boot prints I'd tracked the other day."

"How do you know the prints were his?"

"After I'd lost him, I took a harder look at the tracks he'd left behind. The heel of his right boot has a deep gouge that leaves a noticeable impression. It's how I knew the campsite was his, but the fire pit was cold. He's on the move."

She'd tracked him by following a gouge in his boot heel. *Clever.*

"So he's not staying anywhere long and not building a fire that can be seen from a distance. He's hunting."

"Yeah, us," I said.

"Matson is a poacher. He hunts and knows how to stalk his prey. With us hold up in Nate's cabin, we're easy pickings. I searched around the cabin's perimeter and found the same boot prints along the tree line. The tracks were fresh. He's been out there, watching us. I swear, there are times I can feel him."

"Now who's the psychic?"

"Touché."

"No sign of my phone? He didn't trash it?"

"Not that I saw, but maybe that's a good thing. Your team might have their beacon after all."

"Yeah, I guess, but we can't count on that," I said. "As soon as it gets dark, we gotta sneak out of here and hope he doesn't see us. Maybe we'll get a head start before he comes after us."

Justine stared at me and flexed her jaw tight.

"What?" I shrugged. "You've convinced me we should stick together. That makes sense, and like you said, we're easy targets here. If he's stalking us and came close to the cabin, it's only a matter of time for him to test us."

Justine wandered toward the window in silence. She kept her back to the wall and peered outside, careful not to show her face. After a strained moment she glanced at me. I wasn't sure I liked her expression. She made me glad she was on *my* side.

"This guy is crazier and meaner than I remembered. If he's the one who killed Nate, both of us know what he's capable of," she said. "Now that I know he's been coming close, I'll stand watch and keep a rifle handy."

"I can help with that."

Justine cocked her head and stared at me.

"You just admitted to me that you're hallucinating. I'm not sure I can trust you with a gun. You almost shot me."

"Nothing personal."

Justine smirked.

"Oh, good. I feel much better," she said. "Okay, we'll head out tonight, but we're traveling light. I'll consolidate our gear into one pack with only the essentials. And you're getting sleep before we go. No arguments."

"None."

"We won't stop once we get out of here." With her gaze fixed on the trees beyond the clearing, she talked as if she were making a mental checklist. "No sleep. No fire. No real food. Take the time it took for us to get here and double it. Hell, triple it for your injury. I know the trail. That'll help since we'll travel in the dark."

"Sounds as if you're trying to convince yourself this'll work."

"Call it the lesser of two evils. After my recon of Matson and where he's been, I'm not sure we have a choice." She walked away from the window and went to her first-aid kit. "But you'll do what I say. No questions. A pain med will help you sleep while I pack our gear. I'll wake you when it's time to go."

I stared at the pills she had in her hand as she came toward me. I understood her point. I'd have to rely on her to get me through this now. She knew the trail. She knew Matson, but that didn't mean I had to like it. I already had trouble stemming the tide of my strange and worsening visions. Taking pain medication could make my imaginings worse, but she wasn't giving me a choice.

I had to rely on her.

After I took the tablets from her hand, Justine gave me the canteen and I swallowed the meds. I settled into the pillow and she tossed a blanket over my chest and sat next to me.

"Don't fight it," she whispered and ran her hands through my hair. "I've got you. Count on me and I'll get you out of here. I promise."

As the meds kicked in, I flashed back to nights when my mother sat next to me, comforting me after I had a hellish dream. I was adrift in the past and the present, with Justine bridging the gap.

"I gotta find this guy. I have to." I shut my eyes and let my mind go.

"Maybe you already have found the one who killed Nate, Ryker," she said. "But I'm not as worried about Matson, as I am for you. Right now, getting you off this mountain is my priority. You're the only one who matters to me."

She sat with me until the drugs took a firm hold and the numbness spread through my body. The room did a slow spiral as I sank into darkness. I listened to the sounds of Justine at work.

I prayed I wouldn't dream.

***

BAU headquarters
Quantico, Virginia
Hours later

Hutch stared at the computer screen in stunned silence. He'd tested his theory on how the UNSUB could've identified and stalked his victims by using Nathan Applewhite as ground zero and he worked back using the killer's timeline and what he knew of the other victims. He let his mind be open to the way a killer might think, the scary way Ryker did.

He didn't like how it felt.

"What's wrong? You look like you've seen a ghost." Cam stood at the threshold to his office with her arms crossed. She had a smile on her face until he glanced back and didn't answer her.

"I'm serious. What's up, Hutch?" She pulled up a chair and sat next to him.

"I've got a pretty solid theory on how our UNSUB picks them out...and how he hunts them." Hutch glared at his monitor. "I mean, I expected this to eventually happen. The way technology is advancing, it was bound to, but seeing it work is...frightening. Anyone with the right motivation can do this."

"You're scaring me, love." She put her hand on

the back of his neck and stroked his hair. "Look at me."

Hutch took a deep breath and did as she asked. Whenever he looked into Cam's eyes, it reminded him the world wasn't completely filled with the sick fringe dwellers his team hunted.

"Tell me what you found," she said.

It didn't take him long to run Cam through the basics of what he'd discovered. She was intuitive and smart and connected to the way he thought, but when he was done, she fell silent. She slumped in her chair and stared at the last image he had on the screen. Her eyes were watering and she looked emotionally drained.

He didn't push her to say anything. He'd felt the same way. After a long moment, she fixed her gaze on him. The usual glint she had in her eyes was gone.

"How can people create something like this and not realize how the predators of the world would abuse it?" Cam's voice sounded fragile. "Don't they know people can be messed up and...damaged?"

Hutch heaved a sigh and said, "Broken people are dangerous, because they know how to survive."

Chapter Twelve

BAU headquarters
Quantico, Virginia

Jitters from her caffeine overload weren't helping as Lucinda sat with her team in a conference room outside her office. She was anxious to get started. They would pick up where they'd left off and explore Hutch's idea on the UNSUB's change in victimology. Cam and Hutch had set up a laptop presentation and had asked for Sinead to attend the briefing. After Lucinda noticed the grave expressions on the faces of her ERTs, she let them work in silence. Sinead caught her eye, but picked up on her cue and didn't break the somber mood.

"I tested the theory I had on how the UNSUB could target and hunt his victims, based on the idea Nathan Applewhite earned a special spot on the last Totem for a reason," Hutch began. "I don't know what that reason was, but I think I know how the others got tagged... literally."

Lucinda leaned onto the conference room table and narrowed her eyes at the visual presentation Cam had started. An on-screen capture of Nathan Applewhite's social media page filled the screen in the darkened room.

"Applewhite had a Facebook page that he didn't use much. Brian Dunkirk and Michael Wesson had other social media sites, but when I couldn't find common ground, I was stumped until I went about this a different way," he said. "What if the reason we can't find the way our UNSUB hunts his victims is that he's doing it online and is using software that can be downloaded to any phone or used online? There'd be no trail unless someone is looking for it and his targets would appear random, but after I remembered an app that I'd read about, something clicked for me."

Another slide came up with the website for a software app Lucinda hadn't seen before.

"There's a few versions of this around," Hutch said. "They're called Augmented Identity apps, but the one that's most popular and reliable is called *FaceTrax*. It's an app you can download onto any smart phone or on your computer."

"Oh, yeah. I've heard of this." Sinead nodded.

"What does it do, Hutch?" Lucinda asked.

"Say you're in a bar and you see someone who interests you across the room."

"That would require you to have a life," Lucinda said. "But yeah, go on."

Hutch shot her his quirky smile and went on.

"All you have to do is point your smart phone camera, take a picture, and run their image through *FaceTrax*. If they're posting anywhere online, this app will pull up their name and every social media link they have. Whatever they post is yours to data mine."

"God, you're kidding me." Lucinda slouched back in her chair and shook her head. "People post everything online these days."

"Yeah, it's the perfect stalker tool. It's fast and can be virtually anonymous," he said. "So the common ground that links our victims could be this app."

"Anyone can do the software download on their computer at home, too?"

"Yeah, they don't even have to go to a bar. Having a life isn't a prerequisite. That's how I think an app like this worked with Applewhite and our UNSUB. TK already had photos of Applewhite from his Facebook page, but I think he had to know him, too. That kind of rage doesn't just happen."

"How does the program work...exactly?" she asked.

"The facial recognition software creates a 3-D image of a face and transmits it across a server where it's matched against an identity maintained in a database. A cloud server conducts the actual facial recognition and sends back the name of the person as well as links where they do their social networking. From there, the person's face and identity can be tagged and whatever they post online is fair game. To anyone with a criminal mind, this could lead to identity theft, fraud scams, hacked bank accounts—and yes, stalking."

"How do you know our UNSUB uses an app like this?"

"I don't, but it's a strong theory because I downloaded the app and ran it on Applewhite, Dunkirk, and Wesson," Hutch said. Cam brought up a new slide and a linear grid appeared over the photos of the three dead men. "This is what the program would see. It takes out all the distractions of the features and breaks it down to the basic elements of facial characteristics, called recognition algorithms. As you can see, the face grid patterns are very similar."

"The UNSUB would've started with Applewhite as a template and searched for similar faces," Cam said. "From there our killer would get a retrieval of guys who look like the original—an a la carte menu of choices, pre-screened by criteria our UNSUB looks for, such as age, address, whatever."

Sinead nodded and said, "The newer Androids, iPhones, and cameras with at least five-megapixels are compatible with this app. It's pretty universal and accessible to your basic pervert."

"Don't get too caught up in the smart phone

angle. Our guy can use any computer he has access to and hunt online, privately. He wouldn't have to own a smart phone or even act like a tech savvy guy. In fact it would be a good cover if he wasn't," Hutch added. "He could troll for victims whenever he scored online access, then go about living his life and executing his plan once he knows where they live. He could have a list to cherry pick from whenever he's ready to hunt them, but basically our UNSUB could be *anybody*. He wouldn't even have to own a computer, only have access to one when he needs fresh targets."

"Yeah, you're right," Sinead said. "Damn."

"If being hunted by a stranger isn't scary enough, here's something that will make your skin crawl," Cam added. "You might think the U.S. Department of State maintains the largest collection of images in a facial recognition database, but it doesn't even come close to the one-hundred eighty billion photos posted on social media sites, like Facebook, Google, ImageShack, PhotoBucket, Instagram, and Flickr."

Lucinda was stunned by the implication. She knew the internet had been a fertile ground for criminals and scam artists, but if serial killers could anonymously stalk potential victims online and in encrypted privacy, that meant no one would be safe. Even if a person didn't post to social media, if their friends or family did, that meant those shared photos could make them a target without them even knowing it.

Unbelievable.

"We live in a world where any of our private information can be tracked through a random photo taken on the street or in a bar," Lucinda said. "Our credit scores, sexual orientation, religious affiliations, places of employment, our loved ones and friends, all of it can be traced through what we post ourselves. Online companies and automated data miners bundle the consumer data and reap the financial benefits without any objection from the vulnerable users who use their 'free' services."

"In a nutshell, yeah." Hutch adjusted his glasses. "Scary world."

"This is good, but how can we use it to get ahead of our UNSUB?" Lucinda asked him.

"We can run Applewhite's photo image—our way—and look for potential victims who live in Seattle."

"You mean hunt victims the way our UNSUB would?"

"Yeah, exactly. We can attempt to build a target list he could already have at the ready," he said. "Once we get closer to identifying our UNSUB, factors like what kind of phone he has and his access to computers and use of online social media, can help narrow the field. We're still a long way from identifying our killer, but when you consider our UNSUB is hunting anonymously online and we have a pretty good idea how he's doing it, we can search for certain patterns in social media use and take a harder look at the people who followed our dead guys."

"That's a lot of cross checking," she said.

"That's where Sinead comes in. Cam and I could use her help. We can work from what we already have, through Applewhite, Dunkirk, and Wesson."

"I'll be contacting the software companies who have this type of Augmented Identity app to see how cooperative they can be on sending us details of their downloads," Cam said. "Even having proxy server locations can help. We can cross-reference the servers of visitors to the profiles of our victims to narrow our search."

"This is a big job, but I think you're on to something," Lucinda said. "Sinead, do what you can."

"Yeah, I'm on it. Whatever you and Cam need, Hutch," Sinead said. "But if our UNSUB is hiding his online activity, this could turn into a search for Waldo. He could use dozens of proxy servers to mask his ID. Even your basic kid knows how to ping off one proxy server to get around blocked sites, but a more sophisticated user could use dozens of servers that he can vary. He could use encryption and even go through servers in foreign countries that would refuse to give up user IDs. This could be a big dead end, but I like the idea of stalking our UNSUB online. He may not expect us to find him that way. Payback is a bitch."

"I like your attitude, Royce," Hutch said. "Let's go. We got a long night."

Before Hutch left the room with the others, Lucinda stopped him.

"The question you asked me before about the UNSUB—that if he's hunting anyone who looks like Applewhite, who will he target next—I've been thinking about it."

"And?"

"He's killing the pretenders now. The surrogates. It's like he's murdering Applewhite over and over, annihilating anyone who reminds him of Nathan. That's a great deal of rage."

"In the body of an organized and functioning predator," Hutch said. "You ever hear back from Ryker?"

"Not yet. I'll let you know when I do." She sounded more optimistic than she felt.

As Hutch left the conference room, with Sinead negotiating for him to buy pizza, Lucinda went back to her office with her mind on Ryker. He hadn't called in and no one could reach him.

Something was wrong.

She had a long night ahead, too. Sinead had

given her Ryker's coordinates, the one she'd recorded the last time they'd spoken to him when his SAT phone was operational. Lucinda also got maps of the location, including the aerial satellite variety. If she didn't hear from Ryker by tomorrow morning, she'd made up her mind to call in favors, set up a recon, and get boots on the ground—*preferably hers.*

***

Prince of Wales Island, Alaska
Ryker Townsend

I dreamed of the ocean. Suspended in its icy depths, I drifted in a slow moving current, pulled along its murky floor. Heavy viscous buoyancy lifted and carried me through long strands of seaweed that clung to my arms and legs. I pictured everything as if I were outside my body. I didn't question why I could breathe underwater. I accepted it as fact.

The water's surface dappled light across my body in shiny ribbons that reminded me of the sunlight streaming through the trees on the hike to the cabin. I let the warmth of the light slide over me and I drew from the calming memory.

But in the distance when I heard a shrill muffled sound, I felt the water surge in great swells that pushed me deeper. Large schools of fish darted in frenzy. In fear. Something came. It churned the water from a distance and disturbed the stillness— disturbed everything.

Even though I drifted helpless, unable to move my arms and legs, I opened my eyes and looked up. A huge shadow eclipsed the waver of light from the surface and made the water colder. I shivered as it crossed over and glided above me with an undulating ease. A Humpback whale swept through the current, feeding on clouds of frantic krill. It killed to survive, yet it cut through the ocean's depths with such grace that I wasn't afraid of it— until it came for me.

The whale opened its massive jaws and sucked at its prey. I felt the pull of gravity and I couldn't move. I couldn't fight it. I fixed my gaze on the water's surface and willed my body to rise. Panting for air, I flailed at the seaweed that held me down.

"Ryker!"

A loud crack jolted me from my stupor. I broke free of the sea grasses and floated toward a bright light.

"Ryker! He's here."

***

I opened my eyes in a panic. I'd gone from a blinding light to nothing but vague shapes that stirred the shadows. I threw off the covers and pushed from the mattress, as if sloughing off my deep sleep would be as easy as tossing a blanket.

What had awakened me?

A loud noise lingered at the edge of my mind—a *familiar* one—the distant echo of gunfire. Had I imagined the crack of gunshots or had that been part of my strange dream? With the cabin steeped in darkness, it took me time to realize the front door was open. The sun had gone down. Soon it would be too dark to see.

Justine was gone.

"Justine?"

I fumbled in the dark searching for my Glock near the bed. When I stood, I racked the slide and hobbled for my crutch.

"Where are you?" I called out. "What's happening?"

When I got to the door, I saw two bullet holes in the wood. Matson had attacked the cabin. The sounds I'd heard while I was too drugged to wake up. The holes in the door were fresh. They were *real*. I hadn't imagined them.

A crashing sound coming from the trees sent a rush of adrenaline through me. Someone was running. I heard Justine ordering Matson to stop, but the sounds kept coming. He wouldn't give up.

"Justine!" I yelled.

I limped on my crutch and rushed toward the commotion in the trees, praying I wouldn't be too late. A thin path cut through evergreen trees. They could have gone anywhere. All I had to follow was the sound. Panting and gasping for air, I picked up my pace, hobbling until sweat poured off me.

In the deepening shadows, every tree looked like Matson. I saw things, heard things, I wasn't sure were real. The fever had returned and the heat of it stirred under my skin. Sweat trickled from my scalp and drained down my spine. Dark *what ifs* punished me. Guilt had its grips into me deep. I struggled to remember what I'd heard, but that wouldn't help Justine now.

She'd gone after Matson, alone. Without me.

I heard more gunfire over the next hill. Two different weapons. *Oh, God. Please.* I pushed through the pain and cursed as I stabbed my crutch into the ground and kept moving. When I heard a woman cry out and scream in pain, I couldn't tell where it came from.

Too far. I wouldn't make it.

Hang on, Justine. Please hang on.

Chapter Thirteen

Prince of Wales Island, Alaska
Ryker Townsend

I chased after the sounds of a fight. The noise recoiled off trees and came at me from all directions, haunting me with cries that *had* to come from Justine. With each passing second my mind tortured me with what might be happening to her. I trudged in the darkness and limped on my crutch, swinging my weight until I nearly fell. My body and head ached as I clawed through thick brush, but when the noise stopped and the night grew eerily still, I lost my last hope of getting to her in time.

The only sound in the woods came from me.

"Justine!"

My voice cracked as I cried out for her. I felt as helpless as the day my parents died, when I sensed my mother taking her last breaths, but couldn't do anything to save her or my father. The terror of that day had returned—the hopelessness of it—and the God awful guilt of not being able to stop it.

Stumbling up the hill, I neared the spot where I thought I'd heard Justine in trouble and raised my Glock. I took aim with my hands sweating and shaking. I kept my eyes alert for anything that moved, blinking back the blur of my failing vision. I put up a front I didn't feel. Something from my past— the sense of being completely helpless—had its grips on me.

I'd fought that feeling my whole life. I never wanted it to happen again. I'd chosen the FBI to put my *gift* to good use, and stay in control over how I would use it, but the sense of being powerless had come back too easy.

"Justine. Talk to me. *Please.*"

I lowered my voice and spoke only to her. She hadn't called out to me. Matson could be hiding, waiting to attack. I griped my weapon, hard, and slowed my heart. I was messed up already, but because of my worry over her I wasn't thinking clearly.

As I approached a clearing, I steadied my breath, ready to shoot. I hobbled in steady measured steps to stay quiet. A pale light flickered through the dense trees and made the deepening shadows play tricks on my eyes. I turned in a slow circle and aimed my Glock, praying she'd walk out from the darkness, unharmed.

That didn't happen.

When I got to the edge of the small opening between the trees, I stepped in something wet and slick. The smell got to me first. Even in the dim light I knew what it was. In the bluish haze of nightfall, a blood pool looked like thick oil as it coagulated and glimmered in the cool air. My eyes trailed over the sheen that was too large for anyone to have walked away from.

Oh, God.

Someone had died where I stood. There were signs of a struggle. A torn piece of red plaid from Matson's shirt had been ripped loose and wedged into the base of a tree. Something else was caught in the rough bark—long strands of blond hair.

"Justine," I whispered.

For a split second I had hope for the strong woman Justine was. If she'd fought Matson, she might've gotten away. The blood could be Matson's, but when I looked closer at the thick pool, I noticed an imprint. A boot with a distinctive gouge in the right heel had left a void pattern in the dark puddle.

No. Please no. I winced when I realized what that

meant.

With Matson able to stand over the blood—after it had been spilled—the blood had to come from someone else. I felt gut punched. I couldn't move. The sounds of the night closed in on me as I strained to sense Justine or pick up on the evil that hit me in my hallucinations of Matson and Applewhite.

I felt nothing. *Nothing.*

I was alone, yet in the presence of death. I knew how to sense death and that feeling was thick and suffocating now. I replayed what I remembered of the gunshots and her cries for help over and over in my mind. I searched for her until it got too dark to see. Guilt had a steely grip on me and I deserved the abuse.

In the silence, death drew nearer and I felt Justine's kiss on my lips. The smell of her skin and the touch of her fingers haunted me. Even with the evidence of a deadly struggle staring me in the face, I didn't want to believe Justine had been killed. She hadn't deserved to die like this. The only reason she'd come with me was for the love she still felt for Nate, and when Matson had chosen to make trouble, she took lead to protect me because I'd been wounded.

But what if she wasn't dead yet? What if she was too weak to call out to me or unconscious and needed help?

I stayed longer to search, even though it had gotten too dark to see. I wanted to believe I had a shot at finding her, but if she was already dead, I'd be making it easy for Matson to kill me. Justine's death would be for nothing. My head and body ached and my ankle throbbed in pain. I didn't want to leave one of my own behind, but if I stayed until morning, Matson could come for me and have daylight to hunt me down, at the cabin or on the trail.

I didn't know what to do, but the blood pool in

the clearing had been undeniable proof something terrible happened to her. Justine had been a State Trooper trying to do what was right. She'd bled out at the hands of a killer. I felt bad, but if I wanted her death to mean something, I had to make it off the mountain and make Matson pay for what he did.

Justine.

After I got hurt, she had been my rock. The island was her home and I had relied on her. I felt lost without her now. I fumbled my way back to the cabin with my excruciating headache blinding me like a migraine and my ankle on fire and swollen.

I was bleeding again.

As I got closer to Nate's, I picked up my pace. My eyes searched every shadow. I pictured Justine making it back to the cabin and needing my help, but when I got there, the place was cold and dark as I walked through the open door.

Still as a tomb, the empty cabin made me feel hollow inside. Nate's hope for a better life for him and his boy Tanner were gone. The love Justine had never told Nate about—gone too. I had an idea what that kind of loss felt like. The tragedy of lives cut short bore deep holes that could never be filled. Violent death ripped apart families and left a wake of emotion and loss that never truly went away. Violence happened to *other* people. When it happened to me, it became a whole new ballgame, without rules.

I grazed my fingertips over the bullet holes in the door, the ones Matson had left when he attacked. Justine had been alone to face a cold blooded killer because I'd been wounded and in a drug stupor.

I didn't need another ghost to haunt my dreams, but this one I deserved. If Justine was gone, her death would be on me.

***

Minutes later

Inside the cabin, I stumbled through the dark searching for one of Nate's lanterns. After I lit one, I saw where Justine had packed our gear before she ran out to chase Matson. She'd done as she promised until Matson took shots at the cabin and everything changed. She'd yelled for me to wake up, but I couldn't shake off the drugs fast enough to help her.

I felt sick.

The fire she'd started in the hearth had died to embers and she'd left the first aid kit and my pills on top of the pack and had refilled my canteen. The Remington rifle and the twelve-gauge were loaded and ready. She must've taken the Winchester.

Seeing what she'd left behind, I knew I hadn't imagined the gunfire or her running after Matson into the woods. Regret over those precious minutes when she was still with me in the cabin—with me being unable to help her—would haunt me like one of my waking nightmares.

I still felt her presence, but she'd become the shadow of a memory. The familiar essence of her was strong enough for me to miss. I sensed with some certainty that Justine was gone.

"Damn it. Why did you go after him alone?"

I shut my eyes. Now I knew how Lucinda Crowley felt when she'd asked me the same question and got no answer. I hadn't been much of a team player, but I knew why Justine might've gone off alone. She'd gone after Matson because that was her way. Even from the first day, she'd raced after the man without hesitation after he ran from Nate's cabin. She'd been fearless and gutsy—a State Trooper doing her job. She went after Matson tonight because she wanted a piece of a guy who could've killed

Nate—or maybe she thought she could end this.

She'd been wrong.

In the dim glow of the lantern, I removed my bandage and checked the damage to my ankle. The dressing was saturated with blood. I winced when I pulled it free from my wound and my eyes watered with the pain. I did my best to clean my injured leg, the way Justine had done for me.

I thought of her as I fortified my dressing for the hike out and prepared to leave.

Stay focused.

Matson will pay for what he'd done to Justine, but only if I got off the mountain. A part of me wanted to stay. I wanted to believe she was still alive, but every minute of not hearing from her left a crater in me. She wouldn't have left me alone, just as she wouldn't have willingly backed down from a fight. The only way I could help her now was to make it off the mountain and track Matson down.

I rattled the bottle of aspirin and poured too many into my palm. I had the shakes, bad. Pills dropped to the floor and rolled in all directions. I picked up what I could, but left the rest. I couldn't see well enough to hunt for them. I dosed up and gulped water from the canteen and thought about Grady Lee Matson.

I'd witnessed the man's anger and saw how fixated he'd been on Nate. The guy had even destroyed the cabin to wipe Applewhite out of existence. Now he systematically hunted anyone who stood in his way. Matson could've drawn Justine out—knowing if he killed her—he'd only have an injured Fed to deal with. I'd be easy prey for a guy who poached on the island and could take his time.

I winced at the thought of becoming a Totem topper like Applewhite—with my team sent to process the scene. To process *me*. Fear gripped me for a split second until anger took over.

I'm a hunter. Not a victim. I repeated the mantra in my head. It helped with the pain.

Matson had terrorized us from the start. If he had connections to Seattle or a pilot's license, I'd stumbled onto the lead I'd come to the island to find—thanks to the strange visions I'd seen of Nate—but I had to survive to stop a killer. More was at stake. I had to stop TK.

After I finished packing and was ready to go, I sat on the edge of the bed and stared across the cabin. I still couldn't leave and I knew why. I was waiting for Justine to walk through the door. In the silence, I turned out the lantern and sat alone in the dark and listened to the sounds of the night. Lightheaded and sick, I drank from the canteen and shut my eyes tight. At first the glimmer of the blood pool haunted me and the smell of it had stayed with me. In denial, I shoved those things from my mind.

Instead I concentrated hard and pictured Justine's face when she was alive. It wasn't tough to remember her quiet intensity and her fierce attitude as a trooper, always ready to do her part. But when she let me see her grief over Nate, her unexpected vulnerability had gripped me the most. I didn't want to imagine her dead now, but I had to come to terms with how it had happened.

The guilt I felt was regret over Justine's life cut short. The man who killed her deserved the blame. That's what I told myself, but it would take time to believe it.

In the dark with the hush of night around me, I welcomed Justine into my memory. I visualized her being with me and imagined the sound of her voice in my head. I knew the hike out would be tough. I'd need her to push me through the pain and I had to cover as much ground as I could in the dark, to make it harder for Matson to hunt me. Justine's strength and her knowledge of the island would get me down the mountain, like she'd promised.

When I sensed her with me, I used my crutch to stand. I shrugged into the gear she'd packed, grabbed my rifle, and headed out the cabin door into the dark.

Chapter Fourteen

Prince of Wales Island, Alaska
Hours later
Ryker Townsend

Moonlight made ghosts of everything as its bluish haze flickered between the deep shadows of trees. Branches became severed arms and tree trunks turned into bloody Totems. I knew it had to be something in me that distorted trees into gruesome stumps, but it didn't make them any easier to look at.

My bountiful mind had gotten good at conjuring nightmares.

I leaned onto my crutch and staggered over the uneven ground as my eyes searched the darkness. At first I looked for things I remembered on the way up as I tried to make sense of the landmarks now. My eyes searched the shadows for Matson. For Justine. For Nate. Even for the face of my mother.

My mind unraveled. I felt it happening and couldn't stop it.

My palms were slick with sweat, making it hard to hold the weight of the rifle. Faint tremors in my hands had become more pronounced. The shakes were new. They came and went, but I couldn't stop them once they took hold. They scared me. I didn't know what they meant.

"Keep moving. Don't stop."

I couldn't tell if I'd said the words aloud or in my head. Maybe it really didn't matter anymore. My fever had returned. Heat stirred under my skin, but with my clothes drenched with perspiration, chills raged through my body. I had worse things to worry about.

When I hit a switchback in the path, I slowed

down. One slip on lose rock or dirt could send me crashing down the hill. I slung the rifle over my shoulder and felt for my Glock to make sure it was secure in my holster. I'd need my hands free to get down the steep hill. Using the crutch in front of me, I took one step at a time, but slow had its hazards.

It gave me too much time to think.

I had to get ahead of Matson and I prayed the man hadn't followed me. In my condition, a head start could mean the difference between life and death. My ankle was swollen and hot because I couldn't elevate my leg. I pushed through the pain with voices in my head. I couldn't stop them.

'No sleep. No fire. No food.'

"What?"

I jerked my head and looked behind me. Hearing Justine's voice shocked me. I'd been walking in silence until her voice came from nowhere. I cringed with the noise and when I gaped over my shoulder, I expected to see her. I *wanted* to see her.

Her voice shook me. Not seeing her killed me.

"It was...nothing. You're seeing things. It's the concussion. Don't...s-stop."

I took a deep breath and leaned into my crutch. Every step became a blur. I wasn't thinking right and I knew it. Noise. I headed for a sound, but I'd forgotten why it seemed familiar. I only knew I had to keep moving.

Take the time it took for us to get here and double it. Hell, triple it for your injury.

I had lost track of how long I'd been walking. One step at a time. That's all I focused on to get me by. I had to keep on the move until daylight. Even then I couldn't stop. If I took the time to nap or rest my ankle, I was afraid I'd never wake up. Matson could kill me in my sleep.

I hoisted the gear on my back and focused on

each step. My pack had been trimmed down to the essentials, but every ounce weighed heavy on me. I stopped and grabbed my canteen. My throat had become raspy and dry from panting. *Stay hydrated. Do it.*

He's fixated on you now. The voice of Lucinda Crowley joined the party. I pictured the worried look on her face after I'd read the note that had made the last Totem personal. *Golden Boy.* I didn't *feel* special. I didn't want to *be* special.

"One step at a time. Just do it."

'You better watch your ass, Ryker.'

"Too late, Luce."

Voices haunted me. Knowing they came from inside me didn't help. Their words cut at me like a razor and night vision played tricks on my eyes. Even the steady drone of the distant river sounded like whispers. That was the noise I followed. The river. The blue green river of gems. The one I walked by when Justine had been alive.

Too bad you didn't stop whoever did it before he got to Nate. What Justine had said to me after we first met had stayed with me.

"I didn't stop him before he got to *you*, Justine."

I couldn't outrun my guilt. Her voice was a double edged sword. I remembered her words that would help me down the mountain, but I also felt the pang of regret knowing I hadn't been able to save her.

I'm not leaving you.

Justine *had* refused to go down the mountain alone. If she had, she would've been alive now. She'd stayed because I needed her. Neither us had known how unstable I'd become. Whatever my visions were, they tormented me enough to make me doubt my own sanity. I didn't know why my hallucinations had gotten worse on the island, but Justine had paid the price for my weakness. My being unstable had consequences that went beyond me. If I had fears about my ability to do my job, what happened with Justine should've been answer enough.

This case has gotten to you, hasn't it? That's why you're here alone and not with your team. There's something about Nate that's got its hooks in you, hasn't it?

Justine had been right. I'd left my team behind and came to Alaska alone for a reason. The UNSUB had targeted me and made the last Totem personal with a note sent to me, but my link to Applewhite had driven me here. Why? My own words to Justine repeated in my head as I trudged on.

Who I am is slowly slipping away and I can't stop it.

Dizzy. I couldn't make the spinning stop. Dark shapes moved and taunted me. Were any of them real? Off the trail to my right, I saw a shadow rush me. It came at me fast. My body went on alert and I reacted on instinct. When I stopped and reached for my Glock, I pulled it from my holster as the voices in my head grew louder. They came at me all at once.

"Shut up. Stop talking."

I swallowed hard and cried out with my heart pounding. Everywhere I turned, shadows lurched through the trees. I sensed a presence in the woods, but I didn't know if I could trust my gut anymore.

Shut up! Just shut up!

"I can't stop this...any of it."

I gripped my weapon tighter and my hands shook. A tremor ran down the muscles in my arms. *Oh, God.* If I took a shot and it turned out to be another hallucination, I'd send up a flare for Matson to find me. I had to be certain the threat was real, but how would I know for sure? *Damn it.*

I wiped the sweat from my brow and my slick

palms before I pushed on. *Stick to the trail.* After the switchbacks, don't get off the trail. Nothing looked familiar in the dark. None of it. The only thing I remembered had been the river gorge. The sound of the rushing water got louder, but it wasn't noisy enough to drown out the voices.

Ryker. Golden Boy.

A whisper came on the wind.

With sweat trickling down my neck, I stopped and jerked my head to the right. The sound from the river made it impossible to hear, but in the darkness of the trees, I saw it. A flash of red. The color triggered danger in my mind.

Matson's shirt.

He'd been with me all the time. He'd stalked me like a hunter. I hobbled off the path and braced my shoulder against a tree. No time to drop my pack. I steadied my hands and raised my gun. The edges of my world blurred and I blinked to shake off the dizziness as I took aim, searching for anything that moved.

Don't shoot...unless he's real.

I slipped my trembling finger onto the trigger and took a deep breath with my brain under assault. The voices wouldn't stop. *They wouldn't stop.* Another flash of red and a shadow came from the woods. A bearded face and a hulking body. I couldn't catch my breath or slow the thrashing of my heart. The voices got louder. Too many to hear who they were. They wouldn't shut up.

Not even after I fired.

Adrenaline rushed through my body and I felt numb. Through the trees I saw a shadow drop and heard something heavy hit the ground. I heard it, even with my ears ringing.

He's fixated on you now. Watch your ass, Ryker.

Crowley's voice yelled above the rest. She

screamed at me now, like something wasn't right and she knew it.

Her voice brought me comfort—like she was with me—as I took my first step from cover. I leaned heavy on my crutch and limped across the trail to where I'd seen Matson lurking in the trees. I still saw the red shirt. The vivid color left a ghost image on my eyes. I wedged my crutch tight to my body with an elbow and raised my Glock with unsteady hands.

It was Matson.

Part of me felt bad for shooting without thinking of the families who needed closure, but I had a killer side that helped me get into the minds of serial offenders. My dark side only wanted him dead for what he'd done to Justine and maybe others. I wanted to see his dead body and know it was over.

I wanted to go *home.*

What I'd seen played over in my head as I stumbled through brush and over rocks to search for any evidence I'd hit something. At the base of a tree, moonlight glistened off rough bark and on the ground, giving it an unnatural sheen. I reached out and touched the tree. My fingers felt something slick and when I looked at my hand, dark wet smudges marred my fingertips.

Blood. I must've hit something.

I wanted this to be over, but an unsettling dread gripped me hard. *The red shirt.* I searched the trees for it. My gaze darted to every shadow. I couldn't slow the frantic beat of my heart. Something wasn't right. I inched closer to where I'd seen the blood on the tree. The nearer I got to the spot, the worse I felt. Blinding light seared my eyes and almost doubled me over in pain. My head throbbed as if a lightning storm raged inside my skull.

"Ahh."

I leaned against a thick trunk and held on. When

my visions cleared and the pain subsided, I opened my eyes and looked down. I heard the sound of thick ooze gurgling at my feet. A bloody pool erupted from the soil and spread.

What the hell?

I cried out in frustration and poked the scrub brush with my crutch, hunting for a body. I fumbled in the dark and looked for anything to explain what I saw as the slick pool leached its dark fingers over the ground. I dropped to my knees. The instant I hit the ground, I raked the weeds with my fingers—and the dark sheen vanished.

It was gone.

"Shit. This can't be happening. Not again." I shook my head and tore at the ground. "What's *wrong* with me?"

None of what I'd seen made sense—except for one thing.

Guilt over what happened to Justine had triggered another of my hallucinations. I had seen the blood again—Justine's blood. I smelled the coppery tang as if it had been real, but when I collapsed to my knees to make sure of what I saw, I felt nothing.

Nothing.

I slumped against the tree, panting in the dark, and grabbed my canteen. It took both hands to hold it to my lips as convulsions spread up my legs and into my chest. I shut my eyes until the tremors went away. *The demons.* I couldn't outrun them. They were always with me. It was bad enough I'd imagined the whole thing, but now I'd fired my weapon and Matson would come for me.

I'd run out of time.

Chapter Fifteen

Annandale, Virginia
Dawn

Lucinda Crowley had given up on sleep and hit the CCT with her Cannondale road bike. Her small one-bedroom apartment had access to the Fairfax Cross Country Trail. The twenty miles of continuous system snaked through forested parks and alongside Accotink Creek that cut through Annandale, south of DC. Sweat drained down her arms as she cranked up the final hill to coast toward her apartment and a cool down. After she hit the crest of the hill, she grabbed the water bottle anchored to her bicycle and squirted her face and neck before she drank.

A long ride normally helped her think, but this time she couldn't shake her worry over Ryker. The haunted look in his eyes had stayed with her. She'd deleted the photo of him at the last crime scene, but the image hadn't left her. What had he seen that spooked him?

The guy was pure ice on the job. She saw his mind work as he took in every detail and his analytical nature made intuitive hurdles like no one she'd ever worked with before. He reminded her of a chess player assessing several moves ahead, but lately he spent more time alone. She'd catch fleeting glimpses of him that bothered her.

Something had its grips in him.

She could work alongside him at a crime scene, yet there'd been an undeniable and growing distance between them as they investigated the Totem Killer case. It had to be more than the UNSUB singling him out in the last note. The change in Ryker had been building. He hadn't been sleeping and even after she'd pushed him to talk to her, he hadn't. That hurt. She thought they were closer—or maybe she wanted him to trust her more.

It wasn't like him to drop from sight during an investigation—especially a case that had plagued him for over a year. Even if something happened to his phone, Ryker would find a way to keep in touch with his team. He wouldn't have shut her out when they had fresh bodies holding the potential for new leads.

She coasted to a stop in front of her apartment and hoisted the lightweight road bike on her shoulder as she climbed the stairs to the second floor. When she got inside, the smell of Korean takeout hit her senses. Last night she'd picked up dinner in a section of Annandale called Korea Town and brought it home. The smell had lingered.

After she put her bike away, she took off her helmet and gloves and checked her cell for messages. She secretly prayed Ryker would've texted her or left her voice mail. To hear his voice saying he was okay—and for him to give her his justifiable explanation for what had happened—would've put her mind at rest, but her life had never been that easy. She wasn't one to indulge in wishful thinking. In her line of work, optimism wasn't a good bet.

She stripped out of her drenched bike shorts and sleeveless jersey and tossed them in the hamper as she headed for the shower in her bedroom. She stood under the hot spray of water and washed her hair before she slathered herbal soap over her wet skin, but she didn't stay long. Her mind was too focused on Ryker. After she toweled off, she got dressed for work and turned on the TV news as she made coffee. When her cell phone rang, she raced to answer it. She didn't even look at the number to see who'd called.

"Cam and Sinead are too good at stalking guys online. I just want to put that out there."

Lucinda recognized Hutch's voice and said, "It's a good thing they're on our side, isn't it?"

"That's one way of looking at it," he said. "Sorry to disturb your morning routine, but we found something in our search last night that I thought you should hear, first thing. Cam's running a background check. We'll have more soon."

"Did you guys work through the night?"

Lucinda grabbed fruit and yogurt from her refrigerator and a couple of power bars from her pantry as she packed her lunch and talked to Hutch.

"Uh, yeah, guess so. What time is it?"

"If you have to ask, you don't want to know."

"Good point," he said. "Bring coffee and something to eat. We're starving."

"You got it. Tell me what you guys found."

"We got a hit on a missing person that matched the Applewhite criteria. His name is Benjamin Stevens, age twenty-five. He's got an address in Belltown, not far from downtown Seattle's waterfront. I looked up that location. His neighborhood used to be low rent, but now it's trendy with shops, restaurants, and clubs. He lives with his mom and takes care of her. She has Multiple Sclerosis."

"Oh, God."

"Yeah, that sucks, infinity times infinity. He's a student at Seattle University under the nursing program. This isn't a guy who'd walk away from his life and go missing."

"I agree. He sounds like a possible target for our UNSUB. When was he reported missing?"

"The same night we were there investigating the scene in the Cascades and found our last Totem, but it took time for the missing person report to show in the system. His mom reported him gone pretty fast though. He'd called her after he left a restaurant where he'd picked up dinner from her favorite restaurant and never came home. The place was only ten minutes from their house. They were celebrating his mom's birthday."

"Oh, no. How terrible."

"Yeah, happy birthday. And before you ask, we're trying to get a sample of his DNA to compare against the body parts we haven't identified. That'll take time, but since our UNSUB tortures his victims before he kills them, this guy could..."

"He can still be alive."

"Yeah, and it gets better. Stevens isn't the only potential victim we have, but that's not the better part. I found something else that's interesting about our boy Ben. After Cam pulled his background, we noticed he had a connection to Klawock, Alaska. He got paychecks last summer when he worked a fishing charter. Thank God he filed his taxes."

"Besides this place being in Alaska, where's Klawock located? I'm not familiar with it."

"Neither was I until I looked it up. It's on the Prince of Wales, the same island where Ryker is. I know how much you hate coincidences and I'm getting a weird energy off this island."

Lucinda sighed and ran a hand through her hair.

"Our UNSUB could be comfortable with his routine," she said. "If he's confident enough, maybe he's expanded his reach from Seattle. This *is* significant."

"A remote island in Alaska leaves few places to hide. It could be the break we've been looking for, to get ahead of our UNSUB, but the clock is ticking if we want to find where he tortures them. We got a good shot at finding Ben if we do."

"Have Sinead focus on Stevens to see if we can find any online thread that leads back to Alaska, an IP address we can physically track down."

"Yeah, done, but what if we're wrong about where our UNSUB lives or what address he uses to stalk them online? He could live in Seattle or Alaska or even Canada, but use Seattle as his dumping ground for bodies. If TK is torturing Stevens, we're running out of time before he ends up in a freezer."

Lucinda shut her eyes and felt her heart race as she held the phone to her ear. Hutch was right. Finding the missing person report for Stevens raised the stakes. If they pursued one lead over another, they could make the wrong decision and cost the guy his life.

The call was hers to make.

"Focus on Stevens. Follow the instincts that put you on this lead, Devin. If it hadn't been for you, we wouldn't even know the name, Benjamin Stevens. Whatever decisions need to be made to find him, they'll be on me."

She had new appreciation for Ryker as their team leader. He let them take risks to pursue the investigation, but when it came to taking the heat and living with the consequences, Ryker bore the weight. She always had respect for his strength, but until this moment, she hadn't realized how well he did his job.

She didn't feel ready to be in charge, but she didn't have a choice.

"If our UNSUB thinks the online way he hunts these guys is safe for him, he could be getting sloppy. Extend the missing person search to Alaska, but focus on Stevens as our priority. We have to assume this guy is alive."

"Yeah. I agree. One more thing," he said. "About Ryker, I gotta ask. Do you think he went to this island on a hunch, for another reason than checking out Applewhite's place? I mean, he even warned us the UNSUB had a new victim. How does he *do* that?" Hutch said what she'd been thinking. "I've seen

Ryker follow his gut to very peculiar places that panned out, but this is the first time he's taken off on his own. Even if the guy needed his overdue share of R&R, why not kick back in Seattle or find a beach? Instead he zeroes in on an obscure island. How does he *know* this stuff? The guy is a Zen master."

"Nothing would surprise me about our fearless leader, Hutch." She sighed. "I'll see you soon."

Lucinda didn't hesitate. After she ended the call with Hutch, she went back to her bedroom and looked for extra clothing, suitable for Alaska, to pack in the ready bag she kept at work. She had a strong hunch on how her day would play out. She should have listened to the warning voice in her head long before now. The way she felt about Ryker, it wasn't always easy to think clearly and keep the personal separate from the professional.

What if he'd been in trouble since the day his SAT phone lost service? Terrible scenarios ran through her head as she packed. In every one she couldn't shake the feeling she'd let him down. Even if he hadn't confided in her, she should have pressed him for more.

The last thing she wanted was to be forced into a decision between her searching for Ryker or Benjamin Stevens and prayed it wouldn't come to that. If it took searching in two places at one time, she could enlist the help of local law enforcement or other FBI agents in the region, but she'd been trained to put the innocent victim first. Ryker would understand if she chose to take the lead on the hunt for Stevens, but that wouldn't make her decision any easier if he'd been in trouble from the start.

She could already be too late.

With a gym bag of extra clothes on her shoulder, she grabbed her lunch and headed out the front door. She had decisions to make, but in the back of her mind, a clock had started to tick down—a clock she should have heard days ago.

"Damn it, Ryker. Why did you go alone?"

***

Prince of Wales Island, Alaska
Dawn

Golden Boy had grown weak. His steps had shortened. He looked exhausted and was mumbling to no one as he hobbled down the mountain. The blood he left on the trail made it easy to follow him in the pale light of morning. No need for night vision binoculars anymore.

"Come to me, lover. Give it up. You're mine now. You just don't know it yet."

Soon it would be time to end Golden Boy's misery. The guy was seriously messed up. Last night he'd fired his gun. That had been a surprise, but what he did next had been fun to watch. He'd dropped to his knees and ran his hands over the ground, looking for something only he saw. It didn't matter what it was.

He'd lost it. He had another hallucination and that's all that counted.

"No more help for you. The trooper is off duty."

A bear trap had set everything in motion. The stars had aligned and everything had fallen into place as if it'd been meant to be. Golden Boy turned into a rat in a maze. He'd followed the path down the mountain. He'd taken a few wrong turns that made it harder on him, but he'd see Point Baker soon. He traversed a ridge that would show him the way, if he knew what to look for.

The sooner he wore himself out, the better. He'd be too weak to put up a fight. If he shut his eyes and rested, he'd pass out. It would be simple to disarm him—and even easier to take him like the others.

To stalk him until he collapsed was only the teaser of what would come.

"Can't wait to get you on my table. I've saved my best work for you."

Townsend was used to being in charge and in control, but that ended the minute he set foot on the island. He'd come to track down leads in his hunt for a killer—and gotten much more. Too bad nobody else would know how close he'd come.

"You'll get what you came for, Golden Boy. My face will be the last one you'll see."

***

Prince of Wales Island, Alaska
Ryker Townsend

With the river gorge behind me now, I didn't have the rushing water to guide me. I'd followed its sound and had gotten down the mountain, but I'd lost the only landmark I'd been sure of. I had nothing to focus on. Nothing I remembered.

I took one step at a time and was bone weary and barely able to hold my head up. My tunnel vision had returned and I'd lost more blood. The weaker I got, the more I relied on my makeshift crutch. The skin on my palm was raw from holding onto the rough bark, and under my arm where the padding hit me, it felt bruised and swollen.

The darkness had turned to steel gray and the morning chill left my fingers and feet numb. I thought of home—and Crowley—and my sister Sarah. *Keep moving. One step at a time.* My clothes were damp with sweat from the fever. I'd been traveling across a ridge with a downward slope. Gravity kept me moving, but I had expected to see signs of Point Baker by now.

Out of breath, I stopped and shrugged out of my pack. It felt good to have the weight off my back and the crutch out from under my arm, but when I bent over to pull out the canteen, a rush of dizziness hit me hard. I collapsed to my knees and cried out with the pain that shot through my bad leg.

"Oh, God."

I crawled toward a large tree beside the worn path on all fours and dragged my pack with me. *Don't stop. Not now.* My body wouldn't listen to my head. I rested against the tree and stared at my messed up ankle. The bandage had soaked through and I'd left a blood trail any hunter could find.

We're gonna catch this guy. I promise you.

In my head I heard the words I'd told Justine at the start of our trip up the mountain and almost lost it. I laughed at my arrogance. When I shut my eyes for a second, I heard the hurt in her voice.

We both know you can't promise that.

She'd been right to doubt me.

"One of us knew."

I fumbled through the pack and retrieved what little I had left for first aid. This would be the last time I could change my dressing. I tossed the bloody rags away and put fresh bandages on. My ankle had swollen to twice its size. With my back against the tree, I popped pills in my mouth and sucked water from the canteen to swallow them.

I squinted into the gray morning sky and struggled to remember the way to Point Baker. I looked to where I should've seen Calder Mountain, the landmark Justine had showed me, but clouds covered it. Nothing looked familiar, not even in the daylight. I shut his eyes to steady my heart and catch my breath.

Get up. You can't stay here.

I wasn't sure if I'd said those words aloud. With

eyes closed, I listened to the birds flitting through the trees and the sound of the breeze stirring the leaves. *Rest.* I only needed to rest. After I'd stopped moving, the damp chill of the morning cut through my clothes. I felt numb, except for the burning in my ankle. When I gave in to my exhaustion, I let my chin drop to my chest and everything faded to nothing.

Even the birds stopped.

Chapter Sixteen

Lucinda had her team assemble in her office minutes after she arrived at BAU headquarters. She'd brought a dozen breakfast sandwiches and coffee and set them on her desk. Devin Hutchison was the first to show, with Cam Devore and Sinead Royce arriving minutes later. They came prepared to work and ate as they reported their missing person search results on the new victimology in light of Hutch's theory that the UNSUB used the *FaceTrax* app to hunt his targets online.

Lucinda stared at the DMV photo in the file Cam had created on Benjamin Stevens. The guy bore a striking resemblance to Applewhite, Dunkirk, and Wesson. He had dark good looks and kind eyes that made her want to know him. On his Facebook page he had photos of an active life. The guy was tall, muscular, and physically fit like the other victims.

After learning Stevens was the primary caregiver to his mother who'd been stricken with MS, Lucinda felt the impact of his abduction. A mother's worst fear is to outlive her child, but Mrs. Elizabeth Stevens depended on her son for her everyday needs.

"Once we found the obscure link to the Prince of Wales Island and a fishing charter employer for Benjamin Stevens, Sinead dug into his Facebook page," Hutch said. "She cross referenced anyone who followed his page over the past year. Tell her what you found, Sinead?"

"Ben is an outgoing guy. He chats up strangers who post to his wall and he keeps in touch with friends he made when he worked for Bayview Fishing Charters in Klawock. I checked out anyone who followed his page from last summer until now, and looked into their IP addresses. I had to make a call and rule them out if they looked legit, but one IP bounced me through a dozen sites before I hit pay dirt on its origin. The name on the Facebook page looked as if it was for a freelance guide service—*Thrill-Seeker*. Everything about this business sounds generic. Even the hunting and fishing pictures on the page are tagged from other charters. No original images and no names to track, but the multiple IPs looked suspicious so I chased it."

"Any luck?" Lucinda asked. "I know you said someone with tech savvy skills could send you on a circle jerk, in search of Waldo."

"Whoever went through so much trouble to hide their ID didn't do it on a whim. They had mad skills when it came to online obstacles, but I have my ways of getting around them. I found a physical address we can check out."

"That's great. Is it a residence? Do you have a name?" she asked.

"No, but the IP address is a public library that's close to the fishing charter place. If they have video surveillance in the library or on Bayview Boulevard where the fishing charter is located, we might get eyes on whoever set up the page ID. The library also keeps record of who uses their internet service, but I'd have to narrow down the timeframe to isolate a user. I can cross check the Facebook login activity for *Thrill-Seeker* to do that."

"It can't be a coincidence that the IP is located close to the fishing charter. It's definitely worth checking out."

"We have more," Hutch said. "Cam?"

"I talked to the detective who's been looking into

the Stevens missing person's case. Detective Frank Edwards is sending me everything he has on the investigation," Cam told her. "He said he put a GPS trace on the guy's cell phone right after he was reported missing. He tracked his phone to a cell tower in Alaska and gave me coordinates in Klawock."

"Maybe the guy needed a break from his mother's care." Lucinda played the devil's advocate. "You said he still keeps up with his friends in Alaska."

"He was headed home with dinner for his mom on her birthday when he went missing. Who *does* that? Plus from everything I've seen on this guy, he wouldn't leave his mom in the lurch, not without making sure she had someone to take care of her."

Cam had explained that Stevens had taken the summer job in Alaska last year to earn extra money for college. He'd taken a break from his mother's care only after her sister had agreed to come for a long visit from Edmond, Oklahoma. Any cop investigating a missing person claim might assume Ben Stevens had taken off, looking for a good time in Alaska again, but on paper Cam thought the guy looked too responsible to leave home on a whim, especially without telling an ailing mother who relied on him.

"Did Detective Edwards send out anyone local to search for Stevens in Klawock?"

Cam glanced at Hutch and took a deep breath before she answered.

"Yeah, they did. It's a small town, like Mayberry small. They never found Stevens or an itinerary for him traveling to the state," Cam explained. "They lost the GPS signal for his cell. Whoever abducted Stevens made sure no one could track his phone. Sound familiar? Applewhite didn't have a known itinerary to Seattle and Sinead said Ryker's phone went offline like Stevens. The coincidences are piling on."

Lucinda felt as if she'd been cold cocked. Her worst fears over Ryker were happening. In her moment of harsh realization, she pictured the faces of the three dead men—Applewhite, Dunkirk, and Wesson—and remembered feeling as if she were missing something vital about the three men.

Hearing the news about Steven's missing cell made her realize why she'd been bothered by the faces of the dead men.

"Devin, do a *FaceTrax* comparison between Applewhite and Ryker."

"What?" Hutch fixed his gaze on her. "You think the personal note from our UNSUB to Ryker made him a target?"

"I'm not sure what to think," she said. "Ryker may have been a target *before* he got the note. Sending him a personal message was probably more to mess with his head. I could be wrong, but humor me and let me know what you get."

Lucinda slumped back in her chair and stared out her window. She couldn't look her team in the eyes. She didn't need Hutch to confirm what she already sensed—that Ryker had similarities to Nathan Applewhite and would fit the victim profile. She hadn't seen it before because Applewhite didn't dress or groom the way Ryker did. Take Applewhite from Alaska and he'd clean up nicely in a suit and tie. If Ryker lived in a remote log cabin, she could easily picture him adapting and she liked imagining him that way, but how she saw him had blinded her.

She hadn't noticed the similarities before because she *knew* Ryker. She saw him in many different ways. His face would never be an algorithm to her, but if Applewhite's looks made him the target of a killer, maybe the same thing had happened to Ryker. The media coverage on the case would've put Ryker online. He didn't need a social media page to make him vulnerable.

"I'll call Unit Chief Reynolds to update her," she said. "She'll want to know about Ryker...and the latest we've got on our UNSUB."

"Ryker has a sister. Does anyone know how to reach her...in case?" Cam asked.

Lucinda sighed. Ryker hadn't kept the fact that he had a sister a secret from anyone on his team, but when pressed he didn't talk about her much. All she knew was that he hadn't spoken to his sister Sarah in years, but her contact information would be in Ryker's personnel records under his next of kin notifications. *In case.*

"Until we know more, there's not much I can tell her, but I'll notify her if it becomes necessary." She prayed it wouldn't.

"Tell me we're going after Ryker and Benjamin Stevens," Hutch said. "We've got an IP address to check out in Alaska—something connected to Ben Stevens—plus we've got the last coordinates for Ryker's SAT phone in the mountains outside Point Baker. We could check out Applewhite's cabin, see if he's there."

Lucinda had spent time last night plotting Ryker's last known coordinates against satellite maps and the possible location of the victim's cabin. The FBI had use of a private charter jet, but once they got to Ketchikan, a different kind of aircraft would make more sense. There were miles between Klawock and Point Baker on the island, but a private helicopter would allow them to move quickly, get into the mountains, and land anywhere, if they needed to.

"That's the plan. Pending approval from Reynolds, I'll want you and Cam with me, Hutch. Make a quick trip home and pack for Alaska, both of you. You'll need more than what's in your ready bag. I'll text you with the departure time."

She had a feeling there was a connection between Ryker being AWOL and Benjamin Stevens going missing—a bad feeling.

"Sinead, reserve the jet with a flight plan to Ketchikan, Alaska," she said. "From there, we'll charter a helicopter to search the island. Check out our options and let me know."

"Will do," Sinead said.

After her team left, Lucinda thought of another way to get in touch with Ryker. She didn't have much hope that she'd get results, given his remote location, but before she called Unit Chief Reynolds she had nothing to lose in trying.

She placed a call to the Alaska State Troopers. After her third transfer, she finally connected with someone who knew Trooper Justine Peterson.

"Do you have any way to make contact with your trooper? She's helping one of ours, Supervisory Special Agent Ryker Townsend, in Point Baker. Actually they were hiking to a cabin in the mountains. We've got the last coordinates before his SAT phone lost its signal. It's been nearly three days since we've heard from him."

"Point Baker is on the northern tip of the island," Trooper Gus Whitmire said. "I can try her cell, but the reception there isn't good, especially if they're in the mountains."

She didn't bother explaining how Ryker's SAT phone should have worked, but it didn't sound as if communication with Trooper Justine Peterson would be likely.

"You haven't heard from her either?" she asked.

"No, but we didn't expect to hear anything. Three days in the mountains isn't unusual for a round trip and from what I hear, she took personal time," he said. "Is there something you'd like us to do on our end?"

"Give me your direct number and I'll let you know."

Lucinda took down his number and ended the call. She'd need help from the locals to cover ground in a hurry, but not without oversight from her team. Any search and rescue operation would have to be contained and kept under wraps. It would be too easy for rumors to fly on a small island.

If the UNSUB lived in Alaska, the last thing she wanted was for an overzealous local law enforcement officer to spook the killer by accident. On his home turf, the Totem Killer could have a network of contacts and ways to leave the state, especially if he had his own plane. He'd know where to run and have too many miles to hide.

A trek to Alaska wouldn't only be about finding Benjamin Stevens and Ryker. Her team's operation might turn into end game if *Thrill-Seeker* turned out to be their UNSUB.

Lucinda braced for her next phone call. She knew Unit Chief Reynolds would support her decision to take the team to Alaska and give her any resources she'd need, but having to update her on Ryker would be the hardest to do. Reynolds had recruited him and cultivated his career in the FBI.

When it came to Ryker, the unit chief would have plenty of questions.

***

BAU headquarters
Quantico, Virginia
Minutes later

Lucinda had rarely spoken to Unit Chief Reynolds directly. Ryker had been the buffer between them. In person, Reynolds had a stern expression and smiled only on rare occasions. Her intense blue eyes were tenacious and intimidating. As far as she knew, the woman never blinked. *Ever.* Even on the phone, the seasoned FBI veteran had a way of making Lucinda uneasy.

"Unit Chief Reynolds, this is Special Agent Crowley. I've got an update on the Totem Killer case that you should hear and I'm looking for travel authorization to follow a new lead, but first I need to tell you about...Ryker."

Lucinda filled her in and gave her the facts. As expected, the unit chief asked questions. It had been hard for Lucinda to hold back her personal feelings on Ryker's growing isolation and her concerns over his mounting fatigue. The guy was definitely haunted by this case, but it wasn't her place to say, or to speculate on his reasons.

Reynolds had a close relationship with Ryker that at times reminded Lucinda of mother and son, although she would never say that to anyone. They had a bond and a way of communicating that went beyond words. Even when they disagreed, Ryker didn't back down when he believed in something and Reynolds encouraged him to speak his mind. Her regard for him was obvious and the respect ran both ways.

Lucinda knew if Ryker were missing and in trouble, their unit chief would be more worried than she would let on. She had hired him. Reynolds would feel responsible for him, beyond Ryker working for her. Lucinda knew the news on Ryker would be tough for Reynolds to hear.

"When was the last time you spoke with him directly?"

After Lucinda told her, Reynolds let silence build until the woman finally sighed.

"That's not like him."

"No, ma'am. That's why I called you. We've

identified another victim who may still be alive...and being tortured by our UNSUB. Our missing person is Benjamin Stevens. If he's alive, the clock is ticking."

Lucinda told Reynolds what her team had found and her suspicions. She stuck to the facts, even if it made her look as if she'd dropped the ball where Ryker was concerned.

"Sounds like you feel responsible for Ryker going missing," Reynolds said. "This is your first time being in charge of the team, isn't it?"

"Yes, ma'am. It makes me appreciate the job Ryker does every day."

"Don't let your doubts make you lose focus. They're a distraction. I agree with your assessment. You have my support...and approval. Your victim Stevens may not have much time. Maybe the same goes for Ryker. Coordinate with the local field office and the state troopers and put me on speed dial. I want to know everything."

"Yes, ma'am. I'll keep you informed of—" Before she could finish, Reynolds hit her with a question she hadn't expected.

"Tell me the truth, Crowley. Have you noticed a change in Ryker's behavior?"

Unit Chief Reynolds had asked a tough question, one Lucinda wasn't prepared to answer. Whether she told the truth or lied, either way could come back to bite her. She didn't know what to say. She wouldn't betray Ryker by undermining him in front of his superior, but lying to Reynolds didn't feel right either.

"He's a private man. He always has been."

Lucinda hadn't lied. She gripped her phone tighter and chewed the inside of her lip. It took all her willpower not to say anything more.

"That doesn't answer my question, Crowley."

"No ma'am. Guess it doesn't...exactly."

The line went silent and Lucinda thought the call had been dropped. She grimaced and closed her eyes, waiting Reynolds out, when everything in her gut told her to keep talking. She'd seen Ryker do it many times, with deadpan flair and without a blink, but she felt every miserable second of her stoic silence.

She wasn't like Ryker or Reynolds. Lucinda was a blinker.

After a very long and weighty duration of dead air, Reynolds finally said, "Ryker has rubbed off on you, Crowley."

Lucinda could've sworn the unit chief had a smile to her voice. She wasn't sure what Reynolds meant by Ryker rubbing off on her, but she hoped the high powered woman had paid her a compliment.

"Find him. Do whatever is necessary and keep me informed," Reynolds told her. "You were right when you said Ryker is a private man, but something about this case has been wearing him down. I'm concerned about him...like you are."

"Ma'am, I didn't say I was—"

"Don't bother, Special Agent Crowley. Ryker doesn't think his silence speaks volumes either."

The line went dead.

Lucinda didn't have to hear Reynolds say the words that the woman would be watching every move she made, but she'd gotten the message.

***

Prince of Wales Island, Alaska
Ryker Townsend

A chill shot across my skin. It came from the pain and burn of a needle jammed into my neck. The only move I could make had been a shrug.

Fight it. Stay conscious.

I fought to open my eyes, but when I did, I only

saw shadows clouding over me like a fast approaching thunderstorm. Bright glimmers of light stabbed my eyes. I thought they were streaks of lightning, but they didn't carry a sound. No rumble of thunder. Only the blinding light.

Don't let go. Stay awake.

"Ryker, can you hear me?"

A hand squeezed mine and I felt a soft touch on my cheek. The voice. I recognized it.

"It's Justine. I'm getting you out of here."

What...happened to you? The question screamed in my head, but I couldn't hear my voice. My brain had turned to mush.

Matson. For a split second I'd thought he had me. I felt his menace everywhere, but my mounting hallucinations could've been made worse by whatever had been in the shot. I'd been drugged with a syringe to my neck, but the shot must've been for pain. Justine had been the one to find me. I took a deep breath and thought of her—*alive.*

Justine.

When I tried to move, I couldn't feel my legs or my hands. I opened my mouth, but nothing happened. No sound. The shot made me numb with every passing second and darkness swept over me. I strained to see what had happened, but everything had turned hazy. A shadow stood over me and I felt a hand grab me and strap something tight across my chest. I couldn't breathe. I wanted to puke, but if I did, I would die. I'd choke on my vomit.

Don't get sick. Breathe through your nose. You puke, you die.

Everything went black. No stabbing light. I struggled to see anything. Couldn't make sense of what happened until I realized. Someone had put a cover over my head.

Breathe. Keep breathing.

Heavy cloth covered my nose. Every time I took a breath, it suffocated me. It felt like drowning.

Justine! I tried yelling her name, but nothing came out. Had I dreamed her?

I fought to stay conscious, but I was losing the battle. Hands took hold and dragged me by the shoulders. My ankle hurt like hell and the miserable groan I heard had come from me, but the pain didn't stop until I was dumped onto a metal frame. The thing rocked on wheels as I was strapped onto it.

Something fell across my chest and my legs. The last strap cut across my neck. I couldn't move. Had I been wrong about being rescued by Justine? Had my guilt about the way she died forced me to hallucinate her being alive?

Matson. Could it be him?

I remembered closing my eyes on the trail, exhausted. I must've fallen asleep. Flashes of red, pieces of my fragmented memory were coming together too late. *Oh, God. No.* Panic seized me. I fought the restraints, but my moves were sluggish. My upper body jerked and I thought my head would explode. The motion. The feel of it, I knew I was on wheels now.

An engine started. *Loud.* Near my head. The size of the vehicle and the way it tilted when someone climbed on, it had to be a four-wheeler. I smelled gas and my stomach lurched as I got pulled and jostled down an incline. The wheels crunched on gravel and kicked up dirt as the vehicle hauled my weight hitched behind it.

Through the fog in my muddled brain, the rumble of the engine turned to menacing thunder. The noise raged in my head and I fought the nausea, made worse by the bumpy ride down a steep grade. With every jolt, the straps cut into me and I gagged.

I let the storm sweep over me—and through

me—to rain down its blustering darkness. The last thing I saw was the dead eyes of Nathan Applewhite.

***

The low murmur of rolling waves came to me first, before I smelled the briny ocean. A chill raced over my body as a crush of seawater sent me tumbling under its weight. A swell of bubbles blinded me until I couldn't tell up from down. I shut my eyes and drifted to the bottom until I sensed the water held a dark presence that churned the depths from a distance. The whale had returned. This time the behemoth scared me. I sensed its brutality aimed at me. I fought to wake up, but couldn't. Seaweed grappled with my arms and legs until I couldn't breathe and my lungs burned.

I heard someone yell. It sounded like me.

Chapter Seventeen

Ketchikan, Alaska
Late Afternoon

"Thanks for the assist. I owe you one." Lucinda Crowley shook the hand of Alaska State Trooper Guy Whitmire without breaking stride on the Ketchikan Airport tarmac.

"Glad to help," the trooper said.

Whitmire was in uniform and stood as tall as Ryker, but had a beefy thirty pounds on him. His burr cut, meaty jowls, and wide jaw made it appear the older man had no use for a neck, except to button his collar.

Lucinda and her team headed for the helicopter they'd chartered to search the Prince of Wales Island. She'd contacted Whitmire en route to Alaska—shared her tentative search plans—and arranged for the man to meet them at the charter service.

"After your last call, I figured you could use another helo to hit it hard before we lose good visibility." Whitmire pointed to a nearby helicopter decked out in Trooper decal. "We got us a new A-star for search and rescue. If you're willing to split your team, she's at your service."

When Lucinda saw the Trooper aircraft, she let out a heavy sigh of relief. She'd have greater flexibility to search the Prince of Wales Island before nightfall. Travel time to get to Ketchikan had eaten up most of the daylight. The time change helped and would give them four extra hours, but she had a feeling they'd need every advantage before it became too dark to do a proper search.

Ryker's last known coordinates—pinged by Sinead off his SAT phone—had been near Point Baker on the northern tip of the island. Their search for Ben Stevens would start near Klawock, further south. For any avenues worth pursuing, her team could cover ground in a hurry with two aircraft.

She prayed it would be enough.

"That's very generous. Thank you." Lucinda glanced at Hutch and said, "I'll hitch a ride with Trooper Whitmire to look for Ryker at Applewhite's cabin. You and Cam take the charter to Klawock and hit the library. Use Sinead to search their computer system remotely while you and Cam look for security and traffic cams. I'll join you as soon as I can."

Hutch stopped and fixed his gaze on Lucinda. Cam mirrored his solemn expression.

"If you find anything, good or bad, we want to know the minute you do," he said.

The gravity of what they'd come to do hit Lucinda hard as she stared at Hutch and Cam. They'd avoided talking about Ryker and what it meant for his SAT phone to be out of commission. It was as if saying the words aloud—that Ryker could be hurt or dead—would make it true.

Lucinda could think of a worse scenario. What if they never found him? What if he simply vanished and they never knew what happened? The reality of that sent her reeling, but she took a deep breath and pictured Ryker—alive.

"I understand. Yeah, you got it. With any luck, I'll have Ryker with me the next time I see you." She grimaced and said, "But the clock is ticking on Ben Stevens. If he's still on the island, we've got to find him. Call me as soon as you know anything."

She had to keep her team focused on the search for Stevens. The guy was definitely missing and had been tracked to the island. All she had on Ryker was his offline phone and a bad feeling. She had enough reason to be concerned and had a duty to look for

Ryker, but she couldn't let her judgment be clouded by her feelings for him, not when another life hung in the balance. If the UNSUB had Stevens, Ben would be brutally tortured until TK killed him. In a shadowy corner of Lucinda's mind, she heard Ben's struggling heart pound as if he were living on borrowed time.

His life could depend on every decision she made. No pressure.

Lucinda tossed her ready bag into the A-Star and climbed in. Whitmire joined her and buckled up. As the pilot prepared for takeoff, she watched her team through her passenger window. After Hutch helped Cam into the charter, he stared across the tarmac and fixed his gaze on Lucinda. She'd seen Hutch's worried face before. He nudged his chin and shot Lucinda a thumbs-up sign before he climbed aboard the charter.

She didn't have to hear Hutch say what was on his mind. She knew.

We'll find him, Devin. We have to.

***

Prince of Wales Island
Klawock, Alaska

By helicopter from the Ketchikan Airport, it took no time to reach Klawock on the Prince of Wales Island. The bumpy ride left Hutch queasy, but his unsettled stomach had more to do with why they'd come.

Lucinda had banked on his notion of how the UNSUB hunted online and targeted his victims. Hutch had faith in his theory, but with someone's life on the line, second guesses were normal. To make matters worse, Ryker fit the victimology profile as Lucinda had suspected, which made his offline SAT phone a bigger worry.

Things had become complicated in a hurry and Hutch felt the urgency to be right.

As the helicopter circled for a place to touch down, Cam shot him a sympathy look. He'd never been good at hiding anything from her. Inside the fuselage, the engine noise was too loud for them to talk in private, so she'd settled on sending him her commiseration without words.

The pilot hovered over a helipad painted on asphalt near the small Trooper facility. The State Troopers had a local office in Klawock, giving the charter a safe place to touch down. From there, Sinead had arranged for a trooper to drive them to the library where they'd tracked the IP address for *Thrill-Seeker*.

On the ride over, Hutch called Sinead to check in.

"We're in Klawock. Send me what you found out about the dates and times the *Thrill-Seeker* was online for social media. We'll cross check that against the library's system access and surveillance cams. Those times will also help narrow the search through traffic cams around the library."

"Just sent the social media date and time hits, Devin," Sinead said. "You should have it..."

An alert sounded on his cell phone that he'd received a message.

"Yeah, got it." Hutch thumbed through his phone. "We'll be working with the troopers on the traffic cam surveillance, but once we get to the library, we'll need you to tap into their computer system on remote to tighten the noose. Maybe our *Thrill-Seeker* left a cookie trail for what he did online."

"If he did, I'll find it. Just get me logged in, Hutch."

"That's my girl. I'll be in touch." He smiled as he

ended the call.

In short order, he and Cam were walking into the Klawock Public Library wearing their FBI windbreakers and duty gear. With a uniformed trooper accompanying them, they caused a stir and every eye in the place locked onto them. Hutch ignored the attention and flashed his FBI badge at the librarian behind the front desk.

"I'm Special Agent Hutchison with the FBI." In a low voice, he introduced Cam and the trooper. "We're here on official business. Who's in charge?"

The stunned librarian stared long and hard at his credentials as if she were committing his ID badge to memory—or spell checking it.

"Ma'am?" He waited until she looked him in the eye. "We need your help. Now."

"Oh, yes. Sorry. I'll get Mrs. Levine."

After the woman rushed around the corner, a kid dressed in a yellow and green UAA Seawolves hockey jersey approached Hutch with a smirk on his face. The boy glanced over his shoulder to his buddies who were sitting at a table, thumbing through magazines.

"Are you here to arrest somebody?" the kid asked.

"That depends. You owe any library fines?"

The kid scrunched his face and pointed to the weapon Hutch wore under his FBI windbreaker.

"You ever shoot anybody with that gun?"

"You mean at the last library? That wasn't my fault."

The boy blinked wide-eyed and his face flushed red. He backed off and left without another word. Camilla stared at Hutch with arms crossed.

"What?" he shrugged.

Cam only shook her head.

When she didn't encourage him with a reply, Hutch leaned against the desk counter and studied the library layout. After he found what he'd been looking for, he grinned at Cam and pointed at several security cameras.

"We got eyes. Fingers crossed those surveillance cams work...and that we hit pay dirt."

***

Prince of Wales Island – outside Point Baker
An hour later

"We're over the coordinates where you last heard from your agent. You see any sign of him or Trooper Peterson?"

The disembodied voice of Alaska State Trooper Whitmire came through Lucinda's headset as the blades off the A-Star helo's rotor whipped the treetops and stirred the dirt beneath them. The movement tricked her into thinking any second she'd see Ryker. She couldn't stop staring out of the helicopter window, praying he'd step out from under the evergreens and wave for a rescue.

"I got nothing," she said into her mic.

"Applewhite's cabin isn't far. You ready to move on?" the man asked.

Lucinda clenched her jaw and nodded as she peered through the deepening shadows under the trees. They were losing daylight.

***

Ryker Townsend

"You're...safe."

A woman's voice whispered through my mind. The gentle timbre soothed me. It came in a breathy sigh as if she were inside my head.

"*I'm here. It's me.*"

Her words overlapped like ripples on glassy

water. I wanted to open my eyes, but I couldn't. My body had no weight. In the distance I heard the hush of waves rolling to shore. The sound tapped into a sliver of memory I couldn't quite place and I smelled the brine of the ocean.

Justine. It *had* to be her.

The instant I felt her presence, velvet fingers touched my brow and traced down my cheek. My face burned under the coolness of her skin on mine. I had to see her. When I cracked open my eyes, a bright stab of light blinded me and a throbbing pain shot from my eyes to the back of my skull.

Shadows eclipsed the light. Wherever I was, I wasn't alone.

My eyes burned and watered from the strain of trying to see. When I tried to move, I couldn't. A kiss pressed against my lips and trailed down my neck. A faint whisper—in words I couldn't understand—brushed by my ear to calm me. A hand touched the skin of my chest and traced down to my stomach.

The intimacy made me flinch, but I still couldn't open my eyes. A woman's face took gradual shape in my mind like colorful brush strokes oozing together. I didn't want the touching to end. I wanted her and needed her to be with me. As I struggled to see who she was, a familiar voice came to me.

You're a bomb that hasn't gone off, but the fuse is burning.

I remembered that I'd replied, *When I blow, I'll think of you.*

When her face took substance and the blur cleared enough for me to see, I finally knew the woman who I'd wished wouldn't leave me. I stared into the face of Lucinda Crowley and I kept my promise.

She filled my mind and I willed her to stay.

***

Prince of Wales Island – outside Point Baker
Twenty minutes later

The A-Star circled a break in the trees where it would be safe to set down. As the aircraft maneuvered for a landing, the ground spiraled into a dirt cloud and tree branches thrashed at the intrusion. Applewhite's cabin wasn't far. Lucinda had seen it before the pilot picked the spot to touch down. The log cabin looked deserted. No smoke came from the chimney. No sign of life.

Seconds before the aircraft landed, she'd released her seatbelt and shifted to the edge of her seat.

"We got first aid onboard, survival gear and rations, and a crime scene kit." Whitmire took off his headset and unbuckled. "We're ready to provide assistance...if he needs it."

The trooper had intended to reassure her, but he only stirred the dread she already felt after seeing the quiet cabin. When the cargo door opened, the trooper helped her out and pulled his service weapon. Lucinda did the same.

Whitmire led the way toward the cabin. The co-pilot, another uniformed trooper named Sawyer, had joined them. No one spoke. They approached with caution, using tactical hand signals to communicate. Lucinda tightened her two-fisted grip on her Glock-19 as they neared the cabin. She strained to hear any sound coming from inside, but heard nothing.

Come on, Ryker. Please...be here.

Lucinda wanted her concerns to be over nothing. She wanted to find him safe, but as she got closer, the hair on her neck stood on end. Instinct sent her a message.

Ryker wasn't alright. Something was very wrong.

Whitmire was first through the door. Lucinda shuffled behind him with her gun raised. Trooper Sawyer took the outside and yelled "Clear" once he'd secured the perimeter.

After Whitmire called out, "Clear inside," Lucinda lowered her weapon and headed for the front door. She ran her fingers over the gouged wood.

"Bullet holes," she said. "Splinters are fresh."

"Yeah. Looked that way to me, too."

"This place has been trashed. Who would do this?" she asked.

Parts of the cabin looked well-maintained, but someone had torn things off the wall, ripped up personal treasures, and tossed Applewhite's possessions in a fit of rage. The way some items were gathered and stacked, it appeared as if someone had cleaned up a bigger mess. Had it been Ryker and Trooper Peterson? If they had made it to the cabin, why weren't they here now?

Lucinda didn't like any scenario that her instincts conjured.

"Someone with a grudge. Looks like drawings from a kid were shredded." Whitmire holstered his service weapon and thumbed through a stack of mementos on a bookshelf. "People on the island are more respectful of someone else's property. They watch each other's backs, but whoever did this, it was personal."

"Someone could've ransacked the place before Ryker and your trooper got here. Maybe they were the ones who tidied up after they saw the mess, but with the bullet holes on the door, I have to say I'm worried. Why aren't they here?"

Whitmire didn't answer. He called out to the trooper outside and ordered him to search beyond the clearing of the cabin.

"For what it's worth, it looks like someone stayed

here recently." Whitmire grabbed the flap of a backpack and fished his hand inside. "This pack has food, gear, and clothes. If I had to guess, I'd say the clothes belong to Peterson. The trooper shirts are her size."

"Ryker didn't have a backpack with him, but he'd have his clothes and personals."

"I'm sure Trooper Peterson had gear enough for a small platoon. Alaskans who enjoy the outdoor life are like that. She would've loaned him what he needed, but where is it?"

The bullet holes in the door, the remnants of a trashed cabin, and now only one pack with no sign Ryker had been here. Lucinda didn't like what that meant. If there was one pack, maybe only Trooper Peterson made it to the cabin.

"The stove's been used, but it's like whoever was here left in a hurry," he said. "When Alaskans leave a place, they put it in order for the next use. And Trooper Peterson would know better than to leave food behind for bears to sniff out. Something's not right."

"There's blood on the bed linens." Lucinda stared down at the mattress after she'd tossed back the sheets. Once she spotted the stains, she looked for more. "Bloody bandages...and there's discarded wrappings from first aid supplies. Someone was injured."

Whitmire joined her search and rummaged through the backpack left behind.

"Peterson would've brought first aid. It's part of our duty gear," he said. "If this is her pack, the med kit's gone. I bet Applewhite had a cache of med supplies, but looks like that's missing, too. Whoever was here took first aid with them. You don't double down on supplies unless you need them. Someone was definitely hurt."

"Maybe that's the reason a pack was left behind. An injured person might not be able to carry much."

"Yeah, good point. We could fly down the mountain to see if they're still on the trail. We have time before we lose visibility. If we don't find them, we could check Justine's place in Point Baker. Maybe ask people who know her there."

"Yeah. Good idea. Let's..."

When Lucinda took a step, her foot crunched on something. She lifted her boot to see white powder residue and more.

"Wait. What's this?"

She dropped to a knee and picked up two white pills she found on the floor by the bed. More were shoved into a crack in the floorboards. *What the hell?*

"They don't look like aspirins, exactly," she said.

Lucinda palmed the pills and showed Whitmire.

"I've seen these before," he said. "They look like Ketamine, normally a tranquilizer used in veterinary medicine, but it's the new date rape drug of choice. On the streets, they call it *Special K*."

"What? Why would Applewhite have a date rape drug at his cabin?"

"Good question," Whitmire said. "Could Nathan Applewhite been given the drug to get him out of here? Traces of Special K could be in his system for up to four days. Anything from his autopsy?"

"We haven't gotten the lab results back."

Trooper Whitmire reached for one of the pills and took a closer look. "We have a drug field test kit in the A-Star. It'll take a minute to test. No sense speculating until we can confirm or deny. We'll at least know what we've got here. Maybe it will tie to Applewhite's autopsy."

Lucinda knew a seasoned officer like Whitmire wouldn't have leaped to a conclusion unless he had a pretty good idea he was right. She followed him to the helicopter with her mind filled with questions.

"But I thought there wasn't a definitive field test for Ketamine," she said.

"Our troopers on the front line needed a way to test for it in the remote villages we cover. We use a modified Scott's test. Scott's failed its intended purpose to detect for Cocaine, but it was adapted to specifically test for Ketamine hydrochloride. It works."

"If someone with two legs is drugged with Ketamine, what symptoms would they manifest?" she asked as they approached the helicopter.

Lucinda watched Whitmire rummage through his gear on the A-Star and retrieve his drug test kit. The picture she'd taken of Ryker in the Cascades, where he'd looked as if he'd seen a ghost, shadowed her memory and wouldn't leave her.

"That depends on the dose, but the victims I've seen were really messed up," he said. "They pass out if they're lucky, but most suffer through severe hallucinations, nausea, vomiting, blurred vision, and insomnia. I've even seen body tremors and convulsions in the worst cases. And if something scares them, the fear is extreme and irrational. But there's no sense worrying until we test what we found. Hang tight."

Whitmire performed the test without hesitation. He'd obviously done it many times. One of the pills found on the cabin floor was dropped into a vial and shaken.

"If it tests positive for Ketamine, it'll change color quick."

In seconds the color in the vial turned dark and from the look on Whitmire's face, she knew what he'd say.

"It's Special K. What in the hell happened here?"

Before Lucinda said anything, she heard a voice

behind her.

"Lieutenant?" The trooper charged with searching the perimeter of the cabin called from the trees and ran until he reached them at the A-Star.

"I found something. You gotta see this, sir."

"What'd you find, Sawyer?" he asked.

"Blood. Lots of it, LT. I found a blood trail near the cabin and backtracked it."

"Show me. Now," she said.

Lucinda didn't wait for Whitmire to give his order. When Trooper Sawyer turned on his heels and ran back the way he'd come, it took all of her self-control not to run by him and take the lead. Bullet holes on the cabin door, bloodied bandages, and now this.

Ryker was in serious trouble.

***

Ryker Townsend

A scream woke me. It jumpstarted my heart and I choked a gasp. The visceral desperation of the cry reached deep and dragged me from wherever I'd been. I wasn't sure if I was dreaming, but when I opened my eyes, I got hit with a flood of misery. My body had saved every ounce of agony after I lost consciousness and it hit me all at once.

The pain felt too real not to be.

The first thing I saw was my body. I hung from a harness and bounced when I moved, like I'd been tied into a parachute dangling from trees. The sway did nothing for my nausea. I'd been stripped of my boots and hung like a carcass of meat. My hands were tied behind me and the harness straps cut into my legs, my shoulders, everywhere. I didn't think I could touch the ground. My numb legs dangled and my bad ankle must've bled. The dressing was clammy and soaked through. When I struggled to hold my head up, I paid the price. My stomach churned bile and the room spun.

But the memory of the scream rushed back to me. The chilling sound made me forget about my pain. I knew the unimaginable desperation. I'd heard that cry in my nightmares. It was the sound of someone dying. I didn't have to see to know, but I looked anyway.

Two by fours in a framework and plastic sheets were everywhere, tinted by the pulse of a red blinking light. I squinted through the crimson shadows of a dimly lit room that looked like a workshop in a garage. Through a blur came shapes. Walls bulged in swells as if the cramped space were made of an undulating gel—like waves in the ocean of my dream about the whale—but that's where the similarity ended. Here I felt a smothering heat. The stale air carried thick vile smells. I didn't want to breathe, but I had to.

Another body hung beside me in a bloodied harness. I couldn't see a face—only a blurry shape. I squinted to clear my eyesight, but nothing helped. How many more were held hostage here with me?

A cry forced my eyes to search for the guy making the noise. The gut wrenching wail had come from a man. Across from me, a shiny metal table reflected the red light that pulsed in erratic beats. Water dripped into a sink and the drops became louder. The incessant noise punished me like the pulsing light, but I stared at the man on the table.

His arms and legs were tied down. His wrists and ankles were bloody. He lay on his belly with a hood over his head. Naked. A strange song came over speakers. Why hadn't I heard the music before? The singer. I remembered hearing the song before, but couldn't place it. Ray Charles? The lyrics were brutal.

Cruel.

A dark shape hovered over the guy on the table. Gloved hands held a surgical knife that glinted in the red light. Every cut, blood ran down pale skin and pooled on the table. Another scream sent chills over me.

"S-stop. Leave h-him...alone."

The words were mine, but they came at me from a faraway place. I strained to see the face of the cutter, but I couldn't keep my eyes open or my head up for long.

The screaming stopped.

Time drifted between the darkness like a curtain opening and closing. At the sound of boots scuffing on wooden stairs and the creak of a door, I knew the cutter had gone. The music stopped. The eerie stillness closed in, broken only by the plop of dripping water.

Had I imagined it? The naked man—and the cutter carving into him—never settled in my mind. Everything felt like the remnants of a bad dream, as if what I'd seen hadn't been real. I blinked to clear my eyes and took deep breaths. Unfortunately for the guy on the table, he had to be real, but nothing stayed in focus for long. When my vision became clearer, the blur had turned out to be a mercy. The victim had been worked on with a blade.

I recognized the carving and the skill of the artist. I'd found the Totem Killer. Or rather, he'd found me. Matson must've heard my gunshot. He'd tracked me down the mountain from the cabin, waiting until I collapsed—until I couldn't put up a fight.

My gaze shifted to the guy on the metal table. His bloodless skin looked blanched and dead compared to the red meat of the scrolled cuts that were carved into his muscles. His butt, lower back, and upper thighs had seen the most work, but the artist was far from done.

I knew what he'd look like when it was over.

"Who...are you?"

No answer. He didn't move.

"Tell me your name?" I said it louder, but everything sounded muffled in my head. "Please...talk to me."

The body stirred. I saw him twitch.

"Ben. My n-name is...Ben Stevens."

I almost hadn't heard him. The way he slurred his words, it sounded as if he were drugged.

"My name's Ryker. Who's the guy next to me? Is he dead?"

"I don't know. I didn't see when they brought him in. Can't see his face."

Ben lifted his head, but he couldn't hold it up. I thought about telling him I was FBI, but considering I didn't exactly look like the cavalry, I kept my creds a secret. Telling him would only strip him of hope. I couldn't do that.

"Do you know where we are, Ben?"

"Y-yeah."

He choked on a laugh or a cry. I couldn't tell which. Were we still on the island? Because I didn't know how long I'd been drugged and unconscious, I had no idea where we were. I prayed he did.

"Hell," he said. "We gotta be...in h-hell."

He mumbled something I couldn't hear, but his sobs told me that he'd given up. He was broken. I wanted to tell him to hang on, to not give up hope, but that sounded like bull shit, even to me. I had no idea where we were. Help wasn't coming. Help was strapped into a harness and on deck for the next spot on the table, after the blood was washed away—after it would be too late for Ben.

I wouldn't have to wonder what the UNSUB did

to his victims. TK wanted me to have a front row seat to every cut, to every degradation. It had to be the reason I wasn't wearing a hood. I didn't want to die, but to see Ben suffer—and do *nothing*—felt like another way of dying. I couldn't save him. I'd watch him get butchered.

Then it would be *my* turn.

"Ryker?" A faint voice whispered to me from the shadows. "That...y-you?"

I stared at the body hanging next to me. The drugs had muddled my brain. I still couldn't see a face—only a hazy trail of blood coming from a head wound—but I recognized the voice. *Oh, God.*

"Justine?"

Chapter Eighteen

Ryker Townsend

"Yes. It's me," Justine said. Her voice was nothing but a raspy whisper.

The trooper had been taken hostage like Ben and me. I shouldn't have been happy to see her, but I couldn't help it. At least she still breathed.

"What happened? I thought Matson killed you. The blood."

"I can't remember much. Not after he hit me over the head. I was drugged and woke up here," she said. "What is this place?"

"I don't know. I hoped Ben could fill in the blanks."

Every word made my head ache. The weight of my body had become my enemy. My legs were numb. The harness cut off my circulation, but seeing Justine gave me hope. Even though I thought of escape and breaking free of my restraints, I wasn't sure I could walk. I was no better off than a steer in queue for the slaughterhouse and it gave me little comfort I wasn't alone. If I couldn't find a way to free all of us, I'd watch Ben and Justine die and share their fate.

I yanked at the rope that bound my hands. It cut into my wrists and blood had made my skin sticky. The tackiness had given me better traction and the damp hemp had stretched, but not enough yet.

"Can you get free?" I asked Justine.

"Don't know. I can...t-try."

She sounded weak and lost—a frailty I never thought I'd hear in her voice. Before I lost heart, I engaged my mind with the case in the only way I knew how. Ben Stevens had been a prisoner the longest. I had to know what had happened to him.

He'd be my Rubik's Cube to puzzle over—and a distraction against my pain.

"Ben? You awake?"

I called out to him, careful not to be too loud. I didn't want to alert our host. When I heard Ben moan, I pressed to get him talking.

"Tell me what you remember. How did he take you?"

Before Ben answered, Justine intervened.

"Why does this matter now?" she asked. "We have to get out of here."

"Ben could've seen something to help us."

"You're still working the case, aren't you?" She didn't sound happy as she tugged at the bindings on her wrists.

"What case? What's she talking about?" Ben asked. "Who is she? You act like you know each other."

"Justine Peterson. She's a State Trooper and I'm with the FBI."

"What? But how...?'

Ben stopped and didn't finish. He narrowed his eyes and stared at both of us. Of my peculiar talents, mind reading wasn't on the list—until now.

"I know we don't look like the cavalry," I said. "But there's not enough time to convince you we're law enforcement. That could take days and sworn testimonies. I need to know what you saw. Tell me how you were abducted, Ben. When and where did it happen?"

Ben lifted his head with effort and groaned. He turned toward me, but my vision hadn't cleared enough. I saw his face through the flickers of the red pulsing light. His eyes were dark hollows that made his face look like a skull, an unnerving sight teetering too close to the edge of prophetic.

"It was on my mother's birthday." He choked up

when he spoke of his mom and I understood his sudden rush of emotion. The bond I had with my mother made me feel closer to him. We were sons who'd been loved. Unfortunately for Ben, I'd been right when I told my team the UNSUB wouldn't wait to take his next victim. TK had abducted Ben the same night after we'd investigated the crime scene in the Cascades.

For his sake, I wished I'd been wrong.

"It happened at a parking lot...in Belltown. Seattle." He struggled for every word. "Outside a restaurant. I tried helping a g-guy with his truck, but he...slugged me."

"Was it only one man?"

"Yeah, I guess, but I...c-can't be sure."

"Did you get a good look at him?"

"Not really. It happened...too fast."

"What did the truck look like? Did it have a company logo?"

"No logo. It was old and rusted. Blue or green, I think. It had a white canopy. The bastard had the hood up, like he had engine trouble. I fell for it."

Like Ben, I had no doubt the raised hood had been a ruse to lure him closer. A good kid like Ben would've helped the man if he'd needed it and the canopy would give TK cover to haul bodies without anyone seeing what he carried. The tire treads they'd found in the Cascade Mountains could've come from a truck. The pieces to the puzzle were making sense.

"Anything else you can remember?"

Ben didn't answer for a long time. I thought he'd passed out.

"A plane engine."

"What?" Justine said. She stopped moving. The mention of aircraft had grabbed her attention.

"Yeah, he drugged me, but..." Ben tugged at his restraints and gasped in pain. "I woke up when I heard..."

"Heard what?" I asked.

"A plane engine. I felt the turbulence. I was tied up in the cargo hold of a small plane. I think the guy flew it."

My own words hit me when I'd talked with my team about how the UNSUB operated. *I'm seeing this guy as a commuter who operates outside his body dump sites....*

Too little, too late. Being right about TK—a killer who lived and operated outside of his dumping ground—gave me little satisfaction as I hung trussed like an animal waiting to be gutted. A small aircraft made sense, but it meant the Totem Killer could live anywhere.

"Why all the questions now?" Ben asked. "How did he get *you*?"

How indeed.

"*I'd like to* know that, too," Justine said as she fought the ropes on her hands.

"Apparently my mental acuity is on par with the average bovine destined for plastic wrap."

"I don't understand." Ben looked confused and Justine only shook her head.

"You're not alone. I suppose that's my point." I winced at the brutal pounding of my head. For Justine's benefit, I added, "I let my guard down and passed out on the trail. I don't remember much."

"Do you think we're still on the island?" Justine asked. She didn't expect an answer from Ben. Her eyes fixed on me.

"Given our abductor is a pilot, we could be...anywhere. What else do you recall, Ben?"

"When I woke up, I...saw him." Ben stifled a sob.

"You saw him?" Justine asked. "What did...?"

She never got a chance to finish, before Ben had questions of his own.

"What did I do wrong? Why did he take *me*?"

His questions mirrored my own, but for different reasons. I'd crossed paths with the man I'd been hunting. Instinct had brought me to the island, but I hadn't been in control. The visions of my gift intensified and had taken over. I'd become a victim—of my secret abilities and of the killer I hunted—and had never seen it coming.

"You did nothing to deserve this, Ben."

I said it as much for me as I did for him, but I had earned my place under the knife. I was the enemy. No doubt the Totem Killer would take his time with me—and not for artistic reasons.

"Don't look for reason in the face of such madness," I said. "That's like...chasing smoke."

Victims and their families always tried to make rational sense of unfathomable violence. A reasonable explanation meant a world of order and human decency still existed. In truth none of that mattered in our predicament.

Not here. Not now.

I let Ben take his time and grapple his way back to answering my questions. Whatever he'd say, I suspected it would be hard on him. The autopsy of Nathan Applewhite revealed the Totem Killer was a ritualistic sexual sadist. I sensed the menace of the Great White shark of human predators had circled the bloodied waters around Ben.

Now death filled the room. The air was thick with it.

Ben had suffered indignities at the hands of a soulless killer and had given up. I couldn't blame him, but I refused to quit on Ben and Justine. *On me.* I gritted my teeth and yanked at the rope that bound my wrists and grimaced with every burn. All I had to do was loosen the binding enough to pull my hand out. If that didn't work fast enough, I had a backup plan for a Hail Mary pass on third and long.

Cake.

Until I broke free of the harness, I'd keep Ben focused. I had to know what he'd seen.

"I don't know about you, but I'd rather not be the next all-you-can-eat buffet for maggots. We're still breathing. Talk to me," I said. "Tell me everything you remember. And for all our sakes, don't leave anything out."

***

Prince of Wales Island
Outside Point Baker

Lucinda stood next to Trooper Whitmire and stared down at a bloodied animal trap. Its metal jaw had been snapped shut with meaty tissue left behind in the teeth of the exposed trap. The ground in the small clearing had been disturbed.

"It's a bear trap, but not in season or legal...ever," Whitmire said. "Poachers, I expect."

The trooper's stern face told her all she needed to know about what he thought of the hunters who would use such an inhumane method to hunt.

"Whatever happened here, the activity looks recent," she said as she squatted near the trap and swatted a swarm of mosquitoes from her face. "The tissue is dried and bugs have gotten to it, but the skin looks fairly fresh. Something got caught in the trap."

"The clearing has been trampled," Trooper Sawyer said. "Hard to tell how many boots were on the ground, but the blood trail leads to the cabin. Someone was definitely hurt."

Whitmire had told her the A-Star had a crime kit onboard. If they needed to field test for blood and tissue—to make sure the samples were human—they had what they needed, but there was one thing they didn't have—*time*. They were running out of daylight to help Ryker and Trooper Justine Peterson.

Lucinda heaved a sigh as she stared at the trap. In the dying light of the day, she noticed a flutter. Something was stuck to the steel and the breeze had caught it.

"Wait a minute," she said. "I see something."

Lucinda leaned in for a closer inspection. Something fibrous caught in the teeth of the trap grabbed her attention and she reached for a small strand of it. When she got a closer look, she let out the breath she'd been holding.

"Fabric...and it's bloody," she said. "If I had to guess, it looks like a thread of denim. I'd bet money the blood and tissue in this trap are human. If that's so, it would explain why we found blood on the trail and in the cabin."

"Yeah, that makes sense." Whitmire fixed his gaze on her when she stood. "What do you want to do?"

"We could do an analysis of the scene—to confirm the blood is human—but we'd lose the sun," she said. "If Ryker and your trooper are in trouble, we'd be wasting time. We need to search for them by air, while we still have good visibility. If we don't find them on the trail down the mountain, we'd have time to hit Point Baker before dark, right?"

"Yeah. Let's do it."

Lucinda didn't wait for Whitmire or Sawyer to lead the way back to the A-Star. She pushed her body to get there first as her mind filled with the horrors of the animal trap. Her gut instinct told her the blood and tissue on the metal teeth had been Ryker's.

She was no closer to finding him and more worried than ever he'd been the one hurt. That would explain why she hadn't heard from him. Even with his phone out of commission, Ryker wouldn't have gone this long without word—not unless something had been terribly wrong.

***

Prince of Wales Island
Klawock

After Hutch gave Sinead Royce the remote access she needed to the Klawock Public Library computer system, he talked her through the sign-on procedure from his cell phone. He made sure she could log into the recorded database in search of *Thrill-Seeker* before he would leave the library with Cam.

"You have what you need, Sinead?" he asked.

"I could use a winning lotto ticket and good news on Ryker—not in that order."

"Yeah, I hear ya. Call me when you have anything on *Thrill-Seeker*. We're looking for crumbs here, Royce, but I can make a meal out of anything. Feed it to me as you get it."

"I'm on it, Devin."

To back their play, Sinead had to work overtime without a clear end in sight. DC was four hours ahead. Even if Sinead had someone on late shift to take over her duties, Hutch knew she would've stayed on. They were a team. No one made a big deal about it. They pitched in and worked together. No whining.

Within fifteen minutes, Hutch and Cam were back at the Alaska State Troopers office. Trooper Dawson Biggers had set up two workstations for them and had offered to make a burger run. Although Hutch was always hungry, he couldn't think of food, not with Ryker missing. Cam felt the same and they both turned down dinner.

Sinead had already sent messages on the dates and times that *Thrill-Seeker* had been logged onto the library system, the occurrences that matched with the Facebook posts on the wall of Ben Stevens. Hutch had a timeframe to work with. It didn't take long before they were scrolling through endless streams of digital recordings of foot and vehicle traffic, to try and make sense of what they had and find a pattern. They needed a lead to chase—a license tag or a face—that could save Ben before he ended up in a freezer.

It took time to search the surveillance recordings for the library parking lot and link the patrons who clocked time on the computer. Hutch sat next to Cam and they talked through what they found. The recordings had time stamps to narrow down the day's activities to speed up their search when they cross-matched everything to the State Troopers' traffic cams to track vehicles in and out of the library.

"It's not top of the line surveillance gear. The quality of the digitals isn't stellar," she said.

"It's all we have." Hutch didn't take his eyes off the screen. "I found a truck that matches with two of Sinead's post times, but the recording is too grainy to get a license. Maybe Trooper Biggers will recognize something to ID the vehicle. It's a small town. Worth a shot."

"I'll get him."

After Cam left the room to get the young trooper, Hutch rubbed his face and took a short break from the strain of a long day and his staring contest with a computer. Not long ago, he and Cam had received a text message from Lucinda.

Haven't found Ryker yet. Headed to Point Baker. Will call soon.

Devin hoped Lucinda had more luck than he had. When his gaze shifted to a window, he noticed the sun would dip below the skyline and it would be dark soon. Any search for Ryker would come to an end for today if Point Baker turned out to be a bust, but he shoved that thought from his head. No sense borrowing trouble.

Positive karma, Hutch. Think bunnies and unicorns, asshole.

"Have a seat, Trooper." Cam rolled up a chair next to Hutch and Biggers sat down. He smelled of onions and French fries.

Hutch isolated the recordings he wanted to share with Cam and Biggers, scrolled through the digitals, and slowed things down to hit the key timestamps. After he made his case for the truck, he stopped on an image of the vehicle in question.

"You recognize anything on this truck to ID it? I know it's a long shot, but the tags are too grainy to blow the image up, not enough to pull registration."

The trooper stared at the screen for a long moment before he shook his head.

"Sorry. Don't recognize it, but I can search vehicle registration and pull a list of blue F-150 owners. Would that help?"

"Yeah, maybe."

Hutch slumped into his chair and gripped the armrests as he stared at Cam. It looked as if they'd have a long night ahead, until Trooper Biggers pointed to the computer monitor with a smirk on his face and mustard on his chin.

"You stumped me on the truck, but do I get points for recognizing who's driving *that* vehicle? I saw it a few times as you scrolled through."

Devin leaned closer to the screen. When he saw what the trooper meant, he wondered if the guy had been joking, but he looked deadly serious.

"Well, I'll be damned," Hutch said.

Ryker's words came to him in a rush when he said the UNSUB knew how to be invisible and blend in enough to make the victims trust him.

"Trooper Biggers. Keep talking." Hutch shrugged. "You have our attention."

***

Prince of Wales Island
Point Baker

The flight of the Alaska State Troopers' A-Star helicopter paralleled the river gorge. The pilot knew the mountain trails and spoke through Lucinda's headset and gave her reassurances he'd cover every possible route down to Point Baker.

So far, no Ryker. No Trooper Peterson.

Not one hiker or campsite had been spotted from the air and Lucinda's stomach churned. They'd lose the light soon. The darker it became, the more the dropping temp leached into her bones. Her fingers were ice cold from nerves. She rubbed her hands together to warm them.

"It'll be dark soon." Whitmire's disembodied voice came over her headset. "Point Baker is small. We'll have time to put boots on the ground and ask questions. I know where Trooper Peterson lives."

Lucinda nodded, but kept her eyes on the mountain trails.

"We can split up," Whitmire said. "You and I can hit Justine's place and have a look see. Sawyer can talk to the residents of Point Baker. You good with that?"

"Yeah. Let's do it."

Lucinda sounded more hopeful than she felt. After Whitmire gave instructions to the pilot on where Trooper Peterson lived, the fuselage of the A-Star dipped to make a landing. Lucinda fought her dark thoughts as the helo plummeted. She'd run low on places to look for Ryker. If he hadn't been at Applewhite's cabin and he wasn't still on the mountain, Point Baker would be her last hope of finding him today.

Tomorrow she'd have to start over and keep her mind open to all scenarios. She'd have to speak to residents in Point Baker to figure out what Ryker had done from the moment he'd arrived. Applewhite's cabin and the clearing where they'd found the blood would have to be properly investigated. Volunteers would be needed to search every mountain trail. She had to consider Ryker could be seriously injured—or dead. Her notion of rescue could turn into a body recovery. That would kill her, but she had to stay strong.

She had Ben Stevens to worry about, too.

She couldn't divert resources to search for Ryker at the expense of Stevens. She would need Whitmire to help with manpower and rescue coordination for both, but she could do with a viable lead on Stevens to justify the increased effort. All they really had on him was Hutch's theory on how the UNSUB hunted online and the last ping off the guy's cell phone in Klawock.

"Is that her place?" Lucinda pointed to a gate as the A-Star landed.

"Yeah," Whitmire said.

The helicopter had touched down in an open field across from a gravel road and an open gate. In the distance Lucinda saw a rustic cabin on a heavily treed lot that backed onto a cove. Through the evergreens she caught the sheen of water reflecting the fiery burn of sunset. Whitmire gave orders to his men and got out of the helo with her. The pilot would stay with the A-Star and Trooper Sawyer would head the short distance to Point Baker on foot and speak to the locals.

"Tell me about Trooper Peterson? Is she...single?" Lucinda asked as she walked through the gate. "I mean, does she live alone?"

"She's single. Don't know about her living

arrangements," he said. "From what I hear she's a good trooper. Beyond that, I don't know much about her."

"Do you know how long she's been in Alaska?"

"Born and raised, I hear." Whitmire pointed to the cabin. "Not many women could live like this. Isolation is pretty damned hard on folks, especially the long winter months. Troopers cover a lot of territory on their own. That's how it works here. Takes a certain breed to do what we do."

"Good to know she's familiar with the island...and the outdoors."

As far as Lucinda knew, Ryker didn't have much experience with camping and roughing it. At least he'd never mentioned it to her. His idea of back to nature was an exhausting run on the trails near his apartment. From what Whitmire said about Justine Peterson, Ryker would've been in good hands—a woman with experience. Lucinda clenched her jaw and glared at the cabin, thinking about him being in someone else's good hands.

When they approached the front porch, Lucinda heard a raspy caw. She squinted into the sky, unsure where the sound came from, until the bird's cry grew louder. A large inky black raven settled onto the pitch of the rooftop with a clatter of its talons. It flapped its massive wings and screeched another warning.

The bird looked menacing and reminded her of the crime scene in the Cascades when Ryker first talked about the Trickster mythology.

"Well, hello there, Poe."

Whitmire did a double take when he heard her talk to the raven.

"I channel Doctor Dolittle." She shot him a sideways glance. "You should try it."

"Ravens give me the creeps," he said. "It's like the dead see through their eyes."

"You should give Animal Planet a heads up." Lucinda ignored the trooper's raised eyebrow and shifted her attention to the droopy flowers of a hanging basket on the porch. "Plant needs water."

"Hazards of the job."

Lucinda understood the trooper's sacrifice of a personal life for her work. She only hoped Peterson's neglect didn't extend to her dogs. The sound of barking grew louder and came from behind the cabin.

"Who takes care of the dogs with her gone?" she asked.

Whitmire shook his head and said, "Don't know. Maybe her neighbor. If she has dogs, they're looked after."

The trooper walked to the door and knocked. No answer and no sound came from inside. Lucinda wandered to a window and peered through the drapes. No lights were on. A big yellow tabby had curled up on a sofa and barely raised its head at the intrusion. The cat yawned and stretched its front paws. Something about the place felt empty, like no one was home. Whitmire must've felt it, too.

He knocked again and called out, "Trooper Peterson? It's Lieutenant Whitmire."

No answer. He tried the doorknob, but the front door was locked. The trooper looked surprised.

"Not many folks lock their doors here," he said. "It's called trust."

"Where I live, it's called opportunity."

When she heard the dogs bark, she wandered toward the side of the porch and peered into the back of the property.

"Dogs sound hungry," she said. "If she has someone taking care of them, wouldn't they have been fed by now?"

"Good question. I'll check on 'em."

Lucinda watched Whitmire step off the porch

and head to the kennels. Through the trees she saw a dim light from the neighbor's house. The island's remote and peaceful setting should've been idyllic, but she had a hard time shaking off what she'd seen. The beauty of the island hid a terrible secret. Lucinda had no doubt Ryker had been caught up in it.

What made you come here, Ryker?

He'd come to the Prince of Wales Island because Nathan Applewhite's life triggered something in him, but whatever he kept a mystery, it had forced him to come alone. It hurt he didn't trust her. His quiet brooding and intelligent nature had drawn her to a complicated man who would always be an intriguing riddle. The Totem Killer had targeted Ryker and taunted him in a message. That couldn't have been a coincidence.

Had the note been an invitation only Ryker understood?

He'd become an even bigger mystery since that day in the Cascades. Whatever she knew of him was only what he'd allowed her to see. She knew that now. A palpable darkness stirred beneath the still waters of his life. He'd sacrificed a great deal—and lived alone with purpose—to keep his secret.

Now he might die because of it.

Chapter Nineteen

Ryker Townsend

As I listened to Ben tell his story, my gaze shifted through the room where we were held prisoner. With my vision only marginally better, my eyes still played cruel hoaxes on me that made me paranoid. The shadowy room flickered in a crimson glow. Blood red reflected off the plastic lining the cement floor and hanging from the wooden frames of unfinished walls. It billowed and crinkled as if it breathed and bore the weight of a sinister presence.

My eyes peered from shadow to shadow until they finally settled on Justine.

At first I thought the menacing sensation prickling under my skin had been triggered by the shock of seeing her again, but it was more than that. It *had* to be. Every sound, every heaving glimmer set me on edge and wouldn't let up. Water dripped in a sink and had become my new torture. No matter how much I tried to ignore it, the incessant noise grew louder and plucked at my raw nerves to punish my aching head.

Between the darkness and my blurred eyesight, I wasn't sure if my paranoia came from the drugs or a fear I'd never faced before. I had to fight the feeling of being a victim—and a mounting dread I had yet to name. My skin crawled with something I should know or remember, but didn't.

None of my misery would come close to what Ben had endured. It took guts for him to talk about it.

"When I woke up, I was on my knees," he said. "My hands were tied over my head. I couldn't move."

I strained to hear Ben through the noise I made. I knew Justine sensed my urgency to break free.

Every second we were alone and able to talk was a precious gift, but Ben's voice had weakened to a haunted whisper and my struggle with the ropes behind my back had turned frantic. I couldn't catch my breath.

"I smelled something...dead," Ben said. "Made me sick. I almost puked, but that's when he came."

He choked and the sudden jerk of his body forced him to cry out. Every word was pure torture for him now. I hated that I'd forced him to relive what had happened, but I had to do it. Instinct forced me to.

"Should you put him through this?" Justine whispered only loud enough for me to hear. "It's not like you're in a position to help. Why make him relive it?"

Her words cut me like a razor. She'd told the unvarnished truth, but that didn't make it any easier to hear. I'd confided my worst fear to her at Nate's cabin—of being powerless and watching someone innocent die—and she reminded me it could happen again. I focused on Ben and took a deep breath. I had to ignore her and hold back my own doubts.

I had to know what Ben knew.

"Close your eyes and tell me everything," I told him. "Nothing is too small."

When the rope loosened from around my hands, I jerked harder. Justine had fueled my adrenaline rush. My raw skin seared as if doused in acid and warm blood drained down my fingers.

"It was dark, but there was this...red light."

"Like the one here?" I asked.

"Yeah, but I saw it through wood slats. It blinded me."

"Wood slats?"

"I was in...a cage. It was cramped, like an animal pen. When I called out, I heard someone coming. I thought...they'd help me, but that's not what happened."

A deep agonizing groan echoed across the room. I wanted to tell Ben to be quiet. Any noise might bring TK down the stairs, but I'd started him on this downward spiral. How could I ask him to hold in his pain?

"Ben, we don't have much time. Tell me what you saw. *Please.*"

"He yanked open the door and came at me. He crawled into the cage on his knees. He had a knife. I thought he'd kill me, but..."

"But what?"

"He cut off my clothes. Then he...touched me. I begged him to stop, but he didn't."

Oh, God. I knew what would come next. I wasn't ready to hear it, no more than he was ready to say it.

"Did you see his f-face?" Justine asked.

When Ben stopped talking, he cried. I wasn't sure he'd answer. I gritted my teeth and fought the bile rising hot in my belly. I wouldn't watch Ben die. *I couldn't.* Even if it meant my sacrifice, I wouldn't watch this boy die.

I thought of my mother and father. The vision of their senseless deaths raged in my head. My demons were always with me.

"Not...r-really," Ben choked. "The light blinded me. All I saw was..." He took a deep breath loud enough for me to hear. "The guy wore a dirty ball cap and torn work coveralls. I think they were *Carhartts.* That's all I saw before he tied a hood over my head."

"A hood?" I asked. "How long did he keep you in that?"

"This is the first time he's taken it off."

"But you never saw him...even without the hood?" Justine said.

"No."

From the way Ben answered our questions, I knew he hadn't made the connection to the significance of why he didn't wear the hood now. The next time he'd see the Totem Killer would be his last. TK would want to witness the life leave Ben's eyes. He had to feel him die with every sense of his being when he drove the knife into his heart until it stopped beating.

Ben had run out of time. We all had.

I thought I could free my hands by working the ropes to loosen them, but that would take too much time. I had one hope now and braced for the agony of a wound I had experienced once before in football, only this time it would be self-inflicted.

"Ahh. Shit." I gasped and tears flooded my eyes as I bit my lower lip to stifle the pain of what I'd done.

"What happened?" Justine fixed her gaze on me and stopped tugging at her restraints.

"Are you okay?" Ben said.

With all that had happened to him, Ben was worried about me. Anyone catching my reaction would've assumed I'd been touched by his selfless concern, but the tears trickling down my face came from the throbbing pain of my dislocated thumb. It took my breath and I winced as I tugged my fingers through the abrasive ropes until my hands were free. My arms hung at my sides like dead weight. The harness that had me suspended from the ceiling had left my whole body numb. I couldn't feel my injured ankle and wasn't sure if I could walk, but I had to try.

Justine stopped struggling and stared at me. When I winced in agony, she shook her head. I couldn't tell if she was pleased I'd made progress or entertained.

"What happened...after that?" I asked.

I kept Ben talking as I grappled with the harness.

The dripping water in the sink mirrored the quickening punch of my heart and the pulsing red light messed with my balance. When I got one shoulder free, I resisted the urge to let him know what I'd done and by Justine's silence, I figured she understood why. If I got his hopes up now and couldn't deliver, it would crush him.

"He injected me with something. I felt a needle in my neck and I woke up here," Ben said. "When he plays this weird music, he comes down and...does stuff to me. *Please*. I don't wanna talk about it anymore."

"Take a deep breath, Ben."

The guy never heard me.

"You can see what he's done to me, man. I'm not walking away from this. I'm dead," he cried.

"Please stop. He'll hear you."

Ben was trapped in the horror of what had already happened to him, his ordeal made worse by what he feared would come. The guy had lost it.

"Oh, God, my mom. She can't see me like this. She'll know what he did to me. I don't want anyone to find my body. Please!"

Ben had already accepted the worst. His only thoughts were for his mother. I shut my eyes and fought the lump in my throat, but I wouldn't let him give up. Not while I still breathed and could do something about it.

"This won't be graceful," I said to Justine. "Don't judge me."

From the confused look on Justine's face, I knew she didn't understand until I shoved through the harness and collapsed to the cement floor. My legs were numb and wouldn't hold my weight.

"What?" Justine whispered. "How did you...?"

I had to crawl to a wooden post and grab something to help me stand. Ben hadn't seen me fall.

He yanked at his restraints, even though it hurt him. His eyes were wide in panic and his breathing came in shallow gasps.

He'd lost all control and I couldn't blame him. He'd been through too much.

"Get me out of this, Ryker," Justine demanded.

I gave up any hope of calming Ben. After I popped my thumb back into the joint, I stumbled toward Justine to help her first. Ben would be next. I found a knife to hack at the rope that bound Justine's hands. Once her wrists were loose, I noticed Ben quit thrashing. When he finally saw we were both free, he fixed his eyes on me and I could see he dared to have faith as I made the first cut into his ropes.

But his fragile hope didn't last long.

A song played over the speakers. I winced with the sudden noise. I recognized the music. The voice of Ray Charles sang "What a Wonderful World" and chilled me.

"Oh, God. That's it. The song. He's coming." Ben turned toward me, shaking. "Now that he has you, he doesn't need me. I'm dead."

I stared at Ben and no words came. I couldn't argue. We'd all run out of time.

***

Prince of Wales Island
Point Baker

The dogs got louder as Lucinda and Whitmire approached the kennels behind Peterson's cabin. The cages were a distance from the residence and connected by a raised wooden walkway that led past a series of kennels framed in two by fours, wire and corrugated metal roofs.

"I can't tell whose property this is—hers or the neighbor. The pens are on the fence line."

"With the walkway leading from her place to the cages, it looks like they share it."

Lucinda drew near the pens and the dogs yelped.

"Shh. Easy now," she said.

Muzzles pushed against wire mesh. The animals calmed down when she talked to them. Each dog had its own cage, but an odd tang made it hard for her to breathe and the buzz of flies and mosquitoes droned to a fevered pitch. The vile stench of death, mixed with the potent odor of animal excrement, filled her nostrils.

Something wasn't right. She pulled her weapon.

The sun had dropped beneath the skyline and the night's chill closed in. A pale red light bulb, connected to a timer, hung over a crude crosswalk between two banks of cages, but there wasn't enough light for her to see much.

Whitmire grabbed a Kel-Lite from his duty belt and flicked it on. Lucinda peered through the dark of the kennels as the trooper's flashlight beam washed over the worn pens and made the filth more ominous. The strays had water and food—enough to survive— but the odor and muddy pens hadn't been the neglect of only a few days.

Lucinda took lead and stepped off the walkway and down into the kennels. She had to stoop to get a closer look into the cramped cages. Loose boards creaked under her weight as she crept through pens and winced from the stench. Ammonia build up from urine made her eyes water.

Every cage was occupied—*except for one.*

Inside the empty stall, Lucinda squinted through the wood slats and saw a rope dangling from a hook screwed into a cross beam. The way the rope had been knotted, she couldn't see how it would've been used on dogs, but something chilling caught her eye.

"What the hell?"

After she made a move to open the cage, Whitmire handed over his flashlight.

"You're gonna need this. Keep it. I have another one."

She used the trooper's Kel-Lite to sweep light through the empty cage before she crawled inside. A thick layer of dirty hay had been strewn on the pen floor and a pile of shredded clothes were tossed in a corner. The stall reeked of piss and something else she recognized—the stench of blood and death after a brutal crime scene.

Lucinda holstered her Glock and unlatched the door to the cage. She crouched low and covered her nose and mouth with an arm as she stooped to a squat and moved inside. Eerie shadows cast a grim pallor on the cage and the walls closed in. When she got a closer look at the rope, she didn't like what she saw.

"The rope has stains," she said. "The pattern is on the inside of the hemp. It could be blood."

Lucinda knew they'd have to test if the blood was human, but when she swung the beam of light toward the pile of clothes, her gut instinct told her all she needed to know.

"There are stains on these clothes. We can't be certain it's human blood until we test it, but I'd bet money it is. The rope. This cage. Something bad happened here." She lifted fabric off the pile. "I see a label off a T-shirt. Men's clothes, I'd say, and they're shredded."

"Someone could've been bitten by a dog. The clothes could be rags they used to staunch the bleeding."

"You really think that?" she asked.

Whitmire didn't answer. He heaved a sigh and cursed under his breath.

"What's it mean?" he asked. "What happened to

my trooper and your agent?"

Lucinda retraced her steps in searching for Ryker. She had puzzle pieces with no answers. Trooper Peterson's cabin looked well kept, but the kennels were borderline cruel for the dogs and she had no idea what'd happened in the cage where she crouched.

"Let's pay a call on her neighbor. You game?" she asked.

"Yeah. I feel real sociable."

Lucinda emerged from the hellish pit of the kennels to take her first full breath. She wanted the fresh air to clear her mind, but it didn't. She was even more worried for Ryker as she gazed into the night sky filled with far too many stars to count. The moon cast its bluish tinge over the evergreens and the still water in the cove. The serene beauty should have settled her. With the dogs quiet, she could even hear the whisper of lapping waves along the shore, but she couldn't get Ryker's face—his eyes—out of her head.

"You okay?" Whitmire asked.

She took another deep breath before she answered.

"Yeah." She nodded. "Let's go."

*****

If Trooper Peterson's cabin had been welcoming and cozy, the hovel of her neighbor looked the polar opposite to Lucinda as she crept toward a dilapidated shack. Windows were boarded and nailed shut. Worn wood planks were stained and rotting and the porch overhang looked as if a strong wind would take it down.

One security light cast long shadows over the property and the front porch had sprouted weeds that ignored the blight of human intrusion on the land.

Beyond that, the ramshackle dwelling didn't look as if anyone lived there. Lucinda wanted to think the place had seen better days, but she doubted it.

After she skulked by an old rusted truck that had found its final resting place on blocks, she stepped over the decaying carcass of a large fish gathering maggots. The air reeked.

"Nice welcome mat," she whispered to Whitmire. "Shades of Ted Kaczynski."

The rat hole had a series of connecting outbuildings like a makeshift compound linked together—a survivalist's wet dream.

"What do you know about this guy?" she asked.

"Not much. His name's Josh Getty. No record. Justine tolerates the guy, from what I hear."

Whitmire shot her a stern glance that had a clear message—*follow my lead*. He shoved his back to a wall to the left of the front door and raised his weapon. Lucinda took the other side and did the same. The trooper pounded on the door and yelled.

"Alaska State Troopers. Open the door." When no one came, Whitmire shouted again. "State Troopers. Open up!"

Lucinda knew they had no probable cause unless they found one. She nudged her head to Whitmire and took off toward the side of the compound to look for a reason to gain entry. The trooper followed as Lucinda headed for the only light on the property, the one she had seen from the kennel. The windows were boarded up like the front, but a door had been left open a crack.

"Here. Got something," she whispered.

She stood to the side of the threshold—careful not to become a target—and grabbed the knob with her left hand. The door didn't give. It had a loose metal latch on the inside. She shot a glance at Whitmire and made her move.

Lucinda kicked in the door with her boot.

"We got an open door," she said. "Better have a look."

"Good idea. Why didn't I think of that?"

Whitmire took lead. He aimed his weapon and his second Kel-Lite to give him a clear line of fire. Lucinda did the same. A smothering stench hit Lucinda as she crossed into the darkness of the shack. She winced at the thick odor. As she became accustomed to the dark, her eyes trailed up a heaping pile of trash that smelled like rotting food. *Oh, God.* She wanted to vomit.

Whitmire maneuvered through a maze of hoarder trash. His flashlight shined onto open cans, broken glass, and piles of old clothes.

A faint patter and a shrill squeak made her stop and freeze where she stood. A cat yowled and caught its prey. The sudden shriek made the hair on Lucinda's neck stand on end and made her skin crawl. She gripped her weapon and swallowed, hard. Not being wrong—for calling the dump a rat hole, literally—didn't make her feel any better.

She caught up to Whitmire and stuck close.

Outside the night air had carried a chill, but inside the suffocating smell and stagnant air had sweat pouring off Lucinda. She stayed close to Whitmire and kept her eyes alert for anything on two legs. Adrenaline pumped through her blood. The shit hole gave her the creeps.

After they reached what looked like the end of their search, Whitmire raced ahead. The beam of his Kel-Lite bounced across walls of trash as he moved. When he came to a larger room, the glow of his flashlight steadied.

"Found something," the trooper said. "Good Lord."

Lucinda stepped into the room and the smell of

blood hit her like a punch. She winced and held her breath.

"I take it, this isn't normal?" she asked. Whitmire only shook his head with his face grim.

A double utility sink occupied one wall next to a long butcher block table with an automated saw at the end. Knives were strewn across the workstation and in the sink. Blood spatter marred the walls and surfaces. She didn't know how hunters in Alaska harvested their kills, but nothing about the sinister room looked normal. The cement floor had a large metal grate in the center and had a slant to make it easy to clean and drain blood waste. The stifling air reeked of spoiled meat.

"This is...overkill, too." Whitmire stood over three commercial freezers that filled the other half of the room and ran his hand over each one. "They're all operating. Lotta freezer capacity for one guy."

Lucinda knew what the trooper had on his mind. The chillers had plenty of space to hide and freeze severed human remains. She stared at Whitmire and clenched her jaw. She knew what they had to do, but after her thoughts turned to Ryker, nausea gripped her.

She fought hard not to picture Ryker frozen in one of the chillers, but that was impossible. Her throat wedged tight and her eyes burned with the sting of tears.

"Do it." Lucinda gripped her weapon and nodded. "Open it."

When Whitmire pointed his flashlight into the first freezer, the shadows in the room shifted and closed around her. The trooper flipped the lid and they both stared into the compartment. The freezer was empty. She prayed they wouldn't find Ryker in the next ones. Whitmire opened the lids on the next two chillers.

"Dark ice in all of 'em," he said. "Probably frozen blood. Other than that, they're empty. No human body parts. Thank God."

After she shifted the flashlight toward the back of the room, she caught the glint of a metal knob and Whitmire shot her a sideways glance.

"Well, the hits keep coming," she said. "Looks like a door back here."

Lucinda raised her weapon and reached for the doorknob with Whitmire at her back. She made eye contact with the trooper. After he nodded, she flung the door open and stared down shadowy steps that trailed into a tunnel. The narrow walls were shored with wood until they connected with a large cement drainage pipe. Beyond the beam of the Kel-Lite, she saw only shadows and flickering light.

"What the hell?"

"The way this place stinks, it could cover up a meth lab," Whitmire said. "The guy could be cookin' product."

"I think by the time we're done, we're gonna wish that's all this guy's been doing," she said.

"I'm calling for back up. No telling what cell reception will be underground."

Lucinda didn't like waiting. Patience wasn't a quality she cultivated. Ryker knew that first hand, but she understood Whitmire's logic in calling for support.

With her gut twisting into a tight knot, she waited.

***

Prince of Wales Island
Klawock

"Did you reach her?" The worried look on Cam's face forced Hutch to bend the rules of decorum on the job. He reached out and held her hand, ignoring the smirk on the face of Trooper Biggers.

"No. She doesn't answer. I rolled into voice mail, but I've already left a message," he said.

Hutch grabbed their jackets and pulled Cam out of the room and headed down the hall toward the front door of the State Trooper's building. When they had their privacy outside, Hutch stroked a hand down Cam's arm.

"I left her a text, but she hasn't responded to that either."

"She's gotta know. I think we're on to something." Cam slipped into her jacket and crossed her arms against the chilly night air.

"If we're right, Ryker's in real trouble. We could already be too late." Hutch stared into the stars and filled his lungs with cold air. "Look, we have our pilot and Sinead gave me the last ping off Lucinda's phone. She's in Point Baker. That's where we go."

"Agreed. Let's do this."

Hutch kissed Cam on the cheek and they went looking for their pilot. He had a feeling there was a reason Lucinda hadn't answered his messages. He prayed he was wrong.

***

Ryker Townsend

A distant and steady thud grew louder over my head. When the menacing noise echoed through the room, billows of dust rained down and clogged the air. The disturbance had come from a level above us. Adrenaline punched me hard. I couldn't control it.

"Someone's coming," I said.

"That song. What a sick bastard." Justine grimaced and stared at the only way into the room—a door at the top of the stairs.

"Yeah. He ruined Ray Charles for me. I should arrest him for that alone."

Ben had been right about the song. A cruel killer like our UNSUB would get off on triggering the victim's fear and set the stage with drama. I'd seen enough of the Totem Killer in my visions to know. I stopped cutting the ropes off Ben. I had seconds to choose. Everything came down to what I would do.

"No! Why'd you stop? Cut me loose." Ben tugged at his ropes. "Don't leave me."

"I won't. *Trust me.*"

My eyes darted through the shadows made by the red flickering light. I had a knife. It would have to do, even though it meant getting too close. I could barely walk and still suffered from whatever drug coursed through my veins. I needed the element of surprise and a vantage point to strike first.

I made my move and Ben panicked.

"Where are you going? Get me out of here."

Ben had embraced his last hope for freedom. I'd seen it in his eyes. Now he counted on me to deliver, until he got a closer look at his savior. I was no John Wayne. When I heard the creak of a floorboard, my heart pummeled my chest. I didn't have time to explain anything to Ben.

"Just...trust me."

I touched his shoulder, but couldn't look him in the eye before I staggered for the stairs.

"What are you doing?" Justine glared at me. "You're in no shape to..."

"That's why you're gonna help me. Find cover and follow my lead," I said. "When he's down, you join the party."

The music grated on my nerves. It wouldn't stop. I barely had time to crawl under the staircase before the door rasped open. The Totem Killer would soon descend the steps enough to see I'd escaped the harness. A pale glow cut through the red pulsing light and spread across the plastic covered floor to settle on Ben like a harsh spotlight. The poor guy couldn't take his eyes off the man who'd come to kill him.

Without the hood he'd see everything.

"Please...I don't w-want to die." Ben shook his head and tears spilled down his cheeks.

I couldn't watch. I had to be the hunter, not the victim.

I couldn't see Justine. I'd wedged my body under the stairs and gripped the knife. My ankle throbbed, but I shifted my focus onto the blade in my good hand. With my pulse punishing the inside of my ears, I struggled to slow my breath.

At the sound of a scuff on the wood landing over my head, I braced my back against the brick wall behind me and tensed. I'd have only one shot to take the killer by surprise. A shadow eclipsed the light and the top step creaked with weight. I gripped the hilt of the blade in my sweaty palm and sucked in a breath.

A hiking boot took the step in front of my eyes. In one motion I grabbed it and held on. When I stabbed his meaty calf muscle, the man cried out and sprawled to the floor on his belly. His head hit the floor hard. The crack of bone on cement sent a chill through me. I raced from cover—ignoring the jolt of pain shooting through my bad leg—and ran to the body.

Blood seeped onto the plastic from where I'd stabbed him, but his head wound bled more. The man groaned and tried to get up. *Damn it!* There wasn't time. I collapsed onto him and braced an elbow around his neck, squeezing his throat with every ounce of strength I had. His body tensed and writhed until I thought I'd lose my grip, but I held tight until his breaths turned into wet gurgles.

"Finish him. *Do it.*" Ben begged me to take the

man's life. "*Kill him!*"

Ray Charles sang of a wonderful world while I fought to squeeze the life out of a stranger. I couldn't see Ben and he didn't have eyes on me, but his panicked cries fueled my murderous instinct. From years of nightmares where I switched places with merciless killers in my visions, I'd experienced the euphoria of blood lust. I had enough adrenaline raging through me to finish him. I squeezed harder and his body grew slack.

It would've been easy to kill him. I had seconds to decide if I'd cross a line I never believed possible—all in the name of self-defense—but from nowhere, the words of my mother came to me. I heard her sweet voice. She filled my head and my heart.

There's no light without the dark.

This time her words carried a different meaning. It wasn't a matter of accepting the darkness of my visions in order to embrace my gift. I had to fight my way out of the shadows and struggle for my way back. I had to *choose* the light. I had to want it. In that moment I realized—a splintered fragment of me had always been broken. It was how I understood the killers I hunted and why I didn't judge them.

Except for the grace of God, could I have been one of them?

I released my grip and let the man live. That mercy should've been a relief. For any normal person—especially someone who'd chosen a life in law enforcement—it should've been, but not for me. I shut my eyes to fend off a surprising assault on my mind. *Oh, God. Stop...please stop.* After I'd let him go, the release sent me into a tailspin of dark visions. I relived my most vivid nightmares in a rush—fantasies of killing that...*pleased me.*

No, this can't be happening. Surely these thoughts weren't mine. They couldn't be. I shut the fantasies down and walled them off in my head—the way I did with every nightmare—and stared down at the man beneath me.

I panted for air and gazed up at Ben. I thought it was over until...

"Look out. He's got a gun," Justine yelled.

She shoved me with her shoulder and knocked me off the man. I hit my head hard enough to see stars. She grappled with the big man in a blur. Everything happened too fast.

"Get back, Ryker," she grunted. "He's got the..."

A loud blast hurt my ears. *One shot. Two.* Justine slumped over the man and didn't move.

"Justine!"

I felt my lips move, but my voice sounded muffled through the ringing in my ears. I reached a hand for Justine. My fingers entwined in strands of her blonde hair, but she didn't move. Blood seeped from beneath her and spread.

"Justine?"

***

What the hell? Lucinda Crowley strained her ears at the entrance to the unexpected tunnel leading under Josh Getty's dilapidated shack. A loud crack bellowed into an almost undecipherable echo. The sound erupted and swelled from the underground passageway, but to her trained ear, Lucinda was certain she hadn't mistaken it.

"I heard a gunshot." She yelled over her shoulder, but Whitmire didn't respond. He was still on the phone, calling for back up. She couldn't wait. Not anymore.

Ryker's face came to her from the shadows. She had to move. *Now.*

"Whitmire, I heard gunfire. I'm going in."

Lucinda didn't wait for his answer. She crept down the wooden stairs into the belly of the tunnel with her Glock pointed into the dark. Her world narrowed to the thin beam of a flashlight.

Chapter Twenty

"What happened?" Ben cried out.

I didn't know what to tell him. I stared at Justine. Her body was sprawled on top of the man who would've killed Ben, but when her fingers twitched and she moaned, I reached for her.

"Justine? Are you...?"

Slow and deliberate, she pushed off the man under her. Blood spatter covered her face and hands and saturated her clothes.

"Are you shot?"

Stunned, she grabbed for her ribs and rubbed her hands over her body.

"No. I don't think so."

Justine moved enough for me to see the guy had been fatally shot. He stared through dead eyes with a slack face and a mouth brimming with blood. He had two bullet holes in his chest. Even though his blond hair and beard were matted in blood, the big man looked familiar. He wasn't wearing old coveralls and a cap, like Ben had described, but I'd seen him before—at Justine's.

I stared down at Josh, her odd neighbor, the one who had always taken an interest in the men she brought home—a man she trusted.

"What the hell?" I whispered. "He's...your neighbor."

Justine shook her head and said, "I don't get it. What about Matson?"

I had the same question. What *about* Matson? He'd clearly ransacked Applewhite's cabin. I'd seen the aftermath and heard it with my own ears. The poacher had run from Justine and stalked us. I'd fallen victim to one of his illegal bear traps and he had a known grudge against Nate—a fixation on him—and a history of breaking the law.

"Could Josh have been working with Matson?" I asked.

"That's the only explanation." Justine shook her head. "But isn't it unusual for two serial killers to work together?"

I reached for the Glock, wiped the blood off as best I could, and shoved the weapon into the waistband of my pants.

"It's not an original notion, but it could explain why our profile had been off."

If there were two killers with different patterns— or one killer with help who could seem to be in two places at once—that would change everything. Two killers sharing the blood lust, one could've tracked us into the mountains while the other held Ben and carried on with his torture.

Ben had been flown from Seattle to Alaska, part of his abduction and the first half of a round trip. After the Totem Killer finished with Ben, he'd be flown home in pieces like choice cuts of grocery store chicken. Seattle was the Totem Killer's dumping ground, but given the slivers of my memory about a four-wheeler, the odds were good we were still on the Prince of Wales Island. Two killers, working in tandem, weren't common, but there was precedent.

"If there are two of them, it means something else, too."

"What's that?" she asked.

"It means the second one is still out there," I said. "We gotta get out of here. Now."

I hobbled up the stairs and peered out the door— our only means of escape. I had to see where we were.

Outside the open doorway stretched a hazy tunnel that looked more like an underground sewer. It smelled of stale air and damp earth. Dim light bulbs flickered as if there was a storm approaching and the surreal lyrics of "What a Wonderful World" blasted over crudely wired speakers, hung with connections exposed. The music made a mockery of our deadly predicament and grated on my nerves.

"Well, I'll be damned," I muttered under my breath.

"What?" Justine asked.

"I thought we were in a...basement. I was wrong."

Our prison had been a simple design like a survivalist's storage bunker, hastily set off of drainage tunnels. I stared down the murky passageways that snaked beyond where I could see. There was no clear decision on which way to make our escape. Ben could barely walk and with my injured ankle, I couldn't carry him, but something else weighed heavily on my mind. It came at me in a rush, like the simmering start to a blistering migraine.

"I'm cutting Ben loose." Justine went for the knife and approached Ben who was still tied and helpless on the Totem Killer's table. I only caught the shadowy blur of her moving in the room when I was seized by something I'd never felt before.

Oh, God. What the hell?

An ache in my head almost doubled me over as a sudden flash of a hallucination assaulted my mind like a razor slicing into tender flesh. It happened so fast, it should've shocked me, but the vision had been a familiar one.

What are you doing, genius? Don't. Not now.

I'd lost it. As I stared into the shadows of the tunnel, I sensed an odd presence. The once blaring music faded and had been replaced by an ominous low rumble in my head. I'd heard it before in my dreams. Out of nowhere a distinctive scent came to me—the heady brine of seawater. My belly tossed as if I'd been caught in a strong ocean rip current that would drag me to the depths of oblivion.

The whale returned to haunt me once more. The beast's distant quake swept through me and brought the feeling of being watched. In a rush I'd been thrust back to the Cascades again.

"No...can't be h-happening." My lungs burned and a crushing weight squeezed my chest.

"What's wrong with you?" Justine called out to me.

I couldn't answer her. Vivid flashes assaulted my brain with greater intensity. Memories of visions I had since I'd arrived on the island ticked through my mind one by one. As they slowed, I found it harder to breathe. *Open your eyes. Stop this.* I had to fight the urge to break off my connection and strained for every glimpse.

The waking nightmare *had* to be important.

Images spiraled like the seductive dance of black ink in water and took shape. When one final image settled into my mind, chills crawled over my skin like a legion of roaches. Another truth welled up in my fertile imagination, taking root from seeds planted by the many nightmares I'd had since coming to the island.

No. It can't be.

I pulled the Glock and winced as my vision cleared. I crept down the stairs, hurting with every step.

"Don't go near him." I aimed my weapon at Justine. "Drop the knife. Keep your hands where I can see them."

It was too late. By the time my eyesight cleared, Justine had grabbed Ben and yanked him to her chest. The kid shook, with eyes wide, and tears streaked his face. She had a handful of his hair and the blade at his throat.

If I didn't do something, he'd be dead.

***

The dark passageway under Josh Getty's shack led to a split. With her back to a wall, Lucinda cut off the Kel-Lite—not wanting to become a target—and peered down each branch. Crudely wired light bulbs were strewn high and sputtered on and off as if there were a storm outside. The power could flick out any second.

Only one thing distinguished the split in the tunnel.

A melody blared in a disturbing and surreal echo—a strange Ray Charles song—and she could've sworn she heard voices, but couldn't tell where they came from. Lucinda flipped the Kel-Lite on again and held it high as she aimed her Glock down the tunnels.

The music played over and over in a torturous loop. She couldn't imagine the horror of the killer's victims. Their bodies would be carved into for days as they were forced to listen to the same song.

She had to block that from her mind. She had a job to do.

Her heart pounded and sweat trickled from her temples as Lucinda felt the pressure of deciding which way to go. She strained to listen beyond the loud music for anything to help make up her mind until she finally heard the murmur of voices. At first she thought she'd imagined them. The sound rose and fell, masked by the music.

She couldn't wait any longer. Despite not knowing where the voices came from, Lucinda aimed her weapon and made her choice.

Please, Ryker. Please be okay.

***

Ryker Townsend

"It wasn't Matson. It never was. You're the Totem Killer."

I clenched my jaw and waited for Justine Peterson to deny what I already knew. She didn't bother and her amusement showed.

"I fed you what you wanted to hear. I didn't need you to tell me anything about your case because I knew exactly what would pique your interest. I teased you with choice morsels and you ate them up."

I saw the cold-blooded stare of the killer I'd been hunting—the clever one who knew how to hide in plain sight by wearing the uniform of an Alaska State Trooper. The corner of her lips crooked into a merciless smile.

I knew she wouldn't think twice about slitting Ben's throat, just to see my pain at watching it happen. I had to keep her talking until I had a clear shot.

"Statistically speaking, you are a rarity, especially with you taking on a partner." I fixed my eyes on hers and forced a blank expression. "You're the artist, aren't you?"

Justine only smiled.

Even as late as 1998, famed FBI profiler Roy Hazelwood was quoted at a conference as saying there were no female serial killers. He'd been wrong. Such uncommon women operated under the radar and were less likely to have criminal history. They killed those closest to them and usually did it through more passive means, such as poisoning or smothering.

The overkill with a knife and the torture had been different. Justine Peterson had set an unusual standard in deviance.

"Drop the knife." I shifted the barrel and aimed

at her face. "Step away from him or I'll shoot."

"I thought she...was a c-cop?" Ben's lips trembled. His whole body shook.

"She's the reason you're here, Ben." Without taking my eyes off her, I said, "What else are you responsible for, Justine? Were you the one who..."

"Had sex with him?" She smiled and kissed Ben's cheek, not taking her eyes off me.

"Raped him. Why lie now? You're not a coward. The least you can do is be honest and tell the truth."

Justine licked her lips and smirked.

"You're right. I dressed like a guy to take what he wouldn't normally give to a man," she said. "I took what I wanted, but Ben got hard. He *wanted* it."

Although the woman had finally let down the mask she'd been wearing, she truly believed what every rapist did—that the victim wanted to be violated.

"No. *No!*" Ben jerked in her grip—unraveling—and I couldn't help him.

I had to keep the focus on me and off Ben. When I inched nearer, she countered and gripped him tighter. I clutched the Glock tight in my hands and edged for a better shot, but I had to keep her talking.

"Did the poaching incident ever happen between Matson and Nate?"

"They had friction, but I may have played a hand in making things worse. I wanted to see what would happen." She grinned. "Nate and I got real cozy because of it."

"Did Matson taunt him with butchered animal carcasses?"

"Nope. Me again. You should have seen Nate's face. I scared the shit out of him and milked it, especially when he thought his kid was in danger."

"The illegal bear trap that got me, did you...?"

"Did I know it was there? What do you think?"

She raised an eyebrow and smiled.

Her smug expression told me all I needed to know. Justine had sent me down a trail she knew had traps and hoped I'd be injured enough for her to gain the upper hand. I'd trusted her and she'd played me. It took all my composure to stay cool.

"What did Josh do for you?" I asked. "What was *his* buy-in?"

Justine looked down at the dead man and laughed.

"He loved me. He took care of me. I gave him a good fuck whenever he wanted it. For that, he rendered the meat and did what he was told. Hallmark doesn't make a card for what we had."

"Very touching. That earned him two bullets." I shook my head. "You're...poisoned candy. Enticing on the outside. Lethal where it counts."

She narrowed her eyes.

"When I found out you were coming to the island, I nearly panicked," she said. "I'd seen you in the Cascades and watched you process the scene. At first I thought you'd followed me back to the island for a reason, but I gave you too much credit."

I let her ego spew. She was talking and I wouldn't stop her. I didn't take comfort in being right. I'd been watched in the Cascades and because of Justine, the odd premonition had lingered when I came to the island.

My gift had tried to warn me. The severity of my escalating visions had never happened to me before. Not the way they'd turned into waking nightmares. I should've listened to what those visions had tried to tell me.

"There wasn't a renovation at the motel, was there?" I asked.

"I wanted you close to me, lover. That's when I started drugging you with Ketamine, a veterinary medicine. It was in your hot tea and in the canteen water, Golden Boy. After that, you were easy to play."

She gave me the litany of symptoms I'd experienced, from my worsening hallucinations and nausea to my blurred vision. As she dosed me more, I'd even had body tremors, convulsions, and an extreme irrational fear. She'd played me like an expendable pawn.

"What happened to Matson? He's dead, isn't he?"

She grinned and ran a hand through Ben's hair. The kid gasped and cringed. There was nowhere for him to go. He couldn't stop her and neither could I.

"Talk about good luck," she said. "Not for him obviously, but when he ran, I went with the flow. I couldn't pass up the good karma, especially when it came to you."

Justine told me everything and bragged about it. Matson's body was in the mountains near Applewhite's cabin. She hadn't buried him. She left him for the animals he poached. Nothing much would be left behind. Exposed as he was, within days he'd be nothing but a pile of bleached bones.

"I tied him up and gagged him the first night. I wanted him to know it was me and sweat over what I'd do with him. The bastard was a macho pig. He never saw me as a threat...until I gutted him. That was Matson's blood you found. The cut boot heel was mine. You trusted me and never checked my story. After you got hurt, you were an easy mark, Ryker."

After I realized Justine had caught Matson in her foot chase on our first night at the cabin, I knew she had been the one to double back and steal my cell phone. She'd seen me use it in the mountains and hell, I'd told her it could be a beacon for my team to find us. I'd even told her how to take it offline. She'd isolated me by taking my only lifeline.

Justine made me second guess everything she'd told me. She'd lied to me about hunting Matson. She told me she'd dosed me with meds and staged the gunfight, using the different rifles to make me believe someone else had shot at the cabin. In my drugged state, she'd set up the whole scenario and faked her death to toy with me more.

"Josh had stayed with Ben while I messed with your head at Nate's place. You really lost it. The *Special K* did a number on you and I loved every minute. I believe you even developed a bit of a crush on me. When you passed out on the trail heading back to Point Baker, it was party time. You were a Christmas present, waiting to be opened."

I ignored the smug look on her face.

"Were you the pilot or was that Josh?"

"We both have licenses. Well, *had*. Dead men don't fly, but I own the plane. I keep it in the cove behind my cabin. Convenient. Private. That's where the tunnel goes, between Josh's shack and the cove. Did I tell you how much I love my job...the independence of it? No one questions anything I do. People here believe me. Trust me. I'm *Teflon*."

"You pretended to be a prisoner. Why? You could've stuck with the plan and killed us."

She hesitated. For the first time, she looked unsure. Justine clenched the knife tighter and jerked Ben's head back. The kid was barely hanging on.

"I wanted to walk away from this, right under the nose of the FBI and the state troopers. Do you have any idea how empowering that would feel? If that happened, I could've done *anything* and gotten away with it. You were my ticket out. No one would've blamed me if I quit my job after my terrible ordeal, packed it up and moved away. I could've started over somewhere new, but you spoiled everything....with your psycho bullshit hoodoo."

"So you killed Josh to place the blame on him and Matson. No one would've disputed you. Hell, I'd been a witness to it, thanks to you."

She glared at me.

"No one would've known about me. You would've bought anything I told you because I'd been a prisoner, too. You were willing to believe Matson and Josh were working together. I planted the seed and you nurtured it with me."

Her voice grew louder in her excitement. She got off on telling me everything.

"I only had to kill Josh, the only one who knew the truth," she said. "I couldn't trust him to keep his mouth shut."

Her gaze shifted down the length of my body and back, sizing me up. I didn't want to know what for.

"It took a lot for me to give up on you. I wanted you on my table, Ryker. Even as I slept next to you in Nate's cabin, I dreamed about carving into you. I wanted to cut a scream loose, over and over. You would've fought against the pain, but I would've won."

Her eyes rolled in ecstasy.

"Even now I can hear your cries. I actually dreamed of seeing your soul leave your body. That's what happens, you know. Dying has nothing to do with a blinding light and angels, not when I have a knife in my hands. That kind of power is...intoxicating."

Oh, God. The thought of her lying next to me as I slept made me cringe.

"Why Nate? Why did you keep him whole?"

She shrugged.

"I don't know what love is. Never have. Never will, but that bastard told me he loved me. How could someone physically perfect, be so stupid when it came to women?" She glared at me, yet from the somber look in her eyes, I knew she thought of Nathan. "He had a pathetic way of showing how he felt about me. Josh did what he was told, but not Nate. He always put his kid first. I got tired of it."

"He was a good father, Justine. He loved his boy."

Her eyes flared in anger and her face flushed red.

"I wanted to butcher his kid in front of him. I swear I would've done it. Every time we had a fight, I hunted and perfected my art, but Nate pissed me off one too many times. He earned his special place on my last masterpiece. I got tired of being second on his list. He ended up on my table, listening to Ray Charles while I worked on him. That song was the one his ex-wife picked for their wedding. I love irony."

I tried not to demonize the human beings I hunted, but Trooper Justine Peterson challenged my objectivity. She'd killed fourteen young men and all because Nathan Applewhite had been a devoted father and didn't put her on a pedestal at the expense of his child. In truth, nothing would have pleased her. Nate's days were numbered because he'd crossed her path.

"You wanna hear another bit of irony? You truly remind me of him. I didn't lie about that," she said. "It's the only reason you're still breathing."

"I didn't know Nate, but I'll take that as a compliment. He was a good man."

"Are you trying to piss me off?"

The simple truth was that I'd let Justine get too close to me. She seduced me and I'd let my guard down. I'd opened up to her in a way I never would have with people I should've trusted more. My gift had tried to help me, but I hadn't seen it until I saw the rush of images played back from the moment I'd stepped on the island. My last vision had forced me deeper into the worsening nightmare of the whale—a dream symbol of the Native art I'd first seen in Justine's living room.

My mind knew what I'd failed to see. The presence of death I sensed had been Justine from the start.

"All these questions, you're trying to understand me, aren't you? How pedestrian. I thought you accepted me as I am. I saw it on your face in the Cascades. You saw the beauty in my work. Why must you taint it all by trying to...explain what I do? Sometimes evil is just...evil. It exists in this world for the masses to appreciate the good. I'm only playing my part, Ryker."

She stared at me from behind Ben as if she were seeing me for the first time.

"You don't look surprised by *any* of this," she said. "Why is that? What gave me away? I thought I'd been...clever."

If there was a good time to filter what I thought and watch what I said, it should've been now, but I'd had enough of her ego.

"Even a clown can get away with murder, Justine. Ask John Wayne Gacy."

The grin faded from her face.

"I've operated in the shadows and avoided the light," she said. "Even when you came to me, you never truly saw me, but you've taught me something very special. I can fool *anyone*. You believed my lies like the others. Not even your psychic powers warned you. You let me *sleep* next to you, lover. I'm sure you think I'm damaged goods, yet I'm the one who knows how to survive...and I'll keep doing it. All I have to do is get past you."

Justine was done talking. She clutched the blade and cut into Ben's neck enough for blood to trickle. She hid behind him like a coward. If I didn't get a clear shot, she could cut his throat and he could still bleed out and die before I got help.

"I won't say it again," she said. "Put the gun down or Ben's dead. You'll be the reason, Ryker. Not me."

I gripped the Glock with my finger on the trigger. Scenarios played out in my head—none of them good.

***

As she crept down the shadowy tunnel, Lucinda heard voices. She stuck to the shadows and inched toward the door, holding her breath as she peeked inside. Ryker held a gun aimed at a woman. She held a knife to a guy's throat. *What the hell?* Her mind placed names on the players, the names she'd heard as she approached. She knew Ryker had taken a stand against Justine and Ben's life was at risk.

Oh, God. Ryker and Ben were alive, but all that could change if she stepped into the room now. The tense standoff could blow up because of her. With her back to a wall, she wiped the sweat off her palms and gripped her Glock in both hands. She filled her lungs and blew out the air to steady her heart.

Lucinda had seconds to decide. She knew what she had to do. She had to be Ryker's partner—and *trust* him.

***

Ryker Townsend

Justine had a knife. I had a gun. I should've had the advantage in theory, but Ben tipped the scale in her favor and she knew it.

"Aren't you curious?" I asked.

"About what?"

"Nathan let me see his death. He let me feel

everything. He *did* love you. He let me feel that, too."

"Shut up. You're lying." She clutched Ben's hair tighter and whispered in his ear. "Love is a lie. We come into this world alone and we leave the same way. Are you ready for your exit, Ben?"

Fresh tears trailed down Ben's face. I didn't have to be a mind reader to know he'd lost all hope. None of that mattered to Justine.

"Don't worry," she said. "I'll send a nice sympathy card to your mother. Something from the heart."

I opened my mouth to say something, but stopped when movement caught my eye. I sensed a presence and I saw something move through shadows. I recognized the face and my mind raced with what I would do now. I needed something unexpected—where Justine thought she held all the cards—and I could turn her ego against her.

"I'm sure you think the Ketamine had something to do with my visions at the cabin, but Nate came to me, more than once, before you dosed me. You said I reminded you of him. I think there's a reason for that. You *feel* him in me."

"I'm not a psycho freak like you and I don't do guilt, Golden Boy. Try again."

"I don't expect you to feel anything, Justine. You'd need a heart to do that. But I thought you should know, because Nathan is here now. He won't leave me."

I cocked my head.

"Can't you feel him? Oh, God, I do. He's..." I looked around the room and her eyes followed every move I made. "He's...*in me*. Still here."

Justine glared at me with laser focus. She had Ben in her grasp, but I knew she had her sights on me.

"I'm the one you want, Justine. Admit it." I

steadied my aim and peered at her over the top of my gun barrel. "Cut Ben loose and let him go. I'll put down the gun and I'll stay. If you want Nate, you'll have to kill me."

To a rational person, none of this would've made sense, but in the pit of her torture room, I gambled things would be different for Justine. She'd seen death many times. Anyone who imagined the souls of the dead leaving their bodies would have a singular take on my proposition.

As for me, my only thought had been for Ben. He'd suffered enough. I couldn't watch him die in front of me. I hoped Justine's ego would do the rest.

"That's a stupid trade, lover. The minute I kill you, I'm on Ben's scent. I'll find him before he makes it out of the tunnel and I'll drag him back here to finish the job. He's not going home to his momma...except in pieces."

"You hear that, Ben? She doesn't think you know how to run. Prove her wrong."

"But...you..." Ben's lips trembled.

"Do it, buddy. I need you to walk out the door and don't look back. Promise me. Do it for your mom."

"Yeah, I p-promise."

The second I lowered my gun and placed it on the floor, Justine grinned and edged the knife off Ben's throat. In slow even measure, she cut Ben's ropes and didn't take her eyes off me. I braced my body, ready to grab the weapon if she changed her mind, but that didn't happen. Ben slid off the metal table and nearly fell. In agonizing steps he hobbled to the stairs, naked and scarred. I felt his pain—his humiliation—and wanted to go with him, but Justine had the advantage.

She could beat me to him with the knife before I dropped for the gun. From the cocky amusement on her face, she knew it, too.

As Ben got to the door at the top of the stairs, he looked back one last time.

"You're gonna see your mom, Ben. Trust me," I said.

The kid smiled and faded into the shadows, leaving me alone with Justine.

"You want us." I smiled. "Come and get us."

Justine's nostrils flared and she lunged at me with the knife. I braced my body—the only thing I could do.

***

Lucinda barely had time to grab Ben and pull him to safety. She heard boots on the ground behind her—Whitmire and his back up—but she couldn't wait for the cavalry to arrive. She stepped into the room and took aim from the top of the stairs.

"FBI!" she yelled, but it was too late.

The trooper lashed out and struck Ryker in the chest with the knife. The sound of the full force blow sent goose bumps raging over Lucinda's skin. She didn't hesitate. She took aim and shot. The Glock bucked in her hands and the blast in the tight quarters made her ears ring. The trooper pitched forward, but she didn't stop her attack.

Lucinda took aim again and waited for a shot that wouldn't kill Ryker. He grappled with Justine. Their bodies rolled across the floor with blood spreading over his chest. For a second, Lucinda saw Ryker look at her—her cue to shoot again. He shoved Justine off him and Lucinda had a clear target. She pulled the trigger.

The trooper's head snapped back. Her skull cracked and chunks of bloody gristle and bone spattered over the plastic lining the floor. Justine dropped to the cement and hit hard. Lucinda tensed her body to take another shot. She knew the trooper was dead, but she fought the urge to empty her gun.

Lucinda shook off her revulsion when she saw Ryker. His chest heaved as he clutched at his knife wound. She rushed to him and dropped to her knees, putting pressure on his wound.

"I'm here. I've got you."

Ryker reached a bloody hand to hers and through a weak smile, he said, "I knew you'd come, Crowley."

Lucinda fought back the tears. *I knew you'd come.* Ryker had trusted her to find him. How could he have been so sure?

"You're safe now. It's over, Ryker."

She repeated those words and whispered only loudly enough for him to hear. The room filled with Whitmire's men. Every word, every move, came and went in a blur. Lucinda couldn't take her eyes off Ryker as she kept pressure on his wound.

"Stay with me," she begged. "I'm here. I won't leave you."

When Ryker's eyes fluttered, Lucinda followed her gut and did something she never would have done otherwise. She cradled his head in her arms and lowered her lips to his. She kissed him as if she had every right. She wanted to remember the taste of his lips as she breathed him in. When she opened her eyes, she gazed down at his face.

Ryker stared at her and didn't say a word. His shock didn't last long. He closed his eyes and collapsed in her arms. If he died, Lucinda didn't want him leaving this world without knowing how she felt. Her timing sucked, but she had no regrets.

Whitmire dropped to his knees and said things Lucinda barely heard. Hutch and Cam hugged her, but she couldn't take her eyes off Ryker until a trooper with med training needed room to tend to his chest wound.

"I'm going with him...to the hospital." She said the words, but they sounded throaty and desperate—the voice of a stranger.

Chapter Twenty-One

Ketchikan General Hospital
Morning

It had been a long night. The sun had been up for hours, but overcast skies kept the sunshine masked behind a dark bank of clouds. Lucinda stared out a window into the steel gray gloom as she sat on a hard couch in a waiting room. People had come and gone. Everything had turned into a vague haze. Too much coffee. No sleep. All she could think about was Ryker Townsend.

Ryker and Ben Stevens had been rushed by helicopter to the nearest trauma hospital in Ketchikan. Rather than fretting over Ryker's surgery and what the doctors were doing, Lucinda made use of her time on the phone. Early morning calls were usually not good news. If things hadn't turned out as they did, the notifications she made would have been gut wrenching agony.

But Ryker and Ben had survived. She wanted to always remember days like this. Not all of her time with the FBI would be as good.

Her conversation with ViCAP Unit Chief Anne Reynolds had been a blur. Emotionally drained, she held it together and kept it professional, fighting the tremble in her voice. When she called the mother of Ben Stevens, she let the tears flow. Ben's mom would never see her cry over the phone and she didn't have a heart of granite. She was a blinker.

It felt good to let go.

"Oh my, God. Bless you. Sweet Jesus, thank you." The woman had sobbed. "I didn't think I'd ever see my baby boy again."

"You raised a remarkable son, Mrs. Stevens."

Lucinda wanted to always remember that phone call. It wasn't everyday she got to tell a mother that her missing son—a young man kidnapped by a known and prolific serial killer—would be coming home. She'd told Ben's mother what she could. Ryker wouldn't have wanted his name mentioned, but Lucinda couldn't help it. If Ryker hadn't followed his hunch—and risked his own life—Ben would've died.

Now Mrs. Stevens sat aboard a plane. She'd arrive in an hour. Hutch and Cam would pick the woman up at the airport and take her to see her son. Fresh tears cooled Lucinda's cheeks as she thought of the reunion Ben would have with his mother.

She wiped her face as a voice nudged her into reality.

"We've got Special Agent Townsend in room four-twenty." A nurse had approached her and smiled. "He won't wake up for a while, but you're welcome to sit with him."

Lucinda hadn't seen the nurse walk up, but after hearing she'd see Ryker soon, she took a deep breath and let the good news wash over her. When she reached his private room, Ryker was asleep. A heart monitor beeped and a bag of fluid hung by his bed and dripped down a tube and into a vein in his arm. She stood over him and watched his chest rise and fall as he breathed. He was pale, but his face looked peaceful. She tried to picture him as a small boy. With him sleeping, that wasn't hard.

Lucinda couldn't look away. She was too afraid it was all a dream and if she blinked, her worst fears would've come true. She had to touch him. Lucinda reached out a hand and cupped his cheek, something she never would've done if she thought he'd feel her fingers on his skin. The minute she felt his warmth, she couldn't hold back the emotions welling inside her.

Lucinda cried and didn't think she would stop.

"Why did you antagonize her like that? She almost killed you." She wiped her cheeks with the back of her hand. "You saw me outside the door, right? I *know* you saw me. That's why you did it. You were only thinking of getting Ben out, because you knew I was there to back your play."

Lucinda knew Ryker had seen her in the shadows of the tunnel outside the door after she'd dared to show her face. She'd taken the risk of stepping from the shadows because Ryker had to know he wasn't alone. But after Justine let Ben go, the trooper went bat shit crazy on Ryker, the last person she thought stood in her way.

Everything happened too fast. She replayed the nightmare over and over in her mind. Ryker had survived Justine's attack, but Lucinda would never forget the meaty thud of the knife as the blade struck his chest.

Never.

***

Ketchikan General Hospital
Evening

Lucinda left Ryker sleeping in his hospital room to hear an update from Hutch and Cam. In the waiting area outside his room, she stood with her team, unable to sit. Hutch and Cam had stayed to dig into Justine Peterson's life. Ryker would want to know everything they found when he'd be ready to hear it, but beyond that, they would build a file on the woman serial killer.

Justine Peterson was no longer an UNSUB. She had a name and soon, they'd know a lot more about her.

"Josh Getty's shack is a treasure trove, if you're

into stockpiled shit fit for rats. We're processing his place for evidence," Hutch said. "HAZMAT suits and gas masks wouldn't keep the filth and stink out. Reminds me of an old roommate I had in college. No lie."

"My skin is still crawling from my visit. Believe me I know what you're saying." Lucinda stuffed her hands into her jeans pockets. "You find anything interesting for our case?"

Hutch exchanged a somber look with Cam and let his partner answer the question.

"We found photos she'd taken of her victims...in various stages of their torture, while they were still alive. With facial recognition, we may have enough to ID them now." Cam's eyes were watery. "She and Josh posed with the bodies and took pictures. I still can't get my mind wrapped around her being law enforcement. If Ryker hadn't come here, we might never have known."

A shiver ran over Lucinda's skin. She crossed her arms and pressed them for more.

"You left a text message on my phone the other day," Lucinda said. "I didn't see it until...afterwards. Was there something you needed to tell me, something you found at the library?"

"Yeah. We searched the library computer for logon times that corresponded to hits on Ben's social media pages. With the help of a local trooper, we tied traffic and surveillance cam images to our *Thrill-Seeker* logons. We put a name and face to our mystery computer user."

"And?"

"Another trooper identified Justine Peterson in a patrol cruiser. She uses an assigned vehicle whenever she comes to Klawock. We have surveillance cams to link her to *Thriller-Seeker*. Sinead dug into her online activity through the library system and we know she had a Cloud account. We'll need a warrant to see what's behind the Cloud, but I bet we'll find her *FaceTrax* app with more connections to our victims. We should get closure for the families...finally."

Lucinda knew firsthand what closure meant to a victim's family. It always broke her heart to give a family bad news, but not knowing anything would be far worse.

"I'm working with Whitmire and the state troopers to wrap up our case. We've got a joint operation now," Lucinda told Hutch and Cam. "The troopers seized Peterson's plane and are processing it. He's also got men searching for Grady Lee Matson's body near Applewhite's cabin. I'll let you know when they find something. We should be in on it."

The pieces to the puzzle of Justine Peterson and Josh Getty were coming together. Whitmire had someone search financial and tax records. The troopers found a truck in Getty's name that the man kept outside Seattle at an airport hangar. If these extra locations panned out, there would be more crime scenes to process for evidence.

If Ryker hadn't risked everything on his hunch to dig into Nathan Applewhite's life, Lucinda didn't want to think how many more victims there would've been.

"How's Ryker today?" Hutch asked.

"His color looks better," Cam said.

She gave them the latest from the doctors. When she was done, she said what she'd been thinking since they found him, but had never said aloud until now. She had to be sure he'd survive.

"He's lucky," she said. "We all are."

***

Two days later
Ryker Townsend

Pain meds worked unless I blinked, or breathed, or my hair follicles grew. I tried not to do any of those things.

Lucinda Crowley kept me company during hospital visiting hours. Hutch and Cam made an appearance and I recalled Sinead Royce's voice over the phone, but Crowley had become my most lucid memory during those first days. I'd narrowly missed a punctured lung and my ankle required pins. I *had* broken a bone.

Crowley brought me contraband food whenever the nurses weren't looking. Shakes, French fries, donuts. I didn't know if she was trying to kill me. I couldn't eat much, but I didn't have the heart to tell her to stop. I'd been grateful for her company.

She bought me peculiar Get Well gifts—whatever struck her fancy—that would make me laugh. My favorite had been a Sponge Bob Chia Pet. She'd planted the seeds in the most inappropriate spots and Bob had already begun to sprout. If Sponge Bob was allowed to reach his full glory, hospital staff would be grateful for me to leave and take him with me.

With Crowley, she distracted me and kept my demons at bay. There were moments I would've laughed if it didn't hurt. She made me happy, but when visiting hours were over, the darkness of the case closed in on me.

In my hospital room at night, I stared out the window and wrestled with my ghosts between fits of broken sleep. I sometimes heard Justine whispering next to me in the dark whenever I dozed off—as if she was lying next to me. I'd wake drenched in cold night sweats, panting until I choked.

Death is powerful. Once someone is marked, no one can stop it, not even you.

Her whisper had brushed my ear. I felt it. I knew she would stay with me until I could let her go, but I needed her. She reminded me how close I'd come.

You're the voice of the dead. You watch over them, but who watches over you?

Who, indeed? I remembered what she had said about living alone. *...there's no one there to stop you.* At the time I'd seen her through the mirror of my life and thought she meant the many ways I'd sabotaged my life by erecting absurd barriers to keep others out.

Now her words carried the weight of a different meaning.

I'd survived and my body would heal, but I'd never be the same. Justine Peterson had changed me forever. I'd accepted and trusted who she was because of her uniform. I could've easily become another one of her victims if I hadn't '*listened*' to my gift and heeded my whale dream.

I wasn't stupid enough to believe I'd ever been invulnerable because I carried a gun and worked with the FBI, but I could've been tortured and killed by Justine. My team would've processed my body, whole or in parts. The thought of that chilled me. Now any victim I'd meet in the future, I'd see my face behind their eyes.

Perhaps that was a good thing. I hadn't arrived at an answer.

Lucinda had spent the morning with me, flipping channels on the TV, saying whatever came to her mind, and sneaking glances at her watch. I'm not a nervous guy, but she could've changed that if she'd kept it up.

"What's wrong? Are you having a Korean food withdrawal?"

"Ah, no, but..."

I scrunched my face and it hurt.

"But what?"

"I made a call," she said. "I'm not sure how you're gonna take it...is all, but I gotta go. We can chat later, if you're still talking to me."

Crowley ducked out before I could dazzle her with a witty comeback. She shut the door to my hospital room, something she didn't normally do. When I heard voices outside in the hall, I knew I was about to find out exactly what she meant. I propped up my pillows and waited.

I have to admit, when my sister Sarah walked into the room, I had nothing to say. I was stunned. I never thought I'd see her again. Sarah's face flushed red. She stood near the door, far from my bed. When she cleared her throat, I didn't rush her. I had no idea what she would say.

"After you left, I felt terrible," she began. "I hurt you. I saw it in your eyes, but I couldn't stop."

"You have your family to think of. I get that," I said. "You don't have to—"

"Let me finish...please."

A tear fell down her cheek and she wiped it away. I nodded and kept my mouth shut.

"You were right about the guilt I have over...the accident. I should've believed you. I should have trusted you and told mom and dad not to go." Sarah broke down. I wanted to hold her, but she kept her distance. "Deep down inside, I think that's why I've shut you out. You reminded me of what I did and I didn't want to face it. I'm not strong like you."

I reached for the box of tissues on the nightstand near my bed and offered her one. She took a handful and kept talking.

"I wanted to punish you...for what *I did*. That wasn't fair. It never was." She choked back a sob. "I can't make up for the years I disowned you, but..."

She wiped her blotched face with the tissues and took a deep breath before she went to the hospital room door.

"I have some special people in my life who I want you to meet. And I want them to meet you."

Sarah opened the door and a man stepped into the room holding a little girl.

"Jake, this is my brother, Ryker." Fresh tears trailed down her cheeks. "I told Jake everything. And I told Amanda she has an uncle."

The little girl with soft brown ringlets and large blue eyes smiled at me and I lost it. I looked at my sister and mouthed the words, 'thank you.' Whatever past we had, I would put it behind me and start fresh.

As I stared into Sarah's eyes—the eyes that always reminded me of our mother—I felt the love of my mother and father. I think Sarah did, too.

***

Ryker Townsend

As morning visiting hours approached on my fourth day in the hospital, I found myself eager for Crowley to appear. *Lucinda.* It would take time to get accustomed to using her first name. Lucinda gave me something to look forward to. I didn't have to wait long. She came early and had an armful of gifts. I smelled baked goods and my stomach growled. My appetite would be good today.

"Before you regale me with whatever adventures you've had this morning, I have something to say."

She narrowed her eyes and set down the bags.

"Okay. I'm listening."

I heaved a sigh and fixed my eyes on her. She gave me courage to say what I needed to.

"I stared at this idiot the other day...for a long time." I chewed the inside of my lip and stayed the course. "As he looked back at me in the mirror, I realized you'd been right. I shouldn't have shut you out like I did. I could've died because of...this thing with me. We need to talk. Actually I need to talk and it would help if you listened so I don't feel like a total idiot."

"I can do that."

I told her everything and she made it easy. She listened and didn't push me. I told her about what happened with my parents and why my sister Sarah hadn't wanted anything to do with me. I shared how I feared the FBI would not understand my gift. That's why I'd kept everything a secret and still wanted to. Without my job, my life and my visions would be wasted and I'd feel like a freak even more than usual.

"So this thing you do...you get visions...like a psychic?"

"You said the '*P*' word. I may never forgive you."

"Try, Ryker. I'm just trying to get my head wrapped around all of this."

"Yes, I understand. I get these odd nightmares. My mother called them visions. They're important for my work, but I live in fear I'll lose my job because no one will understand. They'll treat me differently and talk behind my back."

"They already do that."

"Good to know."

"So except for my stellar reputation as a highly sympathetic human being, why me? Why did you suddenly decide to tell me? Not that I'm complaining."

I knew exactly why I had decided to share my secret with Lucinda, but she had been the one to kiss *me*. Before I went any further, I had to understand why she'd done it.

"Before I answer, I need to know why you kissed me."

"Yeah, about that kiss," Lucinda stammered. "I'd been...worried. Call it a heat of the moment kind of thing. I mean...hell, I thought you were dead."

"Is this multiple choice? Do I pick one?"

"You're not making this simple."

"Simple isn't something we do, is it?" I meant it as a rhetorical question, but Lucinda furrowed her brow to ponder it as if I'd asked her to explain Einstein's theory of relativity. She had a hard time looking at me.

"Now...about that kiss," I said. I made the mistake of taking a breath and Lucinda took advantage of the two second lull.

"Yeah, about that," she said. "I promise it won't happen again. I barely remember doing it actually. I mean, it wasn't like I...ever thought of kissing you before."

"Lucinda."

She ignored me.

"You're my b-boss," she stammered. "I thought you w-were—"

"Lucinda."

"...dead, but you're not, so everything can go back to normal."

"Yes, if I were dead, we would have to redefine our relationship." I nodded. "I see your point."

"Should I stop talking now?"

I shrugged and said, "I would never suggest it. I'm rather enjoying our...conversation."

"Conversation takes two...generally."

"Yes, another excellent point. If I may, I have something to say."

She crossed her arms and said, "By all means, proceed."

"You once accused me of being a bomb about to go off. You said I had a fuse burning. And me, being an asshole, I told you the day I imploded, I would think of you." I heaved a sigh and fixed my gaze on her. "Well, when I was drugged and thought I would die, I *did* think of you."

"Thought...what exactly?"

"I thought of you and I felt...safe. And—"

"And what?"

"I may have thought about...kissing. Of course I can't be held responsible. I was under the influence of a powerful hallucinogen."

"Is that the screech of you backpedaling?" She grinned. Her smile didn't last long. "But I work for you. If we want something more, we can't—" She didn't finish. Lucinda shook her head and said, "I'm not sure what this is, but it could turn into...the beginning of the end."

"Or it *could* be just the end of the beginning." I reached for her hand and entwined my fingers in hers.

Lucinda didn't have anything to say. Her eyes welled with tears she didn't try to hide and she squeezed my hand. I didn't know where any of this would lead, but I did know I could trust her with more than my secret. I would trust her with my heart.

If she didn't hock it for grocery money, I liked our odds.

The End

About the Author

Bestselling, critically-acclaimed author Jordan Dane's gritty thrillers are ripped from the headlines with vivid settings, intrigue, and dark humor. Publishers Weekly compared her intense novels to Lisa Jackson, Lisa Gardner, and Tami Hoag, naming her debut novel *No One Heard her Scream* as Best Books of 2008. She also pens young-adult novels for Harlequin Teen. Formerly an energy sales manager, she now writes full time. Jordan shares her Texas residence with two lucky rescue dogs.

Connect with Jordan Dane:

Website: http://www.JordanDane.com
Twitter: http://www.twitter.com/JordanDane
Facebook:
https://www.facebook.com/JordanDaneAuthor
Pinterest: http://pinterest.com/jordandane/

Thriller/Crime Fiction Blogs:
The Kill Zone http://killzoneauthors.blogspot.com/

Bibliography

Avon/HarperCollins titles:
No One Heard her Scream (Apr 2008)
No One Left to Tell (May 2008)
No One Lives Forever (Jun 2008)
Evil without a Face (Feb 2009)
The Wrong Side of Dead (Nov 2009)
The Echo of Violence (Sep 2010)
Reckoning for the Dead (Oct 2011)

Young Adult novels:
In the Arms of Stone Angels (Young Adult, Harlequin Teen Apr 2011)
On a Dark Wing (Young Adult, Harlequin Teen Jan 2012)
Indigo Awakening (Young Adult, book 1in *The Hunted series*, 2012)
Crystal Storm (Young Adult, book 2 in *The Hunted series* 2013)

Young Adult anthologies:
Nyx in the House of Night Anthology- *The Magic of Being Cherokee* essay (Smart Pop books, Jun 2011)

Cosas Finas Publications:
Blood Score (July 2013) – Crime Fiction Novel
Sex, Death and Moist Towelettes – Short Story Anthology
One Author's Aha Moments – Non-fiction author craft book with a focus on writing YA